It was a first for Mitch Rose.

Never before had he felt so sure, so determined, as if making love to this woman was what he'd always been meant to do.

Lowering Darcy to the bed, he explored every inch of her, marking her with his touch, his mouth.

Come morning, reality would be knocking at the door. Come tomorrow, Darcy would leave him and his family and sleepy Rose Arbor behind. Tomorrow she would return to her high-powered life in the city.

But tomorrow would come soon enough.

Tonight, Mitch meant to make certain that Darcy took a powerful memory along.

No one else, he vowed, would make her feel such joy, such exultation.

No other man would ever love her as he did tonight....

Dear Reader,

May is a time of roses, romance...and Silhouette Special Edition! Spring is in full bloom, and love is in the air for all to enjoy. And our lineup for this month reflects the wonder of spring. Our THAT SPECIAL WOMAN! title, *Husband by the Hour,* is a delightful spin-off of Susan Mallery's HOMETOWN HEARTBREAKERS series. It's the story of a lady cop finding her family... as well as discovering true love! And Joan Elliott Pickart continues her FAMILY MEN series this month with the frolicking *Texas Dawn*—the tale of a spirited career girl and a traditional Texas cowboy.

Not to be missed is Tracy Sinclair's warm and tender *Please Take Care of Willie.* This book is the conclusion to Tracy's CUPID'S LITTLE HELPERS series about matchmaking kids. And speaking of kids... *The Lady and the Sheriff* is Sharon De Vita's latest heartwarming installment of her SILVER CREEK COUNTY miniseries. This story features Louie, the kid who won readers' hearts!

May is also the month that celebrates Mother's Day. Cheryl Reavis has written a story that is sure to delight readers. Her FAMILY BLESSINGS series continues with *Mother To Be.* This story is about what happens when an irresistible force meets an immovable object...and deep, abiding love results.

Finally, we round off the month by welcoming historical author Barbara Benedict to Silhouette Special Edition. She makes her contemporary debut with the lighthearted *Rings, Roses...and Romance.*

I hope you have a wonderful month of May!

Sincerely,

Tara Gavin,
Senior Editor

Please address questions and book requests to:
Silhouette Reader Service
U.S.: 3010 Walden Ave., P.O. Box 1325, Buffalo, NY 14269
Canadian: P.O. Box 609, Fort Erie, Ont. L2A 5X3

BARBARA BENEDICT

RINGS, ROSES... AND ROMANCE

SPECIAL EDITION®

Published by Silhouette Books
America's Publisher of Contemporary Romance

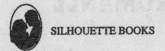

SILHOUETTE BOOKS

ISBN 0-373-24104-6

RINGS, ROSES...AND ROMANCE

Copyright © 1997 by Barbara Benedict

Printed in U.S.A.

BARBARA BENEDICT

Weaving a story has always been part of Barbara Benedict's life, from the days when her grandfather would gather the kids around his banjo, to the nights of bedtime tales with her own children. To Barbara, starting a story should be like saying, "Come, enter a special new world with me."

Her ten books and two novellas are set in varied places and time periods, but this is her first contemporary romance.

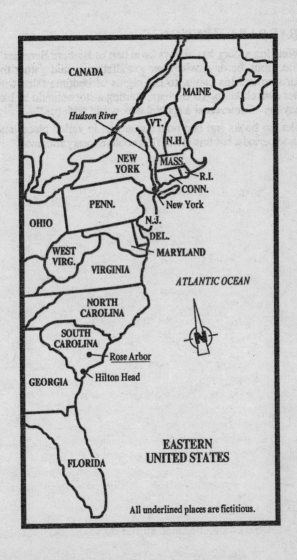

CANADA

MAINE

Hudson River

VT.

N.H.

NEW YORK

MASS.

R.I.

CONN.

New York

PENN.

OHIO

N.J.

DEL.

WEST VIRG.

MARYLAND

VIRGINIA

ATLANTIC OCEAN

NORTH CAROLINA

N

SOUTH CAROLINA

Rose Arbor

GEORGIA

Hilton Head

EASTERN UNITED STATES

FLORIDA

All underlined places are fictitious.

Chapter One

Come Smell the Roses, the sign had invited.

A romantic proposition, but she had a destination to reach, a schedule to maintain. As her fellow workers in the Finley-Binch Advertising Agency would say, Darcy MacTeague was a real go-getter, fast track all the way. Bright, ambitious and ever busy, she'd made a good life for herself in New York. Darcy had set her future on a solid, dependable, predictable path, and it was far too late in the game to be straying from it. She had no time to stop and smell any roses.

She knew it was time she got back to the interstate, so why keep driving along this rutted road, deeper and deeper into rural South Carolina? Because some amateurish sign, seen at the last rest stop, had stirred up long-dormant memories?

Come Smell the Roses, it had beckoned. *Come to Rose Arbor and Rediscover the Gracious Past of the Antebellum South.*

The sign with its fuzzy picture of a mansion with columns and white-railed porches, had stirred up vague, long-dormant yearnings. Darcy felt as if she were twelve again, on her way to the Virginia farmhouse for the brief, happy interlude that turned out to be the only real vacation she'd ever known.

Until now.

It had been a crazy impulse, driving down to South Carolina in her new car. Everyone had told her so—her mother, her friends, Peter Arlington, the guy she'd been dating—but when the Tavish Corporation had scheduled Tuesday's meeting in Hilton Head, Darcy had seized the excuse like a lifeline. It had seemed vital that she go somewhere, that she see something of America, before the combined burdens of car and mortgage payments kept her chained to the city.

Not that she regretted buying her Lexus. She smiled as her gaze swept the posh interior, inhaling the scent of sleek leather, the aroma of wealth and security. After long years of hard work and loneliness, this car was the badge of her success. Like the diamond studs she wore in her ears and the upscale condo she was about to purchase, it was her testament to the world that Darcy MacTeague had made it, that she could stand on her own.

Yet, if she truly sought stability and security, why was she taking this insane detour?

She had reservations at Hilton Head, and the handsome Peter Arlington awaiting her there. Their work-related weekend getaway at a first-class resort should beckon her, not some unknown, out-of-the-way bed-and-breakfast. In truth, the term "gracious past" could prove more ominous than romantic. Darcy didn't know if the antebellum period had enjoyed the benefits of indoor plumbing, but it certainly had never included air-conditioning.

Looking at the heat shimmering off the cracked and blistered road ahead, she was doubly glad to be in the cool cocoon of her Lexus. She knew she should turn back, but she told herself there was no real need to leave the car. She only wanted to *see* Rose Arbor—she didn't mean to sleep there. She'd just drive past the house, take a quick peek and then hurry on to Hilton Head. After all, the whole purpose of the drive had been to work out the kinks in the Lexus, see a bit of the country and prove she was still in charge of where she went and when she went there.

She'd take one more curve. If she didn't find Rose Arbor, she'd head back to the interstate.

But as with the bear climbing the mountain, each small hill led to yet another shaded bend in the road, revealing only an enticing hint of the fields beyond the trees. One curve led to another, taking her deeper and deeper into unfamiliar territory. With the kudzu twining around the stately oaks, and the Spanish moss clinging to the gnarled branches, it made for an alien environment. Darcy felt as removed from this world as if she'd landed on another planet.

She felt an abrupt need to glimpse concrete and steel, the signposts of the city. Clearly, it was time to turn back. Time to return to the safe, predictable route she'd mapped out for her life.

Yet, as her hands tightened on the steering wheel, a sudden damp chill filled the interior of the car, as if a cool mist curled in through the vents and seeped into her bones. With the drop in temperature came a sense of need so compelling, Darcy's every nerve ending tingled.

A murmur of air brushed over her. She heard the words *Help us* whispered softly and urgently in her ear.

Startled, she jammed on the brake.

The Lexus veered to the left, just as two young boys darted out of the bushes to her right, chasing a decrepit goat across her path. Handling the car as if she drove a Mack truck, she managed to miss all three, but in so doing, lost total control of the vehicle.

The Lexus rumbled and bumped, making screeching noises as it swerved into the ditch. Helplessly clutching the steering wheel, trying desperately to save her new car, Darcy felt its final protest as it careered into the wide solid oak before her.

Using the back of his hand to wipe the sweat from his forehead, Mitch Rose leaned on his pitchfork as he tried to figure out what was nagging at him. Every now and then in his life, he'd get the strangest sensation, some sixth sense of urgency, and it invariably propelled him to act.

He glanced at the sky but he didn't need to see the late-summer haze to feel its heat and humidity. The weatherman had been talking about a possible hurricane headed their way, but the sky remained cloudless, with not even a breeze to stir the air. No, it wasn't the weather that had him so edgy.

It could, of course, just be stress. This weekend was bound to be an ordeal with the ever-demanding Roy Hackett—fast-food king—and his clan descending upon them for their annual family reunion. Mitch had to get dressed to greet them, but first he had to load this wagon with hay for the Labor Day picnic, decorate the garden for the garden society competition and set things up for Mel's birthday.

Speaking of which, where was his daughter?

He spun around, looking to the porch to see if Melissa was up there flirting with Dex Bradley, the local teenage Lothario. Mitch didn't spot Mel, but he noticed the twins were no longer working at the old water pump. Great. He'd been after those boys all week to put it back together. Scanning the yard for them, he made an even more unwelcome discovery.

The gate to the pen stood wide open.

Open gate, missing goat—he had all the ingredients for disaster. If he'd told the kids once, he'd told them a hundred times to make certain they left the pen locked. The blasted goat's last excursion through the neighborhood had cost him two hundred dollars and a full hour of apologizing to Hester Macon.

Stabbing the pitchfork into the ground, Mitch started down the driveway, calling his sons' names, his uneasiness deepening with every step. He couldn't say exactly what was wrong, only that he had a compelling need to find his kids instantly.

In the distance, a car gave a big-city-taxi honk as Mitch reached the road. Breaking into a run, he heard the squeal of brakes, the roar of an engine out of control.

Heart slamming into his throat, adrenaline pumping straight to his brain, he ran down the road toward the sound. Spurred by mind-clearing fear, his legs moving in extra-fast motion, he raced to reach his boys in time.

Even as the ground vibrated with a final, decisive crash.

Chapter Two

Dazed, and vaguely happy to be alive, Darcy pushed away the air bag to reach for the handle. The door opened slowly with a scraping, metallic sound, then refused to budge further. As she struggled with it, the heat slammed into her like a second collision.

I hate humidity, she thought hazily, closing her eyes as she leaned back against the seat.

"Wow!" one of the boys gushed, his voice trembling with awe. "Did you see that?"

"Yeah, that old oak was like a magnet." From their voices, she could tell both boys were approaching the Lexus. "One minute she's driving along, and then wham! She's stuck like glue to a tree."

They didn't sound injured, she thought with relief. If nothing else, at least she'd managed not to hit them.

"Is she bleeding?"

Darcy opened her eyes, realizing that this was a question she should have been asking herself. Scanning what she could of her body with the air bag in the way, she found no blood, though her silk outfit could be in serious trouble. Five minutes more in this climate and her suit—not to mention herself— would be ready for the Dumpster.

"I don't see any bleeding," the other boy answered as they peered in the car window. "I hope she's okay. We'll be in *big* trouble if she isn't."

Turning her head, Darcy looked from one boy to the other. They must be twins, she decided, somewhere around ten. Hair the color of straw poked out above their cherubic freckled faces; their lean yet healthy frames were clad in faded Levi's, Power Ranger T-shirts and a generous layer of dirt. Even to Darcy's dazed mind they were a perfect blend of boundless energy, unending curiosity and barely suppressed mischief. Dennis the Menace in duplicate.

"Ky, you think it was Lady?"

This last was uttered in a stage whisper, the boy's wide blue eyes more awed than frightened. Their gazes strayed to the goat, munching contentedly at the weeds on the other side of the road. Eyeing it, Darcy could think of a good dozen other names for the scrawny creature, but Lady would never be one of them.

"Ky, J.J., are you okay?" A third blonde came running at them down the road. Though female, and several years older, her resemblance to the pair was undeniable. Full of the same intimidating intensity, all the teenager lacked was the impish grin.

Though it was hard to tell her expression with the huge wad of gum in her mouth.

Stopping before the boys, the girl looked from the goat to the Lexus, then to Darcy. "Wow, you guys really did it this time," she said, blowing a bubble and popping it loudly. "Dad's gonna kill you for this."

Their gazes returning to the disreputable animal, both boys tensed, their suddenly pale features suggesting that homicide was not an unreal expectation. Just what sort of a monster was their father to put such fear on their faces?

Darcy didn't have long to wonder. Blond and intense, a living example of what his boys would look like in thirty years' time, the man burst out of the bushes like a conquering hero. No hint of mischief on his fair features—every inch of his tall, athletic frame was poised to do battle.

His attention went straight to the boys. As he studied them, some of the tension went out of his posture, relief playing like a wide-screen movie across his rugged face. The only way he'd ever kill those boys was by hugging them too hard, she realized. A distinct possibility, considering what excellent shape his upper body was in. As for the lower...

He turned to Darcy then, fixing her with a sky-blue gaze so intense, it seemed to pierce right through her skin. Some part of her mind heard him ask if she was hurt, but the rest of her tingled alarmingly.

He strode over, grabbing the door and yanking it all the way open, paying no heed to its loud protest. Leaning inside, he shoved the air bag out of the way to look at her. "Are you all right?" he repeated, his gaze probing hers. "Any bleeding, broken bones, serious pain?"

She shook her head. "I'm just a little woozy." She didn't bother to add that his nearness might be as much to blame as the accident.

"Then let's get you out of here," he said in a tone that left no room for argument. "Unhook your seat belt."

To her dismay, her hands shook so, she couldn't get enough force to push down the clasp. Seeing this, he leaned over her to do it himself. He smelled of hay and fresh air, she noticed, and like the boys, had need of a haircut. She found herself tempted to trace her fingers along the damp strands tickling his collar.

As the seat belt clicked open, she braced herself, trying to find the strength to stand up and get out of the car, but again, he took care of that for her. Sliding one arm behind her back and the other under her knees, he lifted her from the car very much like the conquering hero.

It was ridiculous to let him carry her. She was more than

capable of standing on her own, yet it seemed suddenly easier to lean her head on his strong, capable chest and let the rest of the world go on without her. The urge to lean on this man, to rely on him, was nearly overwhelming.

"Daddy, what are you doing?" the teenager asked with a note of petulance. "You're not planning on carrying her all the way to the house?"

"I'd say that depends on her. Do you need me to?" He looked down at Darcy, his incredible blue gaze searching hers, making her conscious of how dangerously close she was to his face—a far too handsome face, with its firm chin, aquiline nose, strong inviting mouth. A few inches more and she could be touching his generous lips with her own.

Feeling the full heat of his grasp through the silk of her suit, she realized how dangerously close she was to being turned on by a complete stranger.

"I don't need anyone carrying me," she said, painfully aware that it had taken some moments to formulate an answer. "I'm perfectly able to walk on my own, you know."

Her agitation made her answer more prickly than she'd intended. His half grin faded, and with it, the warmth in his eyes. Firmly, he set her on her feet in the middle of the road.

As her knees wobbled beneath her, she found she was able to walk on her own, yes, but far from perfectly. Her would-be rescuer reached out with a steadying arm. "Are you sure you're okay?" he asked with gratifying concern.

"She might be," the taller of the twins said with a shake of his blond head, "but you can't say much about the car."

"Not how it's wrapped around the tree," the other added solemnly.

As their assessment sunk in, Darcy turned to view her new Lexus. Or rather, what was left of it. Its front end had wrapped around the oak and steam now hissed out of the radiator. With its ice-blue surface bathed in mud, it looked less like the silver-winged chariot she'd once imagined it and more a dying warrior gasping his last breaths.

"My beautiful new car," she cried in anguish. "What will I do now?"

"It's only a car." Dropping his hands, the man studied her with a puzzled expression. "The important thing is that no one is hurt."

"Important to whom?" All at once, it was too much—the accident, the heat, this tall, disturbing man right there in her face. She shook her head, backing away. "That vehicle means I can go where I want, when I want, without ever having to depend on anyone else to get me there."

"All I meant," he said quietly, "was that you can replace a car."

"You think it's easy to replace a car like that?" she asked, staring at his faded denims and frayed chambray shirt, deciding that his idea of transportation must be some outdated, gas-guzzling truck with shotguns hung on a rack. "I waited months for the right color, the right accessories."

Her voice cracked. Fearing even her self-control had been damaged in the accident, she clamped her mouth shut. It was foolish, trying to explain to this stranger. What did he care if the Lexus was the first car she'd ever owned, bought with her own money?

Not that he stayed around to listen, anyway. Frowning, he walked over to the Lexus and began inspecting it.

She had to regain control of things, she thought desperately—it was the first rule in business. If this man threatened her mastery of the situation with his sweep-right-in-and-take-charge attitude, she had to show him that Darcy MacTeague was not some silly piece of fluff he could boss around. Sucking in a fortifying breath as she followed him to the car, she demanded the location of the nearest phone. "I need to report this immediately," she said, assuming a brisk, efficient tone. "To the authorities and my insurance company. I'll also need a tow truck, as soon as possible."

He barely spared a glance at her. "This isn't the city. You'll find folks here tend to have different priorities."

"Are you saying you don't intend to help me?"

He squatted to survey the damage to the front end of the Lexus. "All I'm saying is that there's a good chance neither Jem Marbley nor his tow truck will be in the garage today. Being a holiday weekend, old Jem's probably off to the lake to do some fishing."

"I'll call another garage then."

"*Another* garage?" Standing, he walked around to the passenger door. "In Seven Corners?"

She hazily recalled driving through the village and thinking it might more aptly be named Seven *Houses.* "There are other towns nearby," she insisted, her Italian-leather heels sinking in the mud as she trailed after him. "There must be a dealership somewhere."

"Yeah, but with the holiday traffic, it'll take them a while to get here. All supposing, of course, they haven't already shut down for the night—even the weekend."

"Fine," she said, her voice tight with strain. "I'll phone and get a rental."

"Maybe."

His shrug said, *Good luck,* both of them knowing the likelihood of finding anything roadworthy this late on a Labor Day Friday. Fleetingly, she considered public transportation, but the idea of being jostled for miles on a bus made her shudder.

She repeated her request for a phone. "You do have them out here, don't you?" she added testily.

Behind them, the girl made that snort of disgust only the teenage female can master. "Like I'd live anywhere without a phone. This isn't Mars, you know. How come you don't have one in that fancy car?"

"Mel!"

"Daddy, I hate that name and you know it."

The man left Darcy by the car as he joined his children in the road. "All I know, young lady, is that you were taught better manners."

The teenager crossed her arms across her chest rebelliously. "She started it. She was rude to us first."

The girl might have a point, but Darcy wasn't about to acknowledge it. She'd watched enough sitcoms to recognize the classic battle between generations, and the last thing she wanted now was to become embroiled in some domestic spat.

Instead, she tackled what in her opinion was the more important issue. "I need to call someone," she interrupted as she marched over to the group. "He'll be waiting for me at Hilton Head and I must warn him there might be a little delay."

As the man pulled his gaze from his daughter to study Darcy, his blue eyes took in everything, from her Armani suit to the gold Swiss watch at her wrist. "I'd say it's a safe bet you'll be more than a *little* delayed," he said, both his tone and gaze growing cooler.

Struck by the enormity of her situation, Darcy saw that getting a tow truck might be the least of her problems. With or without this Jem Marbley's help, she wouldn't be driving her car to Hilton Head—or anywhere else—for some time to come. She could be stranded here, lost and alone, at the mercy of this man, his uncaring children and that disreputable goat.

"Listen, I'm sure we can work this out," he said, his tone softening as if he'd seen her panic. "The kids can take you on up to the house to use the phone, and if worse comes to worst, you can bed down here at Rose Arbor for the night."

"Rose Arbor?" Darcy could only gape at him. Was it coincidence, or merely dark irony, that she should find the house from the sign this way?

"It's our family bed-and-breakfast," he said with blatant pride, before again eyeing her suit with a frown. "Not what you're used to, maybe, but we offer a clean bed, a decent breakfast and lots of down-home Southern atmosphere."

Memories of her childhood vacation in Virginia crowded in on her. The big old farmhouse, rooms filled with laughter, the scent of apples baking in a pie.

"Listen," the man went on, "I know this isn't pleasant. For any of us. But what say we start all over, Miss—"

"Ms.," she corrected automatically.

His smile didn't falter, but it tightened considerably, leaving her to wonder if he was one of those macho reactionary types who resisted all signs of feminine independence. "Just call me Darcy," she said stiffly. "Darcy MacTeague."

"Yeah, well, I'm Mitch Rose."

When he offered his hand, she wanted to ignore it. She might engage in the obligatory handshake every day in her line of work, but something about this particular male made her shy away from physical contact. Just looking at him put her on edge.

Yet avoiding him would give him an advantage, and he had far too many already. Assuming a businesslike air, she meant to give his hand a quick, no-nonsense shake, but the moment she felt his warm, sure grasp, it happened again—that strange, compelling temptation to hold on tight and never let go.

As if he felt it, too, and was no more happy about it, he frowned at her over their joined hands. Something sparked between them, something that had nothing whatsoever to do with business or maintaining control. Far too intensely aware of all solid, sexy, six feet of the man, Darcy yanked her hand from his grasp.

Dropping his arm to his side, he muttered a "Welcome to Seven Corners." He spoke the rhetoric, right down to the slight Southern drawl, but the old-fashioned hospitality was as forced as his smile.

"These are my sons, Schuyler and Jonathan," he went on, turning to the children Darcy had forgotten were there. "And the grumpy young lady is my daughter, Mel...Melissa."

The teenager acknowledged the introduction by glaring and popping another bubble. The twins crowded around Darcy, demanding to know how it felt to be stuck behind an inflating air bag.

"Not now, kids," their father chided. "Ms. MacTeague has enough on her mind." He nodded back at the wrecked Lexus.

Both boys looked instantly guilty as they glanced at the

goat. "It wasn't us this time," one protested, while the other added quickly, "I swear, it was Lady."

"Not that nonsense again." With a pained expression, Mitch ran a hand through his blond hair. "I thought you two meant to start taking responsibility for your actions. If the goat got loose again, it's because one of you didn't latch the gate properly. Not because..." Glancing at the wreck, he inhaled deeply as if hoping to draw patience from the air. "This time it's serious, boys. Someone could have been badly hurt."

The pair hung their heads, trying to look chastened, but it was Darcy who absorbed the brunt of his words. She'd been so busy worrying about her own problems, she hadn't stopped to think of how the accident might affect these people. She should reassure them that she didn't mean to sue, or press charges, especially not when in truth, she *had* been driving a bit too fast for a country lane. "Don't yell at your sons," she told Mitch. "If anything, blame Lady. She's the one who cut across my path."

All four turned to gape at her as if she'd just announced an alien invasion.

Puzzled and slightly exasperated, Darcy added, "Look, just get me to a phone and I won't even mention that I ran into her."

The children now stared at each other as if *Darcy* were the invader.

Their father shook his head in annoyance. "Can we sort this out later? If you'll excuse me, Ms. MacTeague, I have a thousand chores I need to get back to. Please feel free to use our phone, and if things don't work out, remember, there's always a welcome at Rose Arbor."

"Thank you for the offer, but I'm sure taking you up on it won't be necessary." Noticing his frown, she realized she needn't have said it so smugly.

"Mel," he said, turning suddenly to his daughter, "will show you up to the house."

"Why me? They're the ones who got us into this mess,"

the girl said huffily, pointing at her brothers. "Let them show her."

The teenager's reluctance couldn't have been any more insulting, a fact her father didn't fail to notice. "Mind your manners, young lady," he cautioned. "Besides, you need to be heading home to get dressed, anyway. The next tour starts in less than an hour."

The girl groaned. "Ah, Daddy, I hate wearing that stupid wig."

"Humor me. Just help me get through the Hackett reunion, and maybe we can afford to hire someone else to do the tours next season. For the time being, though, I need you kids to pitch in and do your part. J.J., Ky, go gather up that..." He looked around, his features grim. "Where has that mangy goat gotten to now?"

The boys exchanged worried glances. Under their breaths they uttered a soft, simultaneous, "Lady."

Their father's mutterings were not repeatable. "We've got to get that dumb beast before it eats anything else," he told them. "Ky, you try next door and J.J. can check out the Ryans' place. I'll head over to Hester Macon's."

He took off running in one direction, sending the boys in the other, leaving Darcy in the dubious care of his wisecracking teenager. Snapping a bubble, Melissa started down the road, taking it for granted that her unwilling guest would follow.

Darcy hesitated, glancing back at her car. She hated to leave her suitcases behind, but it certainly seemed preferable to carrying them in this heat. With a shrug, she decided to leave them in the trunk and worry about their retrieval later.

Catching up to Melissa, she walked in awkward silence for a few minutes before deciding she could at least try making small talk. "So, you give tours?" she asked, seizing upon the only thing she could remember about the girl. "Do you wear an antebellum costume? I just love all those yards of material and the wide hoop skirts."

"The dress is okay," Melissa said with a shrug, "but I

hate the dumb wig. Gramps says it makes me look like Little Orphan Annie.''

Darcy tried not to smile. "And your dad? Does he dress up, too?"

"*My* dad? He's allergic to dressing up. He grumbles like a bear when he has to wear a jacket, and you should hear him when he has to add a tie."

Definitely the rugged, outdoor type. Mitch couldn't be further from the sort of man Darcy generally dated. Nothing like the elegant, refined Peter Arlington. Yet when she tried to summon Peter's classic features, all she could see in her mind were Mitch Rose's startling blue eyes.

"Well, here we are," Melissa announced as they rounded the bend. "This is Rose Arbor."

Fanfare should have accompanied the undisguised pride in her voice. For Darcy, the scene was the sign at the rest stop come to life. Rose Arbor was all she'd expected, and more.

Following the girl up the wide avenue of live oaks, Darcy approached the house with something close to awe. It could be straight out of a movie, complete with tall white columns and gallery railings, Spanish moss dripping from the overhanging oaks. As if the past lived and breathed around her, she could almost hear elaborately gowned belles giggling as they drove up to the sprawling structure in fancy carriages, their hosts greeting them from the wide front porch.

A barn and several outbuildings stood to the right of the house, with a fenced-in pen in front of them, its open gate no doubt the source of the goat's escape. On the immediate left stretched an ocean of color, with marble statues, ornate latticework and delicate trellises. This must be the garden from which the place got its name, Darcy realized.

Come Smell the Roses, indeed.

"Come on, then," Melissa said, breaking into her thoughts. "Let's get to the phone before my dad gets back and starts hollering. This stuff about Lady has him a little strung-out."

Considering the way the Roses gaped at her when she'd

mentioned the goat's name, Darcy wondered if they weren't all a "little strung-out."

But then, could she blame them, living in this quiet little corner of the world? So little must happen here; it would be natural to turn molehills into mountains. In a busier place, nobody would notice the aging animal, but here the goat ate a few flowers and the next thing you knew, he was considered a dangerous fugitive rampaging across the countryside. "I see how the goat might be a trial," she said, "but you can't expect anyone to believe it poses a serious threat. Not when you give it a name like Lady."

Melissa stopped in her tracks, eyeing Darcy with a puzzled expression. "Who calls him Lady? The goat's name is Lester."

In her mind, Darcy could see the twins, their eyes widening as they stared at the goat. "If he's called Lester," she found herself asking, "then who is..."

The girl tilted her head, smiling mischievously as she gestured at the house in front of them. "Why, Lady's our resident ghost."

Chapter Three

A *ghost?* Darcy asked herself, remembering the chill she'd felt right before the accident. The whispered *Help us* in her ear.

No, she thought firmly; she didn't believe in ghosts. She considered the paranormal strictly a Hollywood creation. She'd watched too many movies, that was all, and now her imagination was running away with her common sense. She was too practical to be hearing voices in her head...and certainly too smart to tell strangers about them if she did.

Especially this teenager.

Stiffening her spine, Darcy turned to find that her reluctant hostess no longer stood beside her. Disconcerted, she scanned the porch, but Melissa seemed to have vanished.

She told herself not to be ridiculous, that there had to be a logical explanation. Busy woolgathering, she wouldn't have heard a bomb drop, much less noticed the girl going into the house without her.

Determined to find the phone on her own, she nearly

walked into the screen door as it burst open. Expecting Melissa, she was taken aback by the man standing there, an elderly gentleman right out of a fried-chicken ad, complete with white hair, whiskers and suit. He introduced himself as the boys' great-grandfather and Darcy recognized the gleam of mischief in his clear blue eyes.

"I'm the patriarch," he told her as he extended a hand, "which only means I've managed to live longer than everyone else. So none of this *Mr. Rose* for me. Call me Edgar, or better yet, Gramps. Might I add, my dear, that I find it a distinct delight to welcome such a lovely young woman to our humble home."

His greeting was as warm, welcoming and old-fashioned as the setting. Enough so to have Darcy relaxing her guard.

Perhaps she relaxed too much, for returning his handshake, she felt her arms begin to tremble. Post-traumatic shock, too long delayed, caught up to her with a vengeance. "I need to use the phone," she blurted out, disconcerted by a sudden strong urge to cry. "I must get to Hilton Head," she pressed, horrified to hear how even her voice was shaking. "Right away."

"Now, now, none of that." Making soothing sounds, Gramps took her hands and led her to the porch swing. "You just sit here a minute and let the quiet soothe you. Take some time to absorb what's happened."

Trembling all over, she sat on the swing. "But everyone expects me to be there. They thought I was crazy for driving all this way when I could as easily have flown, and now it looks like they were right. Peter planned to make this such a special weekend for us. He'll be worried that I'm not there." *And angry*, she didn't add aloud. She sensed Edgar Rose would feel as his grandson had, that the main concern was that she hadn't been injured.

Gramps confirmed this suspicion by patting her hand. "There, now, you'll get to everything in time. Fretting about it will earn you nothing but ulcers."

"I can't believe this has happened," she said, more to herself than the elderly gentleman. "I planned this trip for weeks. I wanted it to be perfect. Whatever possessed me to take that detour?"

"No sense blaming yourself for the way life unfolds, my dear. When you've been around as many years as I, you'll find most things tend to happen for a reason."

Unsettling thought. The detour, the crash, winding up here on this porch—was this kindly old man implying it was all preordained?

"I know you were looking forward to your holiday," Gramps went on, "but who's to say it won't still turn out perfect?

He had to be an incurable optimist. Sitting there with her hair hanging in damp strands and her silk suit sticking to her skin, Darcy couldn't see how anyone could consider being stranded in such oppressive heat as perfect. Unless, of course, they meant perfect *hell*.

"Know what I think?" Patting her hand once more, Gramps moved away, toward the door. "You need something cool to revive you. I'll go fetch you a pop, or better yet, a glass of that iced lemonade we serve the guests."

Sipping lemonade on the porch swing was a leisurely activity others enjoyed, something done in movies, or dreams. Then again, everything about this day held a surreal edge. "I'd love some lemonade," she said, rising to her feet. "But I can get it. There's no need to wait on me."

He shook his head firmly. "Just as there's a time to be strong, there's a time when it's better to ease off and let others take over. You rest now and let us spoil you. Why, you've had quite a scare, what with our Lady calling to you that way."

Whatever color Darcy might have regained swiftly left her cheeks. "How do you know about that?"

"Inevitable, a pretty thing like you." Grinning, leaving that bombshell behind him, he ducked into the house.

Our Lady? He'd spoken casually, as if the ghost were one of them, liable to sit down with the family at the dinner table.

"I want you to know," Darcy said as she trailed after him into the house, "that I don't believe in ghosts. I'm sure your story is entertaining, but that's all it is. Entertainment."

"If you don't sound like my grandson." Gramps chuckled as he crossed the large, nearly empty foyer.

Darcy noticed a great deal of wood, from the polished floorboards to the winding oak stairway dominating the rear wall. Ornate cornices lined the ten-foot ceiling and topped the good half-dozen doorways leading to other parts of the house. In the hot, still air, she detected the faint scent of lemon oil, no doubt the source of all that shine.

A long, narrow table, covered by crisp white linen, had been set between two doorways on the far left wall. Gramps went to it, reaching for a frosted pitcher of lemonade. "Our Mitch is nothing if not stubborn," he said as he poured her a glass. "He insists I concocted the story of Lady to while away a lazy summer night. He'd be singing a different tune, let me tell you, if just once he'd sit up with us and watch for himself."

"Are you saying you've actually seen this ghost?"

His lined face took on a dreamy quality. "When the moon is out and the wind blows just right, you can see her pale form pacing across the upstairs gallery. In her hoop skirt and ringlets, she's quite a sight. Every inch the young Southern belle."

"You're teasing me. You *are* making this up."

He handed her the glass. "You'll just have to see for yourself. I hope you'll make yourself at home, while I, much to my regret, must go see about dinner. The phone's over here in the closet," he told her, gesturing to a closed door by the stairway.

"But I'm not staying long," she felt compelled to explain as he strolled to the back of the house. "I'll be leaving the instant I find transportation to Hilton Head."

His smile was as cryptic as his words. "Oh, you'll be staying," he said over his shoulder as he slipped out of sight. "And longer than you think."

* * *

Mitch cursed softly as he ran toward the Macon place. Just what he needed, his boys letting their overactive imaginations get them—and that ridiculous goat—into mischief. Though thinking of the wrecked car he'd just left, perhaps *mischief* was too tame a description.

The MacTeague woman might be reasonable enough now, but get her up there in the city, with her friends and relatives all screaming *sue*, and she'd soon forget about who was and was not at fault. Frivolous or otherwise, the last thing Mitch needed now was a lawsuit. *Please be lenient, Your Honor*, he could imagine himself pleading if they went to court, *but my boys were being chased by a ghost.*

Didn't he have enough on his plate without a female like Darcy MacTeague being plopped down on the middle of it?

He frowned, remembering how strongly he'd reacted to seeing her sitting there, so lost and alone in that car. At the time, meeting her gaze, he'd been filled with a sense of inevitability, as if he'd been meant to find her, save her. What insanity had come over him that he would go dashing to the rescue like that, sweeping her into his arms like some old-fashioned movie-star idol?

And all so she could make it crystal clear that she didn't need—much less want—his help.

The minute he'd set her down and she started rattling off her demands, he'd certainly come to his senses. After all, he knew the type well. The luxury car, the designer clothing, the insistence upon being called Ms.—he'd been married to the same kind of woman for too many years.

Beth too had seemed soft on the outside, only to prove a veritable barracuda when it came to getting her way. Over the twelve years of their marriage, Mitch had tried giving in to make peace, before coming to the inevitable conclusion that he could never make his wife happy. Beth would always be too busy wanting, and needing, and acquiring more.

Though he supposed he should be glad Beth was so greedy. If she hadn't been in such a hurry to marry her rich new husband, she might not have given Mitch custody of their children.

Mitch grinned reluctantly. Those three would make him old before his time, but he couldn't regret bringing them to South Carolina, where they were free from the everyday dangers of the city. Here, he could raise his kids in safety—the occasional self-absorbed city driver notwithstanding—and he'd happily walk on fire to keep it that way. Even if it meant facing the intimidating Miss Macon to retrieve their blasted goat.

Hurrying down her driveway, though, he couldn't help praying the animal had wandered off elsewhere. A retired schoolteacher, Hester Macon had been the bane of many a student in Seven Corners, and Mitch himself had far too often suffered the lash of her razor-sharp tongue. So much so that even now he dreaded the upcoming confrontation.

He found Hester standing at her gate, arms folded militantly across her chest as if daring the goat to enter her garden, while the animal faced her down with a glare of its own. Seeing them together, Mitch was struck by the resemblance. The scrawny, angular frames, their sharp, irritating voices— they made a formidably ornery pair.

"Mitchell Allen Rose," she began, ever the schoolmarm. Mitch hated the way she strung out his name, an act of intimidation she'd used since he was five. "I thought we'd discussed this matter," she continued, nodding at the goat. "What is that creature doing in my yard?"

He considered relating the boys' version about a ghost letting the goat out of its pen, but responsibility got the best of his sense of humor. "Sorry, Miss Macon," he said, trying his most winning grin as he stepped up to grab the goat's collar. "It's been a hectic day at Rose Arbor."

The grin hadn't worked in the classroom, and it didn't work now. "I know what you're up to, boy, and it won't wash. This year, I am going to win the garden society competition."

As far as Mitch was concerned, she was more than welcome to the trophy, but he was tired of telling her so. "I'll talk to the boys," he said as he corralled Lester. "We'll do our best to make sure the goat doesn't get into your flowers again."

She nodded, then narrowed her gaze on him. "I hear there's been an accident up your way. A woman, Dexter said."

Mitch wanted to ask what Dex Bradley had been doing near his daughter, but his exasperation paled next to the fact that Miss Macon already knew about the incident. The major drawback to small-town life was the speed with which gossip traveled. No doubt the talk would have him married to the MacTeague woman by sunset.

As if to confirm this, Hester added, "Dexter says she's quite attractive. I believe he called her a babe."

Though it rankled, Mitch had to concede that Dex Bradley was right. Ms. MacTeague was an extraordinarily good-looking woman. Her soft brown hair, matching warm eyes, the curves not even the masculine cut of her suit could disguise—Mitch couldn't deny that she'd stirred something in him.

All, of course, before she opened her mouth and proved to be a carbon copy of his ex-wife, Beth.

"I thought Dexter's job was to deliver the newspaper," he said irritably, "not report the news himself."

Miss Macon merely raised an eyebrow.

"You can tell Dex, and thereby a good part of the county, that the woman is now making arrangements to leave." Mitch was determined to put a stop to all speculation. "She's city folk, bound for some resort at Hilton Head. She has no need, and certainly no desire, to be hanging around here."

The eyebrow raised another notch. Belatedly, he realized he was letting his bitterness show, which in itself was enough to fuel gossip.

Miss Macon smiled knowingly. "Pity. Would have been nice, having a new face at Melissa's birthday party."

Against his will, Mitch pictured Darcy's face, brown eyes

glistening, soft pouting lips curved in a smile. He found it unsettling, how enticingly the image beckoned.

"It's time you started courting again, you know," Hester added in her primmest tone. "Those children need a mother."

It wasn't the first time he'd heard that refrain, nor the first time he'd bristled. "As much as I'd love to stay and argue with you, I must take the goat and go. Roy Hackett is assembling his entire clan at Rose Arbor for the weekend."

"So I've heard."

Let her vent her disdain, Mitch thought; Hester wasn't paying the bills at Rose Arbor. Granted, Hackett could be a pain, and a bit of a reprobate, but he was also the wealthiest man in the county. If this reunion went well, it could mean increased business for Rose Arbor, maybe even enough profit to carry them into next season.

A quick glance at his watch warned that he had barely an hour before the Hacketts descended on him. Propelled by a sense of urgency, Mitch made short work of his departure. "Roy won't be at the party," he assured her as he led the goat away. "And don't worry about Lester. As I said, I'll be getting after the boys to make certain he won't bother you again."

He heard her "hmmph" but didn't argue. Bullying the goat home, he took extra care in securing Lester in his pen before hurrying inside to change.

Hacketts were already beginning to arrive. Peeking into the front parlor, Mitch saw with relief that Gramps was at the desk, registering guests and handing out keys. Mitch made a mental note to send Mel to help him as soon as she finished her tour.

On his way to the staircase, he noticed a shapely leg extending from the phone closet. He recognized it at once, having carried the woman from her car, though then the leg had been encased in nylon. The fact that it was now bare did strange things to his insides.

She'd removed her jacket, as well, he realized, her sleeveless top revealing arms as bare—and as shapely—as her lower limbs. He had the sudden urge to ease up behind her, to run his hands up and down those arms, those legs...

As if he'd voiced the fantasy aloud, she turned to face him, her expression startled and wary as she continued to speak into the phone. Realizing that he'd been standing there staring at her too long already, Mitch gave a tight smile and turned to stride up the stairs.

He had fifteen minutes for a quick shower and shave, he told himself as he hurried down the hall to the family wing, and no time to waste on a female who would be gone before dinner.

In the main wing behind him, he heard Hacketts running from room to room. From the clatter and clink of glass, it would seem the group had already begun the cocktail hour. Mitch said a silent prayer that the old ice machine would keeping spitting out cubes at least until dinner.

In his room, he took his gray jacket—his most comfortable jacket—from the closet and laid it on the bed. Reaching for a matching tie, he reminded himself that as much as he hated dressing up, he had too much riding on this weekend to quibble over his attire. Besides, it wouldn't be like one of those stuffy formal affairs Beth constantly dragged him to in Philadelphia. This wasn't social climbing. Mitch had a personal stake in looking his best tonight, in doing whatever it took to make the Hackett reunion a success.

He had to be prepared. Beth might have given up custody of the children, but no one knew better than Mitch how quickly and easily his ex-wife could change her mind. Lately, she'd been calling on a weekly basis, asking for Mel. The fact that his daughter chose not to talk about these conversations, combined with Mel's rapidly fraying temper, left Mitch feeling distinctly uneasy.

Should Beth suddenly decide she wanted her children living with her in Philadelphia, he'd have to be ready to fight her in court. He had to show he provided the more stable environment, both emotionally *and* financially, that his children thrived at Rose Arbor.

Whatever it took, he meant to keep all three with him, even if it meant dressing up every night of his life to greet the guests. Even if it meant...

Those children need a mother.

All these years later, Miss Macon was still putting words in his head.

No, he thought firmly. He'd do just about anything for his kids, but he drew the line at matrimony. One awful marriage should be lesson enough, and besides, Darcy MacTeague was too like his ex-wife for comfort.

So why could he still feel how she'd melted against him as he'd carried her from the car? How, for a split second, staring into her deep, brown eyes, he'd felt strong and whole, as if all was well with the world?

Shaking his head, he reminded himself of how rudely she'd demanded he put her down, how her gaze had made it clear that she thought him a hopeless hick.

Giving a second glance to the gray jacket, he decided in favor of the more stylish blue. Though far less comfortable, it was what Beth called his "power suit." Gramps would say it helped him cut a darned fine figure.

He chose the blue to impress the guests, he insisted to himself as he marched to the shower. It had nothing to do with Darcy MacTeague.

As he'd said all too often, Lord spare him from city-bred women.

Chapter Four

Hours later, Darcy still sat in the oak-lined cubicle in which the Roses had installed their public phone. The dainty chair might be padded, the tiny lacquered table might come with a pad and pen, but without a window, she had to rely on the overhead lamp for light and the exhaust fan for air. The claustrophobia would soon drive her crazy if the heat didn't get to her first.

Of course, she could open the closet door, but the steady flow of arriving guests made it hard to hear. Besides, she had no wish to be overheard. Nor did she want to be seen.

Primly tucking her ankles beneath the chair, she blushed at the memory of being caught by Mitch Rose earlier, her legs sprawled out in the hallway as she argued with the long-distance operator. Darcy couldn't have felt more frustrated and less in control as at that instant when she'd glanced up to meet his electric-blue gaze. Had he seen her moment of weakness? Heaven knew, she'd felt exposed enough under his scrutiny, as if she'd removed far more than her jacket and hose. If Mitch hadn't turned to stamp up the stairs, she might have given in to the temptation to hand him the receiver and ask him to help her find a way home.

Here she was, several hours since the accident, right where she'd started—stuck in the middle of nowhere. Infuriatingly, Jem Marbley and his tow truck had proved Mitch right by taking off for the weekend. To make matters worse, the nearest dealership was closed for the night, the Amtrak station was half a lifetime away and the next bus—this, she was almost grateful for—wouldn't roll through Seven Corners until nine in the morning.

And Peter not only wasn't at the hotel in Hilton Head, he hadn't yet left the office. He was still in a meeting, the secretary at the ad agency had told her, but Mr. Arlington would call the very second he could break away.

Break away from what? Darcy had instantly wondered. This weekend was important to them both, their last chance to go over Tuesday's presentation to the Tavish people, so it must be an emergency, for Peter to put such an important account on the back burner. Yet, when she'd asked what was wrong, the secretary had professed to be as much in the dark as she, promising to have Mr. Arlington call at his earliest possible convenience.

Feeling oddly hurt, and a bit daunted by Peter's inaccessibility, Darcy had next tried contacting friends, despite the fact that no one stayed in New York on a summer holiday. Desperate when she could reach no one, she'd resorted to calling her mother, but of course, Rita had been the first to leave town. Darcy loved the woman dearly, but when had her mother ever been around when she needed her?

With a heavy sigh, Darcy picked up the earring she'd removed to talk on the phone and gazed at its sparkling reflection. Long ago, she'd bought the diamonds to serve as a symbol of her independence, to prove that if she wanted something, she could get it herself.

A lesson she might be wise to heed now. Nothing could be gained by indulging in self-pity. Obviously, no one was about to come to her rescue, so she might better figure out what she meant to do next.

One thing was for certain. She'd accomplish little sitting here in this cubicle, glaring at a phone that refused to ring. Deciding she should refill her glass with lemonade and go outside to think, she left the phone closet.

She found the foyer busier than ever, people going up and down the winding staircase with drinks in hand. Several Tiffany lamps had been lit, bathing the room with a soft, romantic glow, enhanced by the deepening dark outside the windows.

Even though the sun had set, humidity clung to the crowded room tenaciously, undiminished by the constant whir of two overhead fans. Determined to get her drink and go outdoors, Darcy hurried to the long, narrow table.

Next to it, a tall, thin elderly gentleman held court. Eyes as sharp as his expression, he seemed to take in every movement of the room as he pontificated about why a hurricane would never hit their little corner of South Carolina. From his pompous attitude, and the constant, dutiful nods of the men gathered around him, she assumed the man was accustomed to having even the weather obey him. Grateful to be ignored, she fetched her lemonade and took it to the porch.

She felt a ten-degree drop in temperature as she stepped out the door, thanks to a slight, stirring breeze. Sitting back against the swing's cushions, sipping her lemonade, she could feel her jangled nerves unwind. She thought about what Gramps had said, that fretting would earn her nothing but ulcers, and wondered if he was right. There *was* nothing she could do at the moment, so why not sit back and enjoy the evening?

Swinging slowly, she let the songs of distant frogs soothe her. Funny, how different the place seemed now that the sun had set. In the dark, everything seemed less irritating and more magical. With the scent-laden air sighing through the leaves overhead, the Spanish moss swaying in the breeze, she could almost be happy she'd taken that detour. She'd never find such peace and quiet in the city.

Not that she'd know what to do with such tranquillity in her hectic life-style, she insisted defensively. In New York, her nights were as structured and busy as her days, and that was how she liked it.

Hearing a sudden, feminine laugh, she glanced down the driveway. Three people strolled toward the arch of light from the porch lamp, a young couple and a man in a smartly tailored jacket and tie. Darcy's gaze stayed with the man, intrigued by his confident gait and assured gestures. Curious about him, glad to find someone more in line with the men she chose to date, she set down her glass and leaned forward to see him better.

At the same time, he turned to gesture back at the house, and as the light fell squarely on his features, she recognized Mitch Rose.

So much for dismissing him as a hick.

Shaking her head as she watched from her shadowed position on the porch, Darcy couldn't believe her eyes. If Mitch hated dressing up, as Melissa had implied, you'd never guess it now. Wearing the tailor-made clothing as if he'd been born in it, Mitch guided the young couple toward the Mercedes waiting in the driveway, acting so calm, assured and in charge, he would be at home at any boardroom meeting Darcy had ever attended.

She leaned back in the swing, trying to regain her own poise, telling herself she had no reason to resent him for not staying in the niche she'd carved for him. She wasn't attracted to this man, this absolute stranger. She couldn't be. Years ago, she'd vowed she would never be like her mother, falling instantly in and out of love, going from one marriage to another. Darcy needed far more than a pretty face and smooth charm; the man she chose had to have solidity, dependability and a firm grasp on the future.

Yet try as she might to stop it, her gaze kept straying back to Mitch Rose. Physical attributes might mean little to her, yet she couldn't deny that he was nice to look at, that his broad shoulders filled the jacket superbly. She continued to watch as, with athletic grace, he strode forward to open the passenger door, every inch the gracious host.

Image is all, Darcy knew from her advertising background, and as such, this must be a pose, Mitch playing the successful businessman to impress his young guests. As he held the car door open, the young woman slid into the seat, gazing up at Mitch with a dazzling smile. His efforts obviously worked on one of his guests, Darcy thought cynically—the woman, at least, was utterly charmed by him.

The intensity of her reaction bothered her. So Mitch felt a need to exert his considerable charisma on the young blonde, what should that matter to Darcy? True, he'd felt no such need in their own encounter, but she should feel relieved, not annoyed. She had neither the time nor interest in a casual flirtation. The moment Peter called, she'd be on her way.

She couldn't wait to be back in the city where she belonged. She'd been raised in Manhattan, knew the streets and the people, felt at home there. Here in the country, she felt lost in the slow, languid pace. Clearly, she was out of her element, and fast losing control. She should do something about it, get up and start making more calls.

Yet she sat where she was, her gaze drawn to Mitch.

He stood watching the car drive off, hands jammed in his pockets, with a pensive, wistful expression clouding his square-boned features. Staring at him, Darcy thought back to a long-ago night when her mother had driven off in a snit after a fight with her third husband. Wearing the same expression as Mitch did now, Simon Conners had watched Rita's taillights vanish into the night, his shoulders slightly slumped, alone with his loneliness and pain. Then, as now, Darcy had watched helplessly, wishing she knew how to bring back the smile to her stepfather's handsome face.

Not that Mitch Rose needed any comforting. A guy like that had to have a woman somewhere. Someone to stand beside him, make him laugh, warm his bed.

All at once, she remembered him carrying her from the car. What girl wouldn't melt when faced with such gentleness and concern? Too well she could recall how his hands had felt on her, how his eyes had traced every inch of her exposed skin, how she'd burned under his clear blue intensity. Letting herself go, she imagined again being swept into his powerful arms, only this time she'd let him carry her inside, up the winding stairway to some canopied four-poster in a cozy, fire-lit bedroom. With the balmy air stirring the curtains, the perfume from the garden wafting through the air, Mitch would lean down to...

The image dissolved as he turned suddenly for the house.

Darcy panicked as she realized where her thoughts had taken her. She couldn't confront him. She'd never been good at bluffing. One quick glance and he'd see every lurid thought as if they were written on her face.

She wanted to flee, but where could she go without him seeing? And what possible excuse could she offer for suddenly darting up and running for the house?

Ring, she begged the telephone. *Peter, you've got to get me out of here.*

Mitch grimaced as he walked to the porch. Though he'd smiled while giving last-minute directions to the newlywed couple, inside he'd been chafing against the noose his tie had become. Climbing the steps, he slipped his fingers under his collar and scratched his neck—a habit that had always irked Beth no end. He'd tried getting her to laugh about it, claiming he was allergic to dressing up, but sadly enough, his wife had never been known for her sense of humor.

Still scratching, he nearly bumped into the MacTeague woman, popping up from the porch swing in a dash for the door. As he reached out to prevent their collision, she came to an abrupt stop before him, frowning fiercely. He thought of teasing a grin out of her, but she felt so stiff and rigid, he doubted she had it in her to crack a smile.

He dropped his hands with a stab of disappointment. It had

felt nice, holding her arms. If only the softness were more than skin-deep.

"I, uh," she said in a voice so low he had to strain to hear her, "was just going inside. I'm waiting for a phone call."

Expecting to be snapped at, he was caught off guard by her hesitant reply. "No luck in tracking down Jem?" he asked, toning down his own response accordingly.

Apparently he hadn't toned it down enough, for her nose went up in the air. "No, it seems you were right about that. He—along with a good half of South Carolina—seems to have taken the weekend off. Actually, the call I'm waiting for is from New York."

It annoyed him, the way she said "New York," as if the island of Manhattan were the epitome of civilization. "Oh? You planning on going way up there to rent a car?"

"I may yet have to." Her tone was as tight as her grip on the railing.

"The invitation still stands, you know," he felt compelled to offer, ever mindful of his manners. "You can always stay here for the night."

She looked uneasily at the door. "Your grandfather seems to think I have no choice."

"You've met Gramps?" Mitch braced himself, already anticipating her complaints. Even for the locals, some of his grandfather's eccentricities took some getting used to, and he could just imagine this woman's reaction had Gramps tried to entertain her with one of his strange tales.

"He showed me to the telephone," she explained stiffly. "He seemed quite proud of the ghost he claims haunts this place."

It was like listening to Beth again, insisting that Gramps was more than eccentric, that he should be put in a home for his own welfare and safety. "So my grandfather has a few offbeat stories," he said defensively. "I assure you, Ms. MacTeague, the man's is completely harmless."

She tilted her head, as if surprised by his outburst. "I

know," she said, surprising him with a wide, beaming smile. "Actually, I found him quite charming."

Just like that, he forgot his resentment, beguiled by the genuine warmth and generosity he found in her smile. "I'm sorry, I guess I'm a tad sensitive when it comes to the old man. He and my grandmother raised me, so I've gotten used to his ways, but most outsiders find them, well, not all are as gracious as you."

Her expression turned sheepish. "I told him right away that I don't believe in ghosts. He tells me you don't, either."

Mitch shrugged. "If you ask me, I think this Lady thing is just an excuse he and the twins use to explain away their mischief. It's a tad too convenient that Lady is always around when they get into trouble."

She grinned, then sobered as she nodded at the house. "He told me he's seen her himself, pacing across the upstairs gallery."

Even her profile is perfect, Mitch thought, slightly bemused, finding it hard to resist the urge to trace her perfect cheekbones, to run a finger along the line of her delicate chin.

"He made me wonder..." She pulled her gaze from the house, fixing him with a solemn expression. "He said something about me staying here longer than I might think."

"Trust me," Mitch said with a chuckle. "Stay around long enough and Gramps will regale you with any number of his fanciful theories."

She visibly stiffened. "I didn't mean to imply that I believed him. Nothing could be further from the truth, of course."

"Of course," Mitch agreed, though he felt a pang of regret. Talking about Gramps, Darcy had seemed soft and warm and friendly, an antidote to his recent loneliness. He hated to see the prickly businesswoman return.

"I'm waiting to hear from my friend," she added primly, raising her chin a notch. "As soon as he arrives, I'll be on my way."

To Hilton Head, Mitch remembered. He could probably

pick out the resort, too, something straight out of "Lifestyles of the Rich and Famous." A woman who wore a silk designer suit in this heat obviously didn't expect to brave the elements.

"And if he doesn't call?" he asked, feeling a perverse need to test her. "What will you do then?"

"Peter will be here," she said, raising her chin even higher. "He's been looking forward to this weekend as much as I."

Hearing the bravado behind her words, Mitch wondered if it was all facade, this woman-of-the-world air, less a case of assuring him she could depend on this boyfriend, and more one of convincing herself. Despite the stiff pose, she seemed suddenly a fragile thing, vulnerable and easy to hurt.

For her sake, Mitch hoped the man would live up to her expectations, yet the more he gazed at her, the more he found himself hoping this Peter would fail. It might prove interesting if she should be forced to stay. No use denying he was attracted to her, that he wanted nothing more right now than to lean down and cover those rosy lips with his own.

"Monday will be our six-month anniversary," she went on. "Of dating." Her gaze skittered to the door. "I have to get to Hilton Head. I can't stay here tonight."

Mitch stared at her mouth as she spoke, fighting the urge to just kiss her, anyway. Was this talk of the boyfriend and Hilton Head an attempt to discourage him, or did he actually see an invitation in the melting brown of her big doe eyes?

"Isn't that the phone?" she said with an odd catch in her voice.

Belatedly, Mitch heard the jingle. He must have missed it, caught up in watching the building cadence of her breathing.

But then, she didn't seem in any real hurry to go inside.

"I really should see if it's Peter."

Peter, Mitch thought, disliking a man he'd never met.

She gazed up at him in confusion. Noticing that he blocked her way, he realized he should step to the side, but a stubborn, more selfish part of him wanted to stay where he was—to keep her where she was—and see what happened. Too bad he'd been raised to act like a gentleman.

It might go against the grain to keep a woman against her will, but he was not all that swift or gracious in moving away. Taking his time, he had the dubious pleasure of feeling her arm brush his own as she slipped past him to the door. Pleasure, since her arm felt every bit as warm and smooth as he'd remembered—dubious, since the touch was far too brief.

Still, she glanced up at the contact, and in the split second their gazes locked, Mitch saw an answering jolt of attraction. Her eyes pulled him in, drank him in, searching his. It took all his good sense and willpower not to ask her to stay.

He was glad that he'd resisted, when with a quick, muttered, ''Excuse me,'' she fled through the door.

Staring after her, Mitch shook his head, feeling as if he'd just stepped off a roller coaster. In the brief few minutes they'd spoken, he'd run the gamut of emotions, from resentment to a strange sense of protectiveness, all coated with a healthy layer of lust.

Something had sparked between them—he could still feel it coursing through his veins—but while he'd been eager to pursue it, she'd thought only of escape. Back to the boyfriend and her busy life in New York.

For which he should be grateful. After all, she'd spared him from making a fool of himself. He'd gone a little crazy for a minute, the heat and the pressures of the upcoming weekend clouding his better judgment, but his mind was cool and lucid now. They had nothing in common. Raging hormones were all that drew them together. If he had any sense, he'd go now and deal with the ever-growing list of chores, and forget Ms. Darcy MacTeague ever dropped into his life.

Mitch was a practical guy, and eminently sensible, yet with a low, muttered oath, he nonetheless followed her into the house.

Chapter Five

Darcy took the phone from Gramps with trembling hands. She wanted to blame her reaction on the excitement of hearing from Peter at last, but her shaking had started long before the phone began to ring.

Inhaling deeply as she stepped inside the phone closet, she told herself to forget about Mitch Rose and concentrate on making arrangements to get away.

It was hard to hear, since every member of the Hackett-family reunion seemed to have congregated in the foyer, but even after closing the closet door behind her, she needed several repetitions to understand that Peter wouldn't be leaving the office for some time. "We found some kinks in the Tavish deal," he explained tersely.

"Kinks?" Darcy asked sharply, her vague fears crystallizing.

"Nothing major," Peter said, switching to his calm, negotiating tone. "Just some details we need to iron out before presenting it."

"I'll catch the next flight to New York." In her mind, she was already trying to figure out how far it was to the airport, if she had enough cash on her for a taxi.

"Darce, whoa. It's not necessary. I've got everything under control, babe."

"You know how important this deal is to me, Peter." He should, having worked with her on it for the past month. She'd put everything into this project, knowing it was her big chance to showcase her talent, to earn that long-overdue promotion. And she needed the commission they'd earn to bankroll her condo overlooking Central Park.

"It's important to us both," he corrected smoothly. "But really, what can you accomplish by racing up here at this time of night? Besides, what about your Lexus? Surely you don't mean to leave a major investment like that stranded on the side of some road?"

"No, but—"

"You'll need to deal with tow trucks and insurance adjusters. You can't leave it to someone else."

He was right. She couldn't trust others to take care of her beautiful new car. Oddly enough, though, she found herself wishing Peter would volunteer to fly down and help her.

But his mind was clearly on business. "Listen," he went on, "I can't talk now, not if I want to fly down there and meet you tomorrow. Ring me in the morning and I'll let you know what time to expect me."

"What exactly is wrong with the Tavish account?" she asked, freshly worried by his air of distraction.

"Stop worrying about nothing," he assured her again. "You take care of things on your end, I'll mop up matters here, and we can compare notes over drinks at the hotel."

"But—"

"Listen, they're calling for me, babe. Gotta run. Talk to you in the morning."

Darcy stared at the dead phone, then slowly lowered it to its cradle, fighting the sense of disappointment. She'd taken great care that she and Peter would never owe each other more than mutual respect, so why did she feel as if he'd somehow let her down?

She stood, telling herself not to be silly. After all, Peter's attraction was that she could count on him to take care of his business and leave her to deal with her own. It was an ideal relationship, a merger unhampered by unreliable emotions like jealousy or love.

If he knew, Peter would be stunned by her reaction. He certainly wouldn't expect her to feel hurt that he'd chosen an important business deal over an unexpected—and temporary—weakness on her part. He'd be the first to remind her that he'd advised against driving to South Carolina in the first place.

Besides, as he would quickly point out, getting ahead meant making sacrifices, putting personal needs and desires last. It was how things were done in the corporate world.

Yet, it was one thing to set rules in New York, and quite another to be stranded in South Carolina, where everyone seemed to be making up rules as they went along. Stepping out of the closet, looking around her, Darcy felt she couldn't be any farther away from her normal environment had a tornado picked her up and dropped her in Oz.

Guests milled around the foyer, spilling out of the parlor next to it, but like the elegant winding staircase before her, no one seemed in any particular hurry to get where they were going. Though they all held drinks in their hands, she could tell this was not the typical New York City cocktail party. She saw no frantic eye movement to see who might be coming in the door next, no subtle jockeying for position. Everyone seemed content with whom they were talking, as if the conversation itself was what mattered and not what they could get out of it.

A nice concept, until she overheard the topics of discussion—everything from bowling averages to the merits of homegrown manure versus man-made fertilizer. It looked to be a long evening.

For like it or not, she seemed to be stuck at Rose Arbor.

And as long as she was, the sensible thing to do, however reluctantly, would be to arrange a room for the night.

Slipping into the parlor, she noticed the long mahogany table set up in the far corner, an ornate French piece painstakingly refinished. A wooden plaque set on its surface euphemistically referred to it as the "front desk."

Behind the table, hoop skirt billowing around her, sat a surprisingly pretty Melissa Rose. An elaborate concoction of ribbons and sausage curls had been plopped on the desktop in front of her, no doubt the much-maligned wig. The pale blue of the multitiered antebellum gown suited the girl, the flounces of lace softened her pose of bored dissatisfaction.

Noticing the boy chatting with her, a good-looking youth with an impish grin, Darcy understood Melissa's sudden vivacity. She'd probably smile more, Darcy thought, if she knew what it did for her looks.

The tall, gray-haired gentleman who had earlier been asserting the unlikelihood of a hurricane marched across the room to the desk. Clearly displeased, he nudged the boy aside and began addressing Melissa. Darcy could only hear snatches of the man's tirade, something about an ice machine that wasn't making ice, but she could see all too plainly the strain on the girl's face as Melissa struggled not to snap back. Darcy stepped forward with some vague notion of offering help.

"Tell me, girl, what y'all mean to do about it," she heard the man demand as he stabbed a foul-smelling cigar in Melissa's direction.

The girl merely shrugged and popped another bubble, but the smile had long since faded. "What *can* I do?" she asked sweetly enough, but Darcy saw the betraying glint in her eyes. "I imagine we'd still have plenty of ice, Mr. Hackett, if y'all didn't drink so much."

Apparently, the teenager had yet to hear the adage that the customer is always right.

"I'm paying good money to stay in this house, Miss Rose," the man continued. "Either you folks fix that machine

or I'll be taking my business elsewhere. As for you, Harley
Hackett,'' he snarled, turning to the boy who had been flirting
with Melissa, ''I expect you to be dressed and ready to go
out to dinner in five minutes flat, or I'll be taking it up with
your parents.''

Both the old man and the boy stamped off—Mr. Hackett
toward the front door, Harley to the winding staircase—leaving Darcy next in line to face the still-fuming Melissa. Not
surprisingly, Darcy received no smile when she stepped up to
request a room for the night.

''I thought you were leaving,'' Melissa said curtly. ''With
your boyfriend.''

''He's been delayed.'' Darcy saw no reason to volunteer
more. ''Now, about that room?''

''Sorry, can't help you.'' Lifting a magazine, Melissa began to scan it with her usual air of boredom.

''Excuse me?'' Unable to believe the girl could be so rude,
Darcy felt her control slip. ''Perhaps you didn't hear me. I'm
asking for a place to sleep, the same room your father offered.
In light of my recent accident, I doubt he'd want you to turn
me away unhappy.''

Melissa continued reading, but her fingers gripped the magazine tighter. Clearly, she'd understood the implied threat.
''It's not a matter of wanting,'' she said, even her tone tightening, ''it's just the way it is.''

''Is it now?'' Darcy heard the bite in her tone, saw the
heads turning in their direction, but all she could think of was
that this surly, stubborn teenager meant to deny her a room
she hadn't wanted in the first place.

''You needn't be afraid you'll be doing me a favor,'' she
said, her own words clipped and controlled. ''I had plans for
this night, none of which involved staying in a ghost-infested
inn miles from nowhere. I could be soaking in a Jacuzzi,
drinking champagne—'' She broke off, appalled by how she
was letting her emotions get the best of her. ''Why not keep
this on a what's-best-for-business basis? If you'll hand me

my key, I'll run off to my room, and I promise, you won't have to see me again.''

Melissa stared at Darcy's outstretched hand. ''Sorry, can't do that.''

''Can't? Or won't? Maybe I should take this up with your father.''

An idle threat, since the last thing Darcy wished was to confront Mitch, but the ever-contrary Melissa took up the challenge. Rising to her feet, blue eyes glittering, she faced Darcy squarely. ''Go right ahead and talk to him. He'll only tell you the same. Won't you, Daddy?''

With dismay, Darcy turned to meet the penetrating blue gaze of Mitch Rose.

Mitch had been watching the war of wills while dealing with the disgruntled Roy Hackett. Roy could try the patience of a saint with his endless demands, especially when he waved around that awful cigar. Still, he was a paying guest, and Melissa should be watching her manners.

Soothing the man's pride by promising to fix the ice machine at once, Mitch had been relieved to hear that Roy meant to take the entire clan to the Sunnybrook Inn for dinner. It should give him several hours to work on the ice problem, and a few moments to talk with his daughter.

As her father, he had to enforce the rules, however much he might be tempted to let this one slide. He knew Mel was stewing over the fact that her mother wouldn't make it here for her birthday, and like any teenager, was liable to take out her hurt on whoever stood nearest.

And right now, Darcy seemed to be smack-dab in Mel's line of fire.

Approaching the desk, he watched the two exchange heated words. The speed with which Mel smacked her gum should have warned Darcy to run for cover, yet the woman wagged her finger as if she was more than capable of holding her own.

He reached the desk in time to hear Darcy's regrets about

the Jacuzzi and champagne. Part of him resented the implied comparison to Rose Arbor, but he remembered her earlier bravado. So Prince Charming Peter hadn't come through in the clutch.

Mel saw him first, clearly looking to Mitch to take her side, but he had an equally strong urge to go charging to Darcy's rescue. "Watch your manners," he admonished his daughter, and then, in an effort to be fair, added with a smile, "Tell me, what am I supposed to tell Ms. MacTeague?"

"That we can't help her, is all. Really, Daddy, it's not our fault if her boyfriend dumped her," Mel added, as if determined to make matters worse.

"He did not..." Darcy tightened her lips, inhaling deeply as she turned to him. "Peter has been detained at the office and I find myself in a bit of a fix."

She smiled, one of those you-can't-fluster-me looks so prevalent in the female business world, but behind the pose, Mitch could see a trace of panic. She obviously didn't want his help, but he offered it all the same. "There's an easy remedy for that," he told her. "You can stay here with us at Rose Arbor. Mel, find Ms. MacTeague a room."

Mel got that look in her eye. "I can't."

"Young lady—"

"But Daddy, isn't anyone listening to me?" As if sensing she'd gone too far, Mel's tone went defensive. "I've been trying to say that we can't give her a room because we don't have any. I just gave the last one to those people from Baltimore. They liked my tour so much, they decided they just had to stay here."

Sold-out? Mitch couldn't stop the smile. Nor could he think of a better way to end the summer season.

"I don't see what's so amusing, Mr. Rose. I've had a long trying day, and now..." Hard not to notice the crack in Darcy's composure; it quivered in her voice. "Now," she tried again, "I find myself with nowhere to sleep."

"I offered you a room and you'll have one." With a full house, Mitch could afford to be generous. "Mel, go on out to the cottage and make sure it has clean sheets and fresh flowers.''

"Daddy!'' Mel looked positively horrified. "You can't let her stay in Grandma Rose's cottage. What if Mom—'' She stopped, her voice breaking with emotion.

Mitch sighed. Poor kid, she knew her mother was in Europe and not likely to appear anytime soon, but being Melissa, she probably already had roses waiting in the living room as a welcoming gesture, hoping against hope Beth hadn't forgotten her birthday again.

"You said the cottage was only for family,'' Mel persisted, the telltale moisture gathering in her eyes.

Mitch ached for the kid, but she had to get used to the fact that her mother wouldn't ever return to Rose Arbor. "For tonight,'' he said gently, "let's just consider Ms. MacTeague part of the family.''

"I can't believe you. I can't believe any of this.''

"That will be enough. Our motto here at Rose Arbor is hospitality, and I'm not about to allow any of my children to stint on it. I'm giving you five minutes to get out to that cottage and make sure our guest will be comfortable, and then I'll start taking away privileges with every minute you delay. Now, get moving.''

Glancing angrily from Mitch to their guest, making it clear that she thought her father had lost his mind, Mel marched off in a huff, her hoop skirt swinging dangerously as she brushed past the Hacketts.

Their number had dwindled, Mitch noticed, most of the clan no doubt already heading for the Sunnybrook. Seeing the half-empty glasses strewn about the lobby, he knew he'd be all night cleaning up after this bunch. At least he'd have a short reprieve before they wandered back in from their dinner. Stumbled in, probably—as a group, they were fairly heavy drinkers.

"Sorry about that,'' Darcy said awkwardly, staring after Mel with a frown. "I was upset at having no place for the night, I didn't stop to think I might be causing friction between you and your daughter.''

"She's a teenager, Ms. MacTeague. Friction's a way of life around here."

Amazing, how pretty she was when she smiled.

"Still, I don't want to make things more difficult. Isn't there someplace else nearby where I can stay?"

The Sunnybrook Inn could probably put her up for the night, but Mitch didn't volunteer the information. "Don't mind Mel," he said instead. "She's just sore at her mother and taking it out on everyone else. In her hurry to get to Paris, Beth has forgotten she promised to be here for her daughter's sixteenth birthday."

Her gaze, warm with sympathy, went to the retreating Mel. "Poor kid."

"Yeah, but it doesn't give her the right to be nasty to a guest in our home."

"Don't be so hard on her." Darcy turned back, her features earnest. "That man wasn't trying to be very nice, either. If Melissa hadn't spoken out, I'd have been tempted to cut him down to size, myself."

Though Roy Hackett might be a tough nut to crack, Mitch wouldn't give much for his chances if these two females ganged up on him. "I wasn't just talking about Hackett," he told her. "I meant, she has no right to be rude to you, either."

"But I'm not a guest here. I mean, I can't be. I can't stay here now. Not in your wife's room."

"My ex-wife. We're divorced."

Watching her stiffen, he wondered what he'd said now to upset her. "She has to accept that her mother won't be coming," he said more harshly than he'd intended. "Mel's no fun to be around when she's in one of her moods," he said, softening his tone. "No matter how we try, everything the boys and I say is wrong. Gramps claims it's a female thing."

"Can you blame her? She must feel the odds are stacked against her with four guys in the house."

"You could better those odds by staying."

Her face remained solemn but a tiny twinkle lit her eyes. "Since you put it like that, I suppose it would be cruel to refuse."

"Not to mention dangerous. There's no guarantee Lester won't escape again. Really, Ms. MacTeague, I couldn't live with my conscience if I let you venture out on that road tonight with a goat possibly on the prowl."

"Clever, Mr. Rose. Shift the burden of guilt to my shoulders. Unfortunately, I'll have to go out there, anyway. I left all my things in my car. My bags, my traveler's checks—"

"You won't need traveler's checks. Your stay here is on the house." He held up a hand when she tried to protest. "I mean it. The least we can do, Ms. MacTeague, is offer a meal and a bed for the night."

"Well, then, if I'm to be part of the family for the evening, shouldn't you start calling me Darcy?"

"If you'll call me Mitch." He held out his hand in greeting.

She stared at his hand as if it would bite her, before tentatively offering her own.

Given her background and general attitude, it should have been a firm, businesslike grasp, but once again, her hand slid warmly into his, settling in as if it belonged there.

She broke contact first, pulling her hand firmly back to her side and taking the warmth with her. "I, er, really should be getting my things."

Mitch couldn't deny that the woman did something to him, but it was hard to tell if the tingling he felt was excitement, or merely some innate alarm system going off in his head. "Give me your keys," he said gruffly to cover his confusion, "and I'll go get your bags."

"I couldn't—"

"You can. Listen, no offense, but you look beat. Why not stay here in the parlor and fix yourself a drink?" He gestured to the makeshift bar laid out for the Hacketts. "Put up your feet and relax. Someone will come fetch you when it's time for dinner."

"But my room. Where will I sleep?"

How about with me? he nearly offered before catching himself in time. What was it about this woman that had him acting like a randy teenager? He was nearing forty, for crying out loud, and getting too old to be horny.

"At the moment, I have to fix the ice machine," he told her instead as he strode to the door. "But as soon as the cottage is ready, I'll show you there myself."

It wasn't until he was out the door and marching to her car that he realized what he'd volunteered to do. The way to the cottage was through the rose garden, a scent-filled, moonlit Eden for seduction.

He hadn't the time, he told himself. He had chores to finish, an inn to run, children who needed his attention. Only a fool would complicate his life further. A sensible man would let someone else show her the way.

He'd tell Gramps to escort her. Gramps, with his Southern charm and wealth of stories could undoubtedly do the job better, anyway.

Mitch, after all, had a date with an ice machine and he meant to keep it. It might prove less pleasurable than taking that stroll with Darcy, but all things considered, it was far, far safer.

Chapter Six

Divorced, Darcy thought as she paced across the now-empty parlor. She should have guessed the man had a failed marriage. She might have, had she been thinking clearly, but she seemed to have abandoned all rational thought since leaving the highway.

She wondered about his wife, and why they'd split up. Listening to Mitch, she'd sensed it hadn't been a pleasant break, but then, what divorce wasn't ugly? From watching her mother separate from five of six husbands, Darcy had learned what could happen when wedded bliss turned sour. Those long-term effects, in fact, were what kept her so wary of marriage. She'd have to be a real nutcase to consider a divorced father of three.

Not that she was seriously considering anyone, of course. She had more important things to do with her life than to get sidetracked by a devastating smile and all that warm, Southern charm.

Taking a seat on the rose satin settee, she gazed at her hand, wondering why it had so betrayed her in Mitch's grasp. By now, she should know herself, predict how she'd react in any given situation, yet ever since she'd met that man, Darcy had behaved as if the world had spun off its axis. She let Mitch confuse her, set her off balance.

It had to stop. She had to retain control of her life. She had to set it back on a comfortable, familiar footing.

As if tailor-made to distract her, a stage whisper sounded outside the parlor door.

"She's not in there."

"She is too. C'mon, I'll show you."

Darcy rose to her feet, bracing herself as Ky and J. J. Rose raced into the room with an air of reckless abandon that she suspected was habitual. At first, she thought she might be the "she" they'd referred to, but they paid no attention to her as they poked behind the damask drapes and peered under the stuffed chairs and mahogany tables.

"I might be able to help," she offered, turning to follow their movements, "if I knew what you were looking for."

"Lady," they said in unison, looking at her as if she were a tad dim.

"Lady?" she repeated, feeling dim. "Oh, do you mean the ghost?"

The twins nodded eagerly, coming over to stand before her, looking like a pair of lost cherubs with their blond hair combed back and their eager faces freshly scrubbed. She noticed the initials sewn on their sparkling white shirts and remarked on them.

Both made a face, explaining that their dad said to get dressed up nice for dinner and all they had clean were last year's school-uniform shirts. The boys expressed only disdain for their "third-grade-baby" clothes, but Darcy was grateful for the initials, since they helped her tell the twins apart.

Though the more the pair talked, the more she saw subtle differences between them. Ky wore the more somber expression, to go with his serious outlook. "Gramps said Lady came this way," he told Darcy. "Have you seen her go by?"

"No." Darcy glanced nervously behind her. They spoke as if at any time, their phantom would just stroll down the hall.

"That's okay," Ky added gently. "Don't feel bad. Most grown-ups we know can't see her, either."

"Not even Dad," J.J. added, showing dimples with what seemed to be his perpetual grin. "Though we don't think he's really trying."

Darcy might not believe in ghosts, but she nonetheless found herself scanning the room. "Is Lady here now?"

Both boys did another quick search, then glanced at each other. "Nope," Ky answered for both of them. "She's gone now."

Both he and J.J. deflated before her eyes. Fearing she might have played a part in discouraging them, wanting to see their endearing enthusiasm return, she decided to stop acting like the logical, reasoning adult and play along. "How can you know?" she asked them, keeping her own voice low and conspiratorial as her gaze darted around the room. "I mean, does Lady leave some sort of vapor trail or something?"

The pair giggled contagiously.

"Lady doesn't do any of that ghost stuff like in the movies," J.J. told her. "She's just...I don't know...just here. Part of Rose Arbor."

Ky gazed at her with his father's intense blue eyes. "She's looking to find her lost love."

Up until now, this ghost business had sounded like a boyish game, even a prank, but somehow, she couldn't picture this pair dreaming up such romantic trappings as lost love. "How do you know what she's looking for? Did your grandfather tell you?"

They looked at each other, then shook their heads in unison. "It wasn't Gramps," Ky answered solemnly. "Lady told us."

"Lady talks to you?"

"Not right out, like people do," he explained patiently. "But she doesn't need words to talk to us."

"Yeah," J.J. added. "We can just *feel* what she's trying to say."

Uneasily, Darcy remembered the moment on the road when she'd heard the whispered "Help us."

"She told us she likes having you here." J.J. beamed up at her, all dimples and angelic innocence.

They were making this up. She could see no reason why some lost soul would single *her* out. Darcy MacTeague had to be the last person this household needed.

Nodding at his brother, Ky turned to her with an expression as sober as the proverbial judge. "And we decided that if Lady likes you, well, me and J.J. will, too. We think we should be friends."

It seemed like the good cop, bad cop routine, J.J.'s winsome dimples offset by Ky's youthful sincerity, and she was simply no match for it. "I'd like that," she told them, surprising herself by how much she meant it. "And since we'll be friends, why not call me Darcy?"

Extending her hand, she was further amazed by how at home she felt with this pair. In her busy life, she rarely met children, much less spent time talking with them, yet these two boys had her wondering if she might have missed something.

They shook her hand—Ky first, with great ceremony, then J.J. more exuberantly.

"I'm honored that you'd tell me about Lady," she added, knowing she should be honest with them, "but I'm afraid I find it hard to believe in ghosts. I guess I'd need to see your apparition myself."

"That's what most grown-ups say," Ky said, nodding sagely in an apparent effort to be fair.

J.J. wasn't about to let her off the hook so easily. "How long will you be staying?" he asked eagerly. "You know, Lady has been showing up more and more lately. Maybe, if you're lucky, she'll even show up tonight."

I should be so lucky, Darcy thought, but before she could repeat her intention to leave early in the morning, Melissa popped her head in the door. "C'mon, you two," she snapped at her brothers. "It's time for supper." Noticing Darcy, she frowned. "Oh, yeah, you, too, Miss MacTeague."

"Call me Darcy."

The offer was wasted on Melissa, who had already turned away. Even if the girl seemed determined to be rude, Darcy saw no reason to rise to her bait. Melissa might not be offering the gracious hospitality her father demanded, but it had been an invitation to dinner, of sorts, and considering how hungry Darcy suddenly felt, she was more than happy to accept it.

All the way to the dining room, the boys danced at her heels, yapping out questions, wanting to know everything about her job in the city and the life she led there. When Melissa rounded on them, telling them to stop being so nosy, the twins eyed their sister with an adult air of overtried patience.

"We have to ask," Ky told her.

"Lady needs to know," J.J. added firmly.

"Lady!" In a huff, Melissa marched across the dining room to Gramps, who was placing a platter of spaghetti and meatballs on a table set for six. Darcy, startled to find herself in this intimate family setting instead of the public dining area she'd expected, only half heard the girl's complaining.

"They're doing it again, Gramps," Melissa was whining to her great-grandfather. "They're telling everybody stuff about their stupid ghost."

Preoccupied with laying out napkins, Gramps merely smiled. "That's nice."

"Nice? People are gonna think we're crazy. You've got to stop those boys before they ruin any chance I still have of finding a boyfriend."

Darcy could empathize. Sixteen was such a difficult age. Everything seemed to threaten your social life.

"Just leave your brothers be, honey," Gramps told Melissa, still distracted by the table arrangements. "They're not hurting anybody."

"I should have known you'd take their side."

"Actually, Melissa, I don't think you need to worry," Darcy offered. "I doubt they've mentioned Lady to anyone but me, and I'm certainly not going to say anything."

Melissa flashed her a look that said, *Who asked you?* before turning again to Gramps. "I can't wait until Mom comes to get me. I'm so tired of being the only female in this stupid house."

"There's always Lady," Ky said brightly.

"And Darcy."

Seeing the girl's scowl, Darcy hastily changed the subject. "Mmm, dinner smells wonderful."

"Come, sit down, all of you." Beaming ear to ear, Gramps gestured around the table.

"What about Daddy?" Melissa asked belligerently. "Shouldn't we wait for him?"

"He's out back wrestling with that ice machine. Since there's no telling when he'll win that fight, he said to start without him. C'mon, sit down and eat. With dinner so late tonight, you've got to be starving."

The boys needed no further encouraging, scrambling into their seats as Gramps took his own. Melissa pursed her lips, apparently realizing she was again outnumbered.

"Shall we?" Darcy suggested to Melissa, gesturing at the table. But if she'd hoped the girl would appreciate the gesture of camaraderie, she was doomed to disappointment. Melissa's sour expression implied that she'd rather join ranks with a snake.

Mitch was right, Darcy decided. With this teenager, friction *must* be a way of life.

Reluctant to make further attempts at conversation, Darcy settled into the business of filling her plate and eating the delicious dinner Gramps had prepared. It surprised her how much she enjoyed the simple, home-cooked fare he offered. Since dating Peter, most dinners had been spent in whatever restaurant was currently "in" for Manhattan's elite, the meal meant more for being seen and making an impression than for nutrition or pleasure.

Peter would be appalled by all the salt and fat in this particular dinner, she thought. She bet he'd be counting the cholesterol in each bite she put in her mouth.

Live dangerously, the devil inside her prompted. *Snatch another meatball and live on the edge.*

"You needn't laugh at me, Miss MacTeague," Melissa said suddenly from across the table. "It's not really funny."

Busy filling her plate, Darcy had lost track of the conversation. "I'm sorry, Melissa," she said, reaching over to stab *two* juicy meatballs. "I wasn't paying attention. What's not funny?"

"This ghost stuff. I don't think it's the least bit humorous that I can't see Lady. And I certainly can't see any reason to stay up half the night waiting for her to appear. I swear, sometimes I wonder if I'm the only normal one in this house. Except maybe for Daddy."

It was on the tip of Darcy's tongue to deny that she'd been laughing at anyone, unless maybe herself, but something in the girl's smug attitude tweaked another devil inside her. "I heard her myself, you know," Darcy said, flashing an enigmatic smile. "Out on the road, just before my accident."

It was a stupid thing to say, and she regretted the words the instant they left her mouth, but never more so than when she glanced up and found Mitch Rose standing in the doorway.

Mitch had the strangest feeling as he paused by the door, as if somehow his world had altered in his absence, shifted focus. The dining room was the same, as was the table, but chatting easily, as if she had always sat there, was the disturbing Darcy MacTeague.

She was still in that sleeveless top, the scoop neck revealing far more than she knew, or probably wanted, as she reached out to fill her plate. At the sight of her generous cleavage, as well as the creamy bare flesh of her arms, he felt a rush of the now-familiar desire speed through his veins. He had the sudden insane urge to go charging across the room, crush her against his chest and kiss her until he'd gotten his fill.

As if to spare him from such insanity, Darcy turned suddenly to Mel, and began talking about the boys' ghost as if she and Lady were the best of friends.

She looked up at him then, linking gazes. In her deep brown eyes he saw surprise, then wariness, and the inevitable defiance.

"I take it we're discussing Lady," he said smoothly, striding over to the table, taking the seat opposite Darcy. "Let me guess. Are we planning another ghost-hunting excursion?"

"Monday will be the full moon." Gramps, the old imp, was trying hard not to smile.

Mitch sat, handing his plate to Mel. "Yeah, well, keep in mind that the weather bureau is tracking a hurricane, possibly heading up the coast. Monday could be a long, wet night." Taking the filled plate from his daughter, he began to eat.

"I didn't think ghosts cared about the phases of the moon," Darcy said, staring at him in a way that left him suspecting she was merely pretending to consider this seriously. "I would think we'd be able to spot Lady any night of the week."

An argument ensued, Mel battling her brothers about the existence of their resident spirit, while Gramps tried to hide his amusement. Mitch couldn't take his eyes off Darcy, fascinated, in spite of himself, by how at home she seemed at his dinner table. Living in New York, she was probably accustomed to dining on elegant international cuisine, yet she relished his grandfather's home cooking as if it were lobster and caviar.

Her occasional comments about Lady likewise caught him off guard. She wasn't the type to accept the subject of paranormal activity so casually. He'd have expected her to sneer with cool disdain, to side with Mel rather than the boys and his eccentric grandfather. Granted, Mel seemed determined to challenge their guest, but instead of taking the bait by snapping back, Darcy asked calm, intelligent questions about the ghost.

How like a female to be so unpredictable.

Watching her interact with his family, he was struck by how long it had been since they'd had a woman sit at their table. Mitch found he'd missed that gentle touch. As too, he supposed, had his children. The boys certainly responded to Darcy's delicate proddings, and even Mel began to tone down her aggressiveness. And more surprisingly, Darcy Mac-Teague, big-city businesswoman, seemed to be enjoying herself immensely.

He liked this new side to her. He found himself wondering how she'd look in casual clothes—jeans and a tank top, maybe, her hair loose and blowing around her face. Taking it a step further, he thought about how she'd look removing those jeans and shirt...

"Isn't that right, Daddy?"

All eyes turned to him expectantly. With a start, he realized he didn't know what Mel had asked or why everyone else was smiling.

"Let your dad eat," Darcy said quickly. "He's got enough on his mind with Mr. Hackett and the ice machine without worrying about some ghost roaming the halls."

She flashed him a look that said she knew he'd been woolgathering. Considering what wool he'd gathered, Mitch hoped she hadn't seen too far into his thoughts.

A good time, he decided, to switch subjects. "At the moment, my main concern is this possible storm. Chances are, it will veer out to sea, but just in case, we have to be ready. Come Monday, the minute the Hacketts leave, I'm going to need you all outside working. The summer lawn furniture has to be stored, the shutters nailed down—all those chores that would normally wait for winter."

The kids joined in a chorus of groans, but Darcy gave a poorly disguised yawn. Glancing at her watch, she acted as if their problems didn't concern her.

Which, of course, they didn't. For a moment there, Darcy

had seemed so much a part of the group that it came as a jolt to remember that she'd be leaving in the morning.

Yawning again, she rose to her feet. "Dinner was delicious, and I enjoyed the conversation, but if you'll excuse me, I'm really tired. After a day like today, all I can think about is a bed." She smiled at each of them, saving Mitch for last. "If someone could point me in the right direction..."

Taking his last bite, Mitch stood.

"No, please, finish your meal," she said with a strained smile. "Just show me where to find the cottage. I don't need an escort."

No, she probably didn't, which made his actions even more incomprehensible. Suddenly, he knew he wasn't going to let her walk to the cottage alone, or with anyone else, either. "The ice machine is over there, anyway," he offered as an excuse. "If I don't have it spitting out cubes by the time Roy Hackett gets back from dinner, none of us will be sleeping tonight with all the racket he'll be making, ranting and raving."

"I don't want to keep you from your work."

Realizing she must feel uncomfortable about being alone with him, he had a perverse, even stronger urge to escort her. "It's my job to see my guests comfortably settled," he insisted. "You kids help Gramps with the dishes."

He was met with a second round of groaning, Ky and J.J. the most vocal. "Start clearing the table," Mitch said sternly. "Maybe keeping busy can keep you boys out of mischief until I return." He gave a mock bow to Darcy, nodding at the French doors leading out onto the veranda. "Shall we?"

You'd think he'd suggested a night of illicit sex, the way she blushed. Come to think of it, he felt fairly heated himself.

"Lead on," she said as she reached him.

Smiling, Mitch pushed through the French doors. Unwitting or not, that was quite a provocative invitation. Staring at her lovely face, her bare arms and legs, he found himself suddenly wanting very much to take the lead.

The question was, would she follow?

Chapter Seven

Strolling beside Mitch, Darcy felt again that sense of being caught in a dream. She had a hazy sensation of another world—of a whole different life—tugging at her, but it was so hard to remember it with the balmy breeze covering her like a warm cocoon, creating a certain fuzziness when she thought about anything outside this garden. Each breath she inhaled took in the gentle, calming scent of the myriad roses surrounding them.

How quiet it was here—no planes overhead, no honking horns, not a siren anywhere. Only the soft, soothing drawl of Mitch Rose's voice.

"My grandparents insisted upon naming every bush they planted," he was saying beside her. "Everyone in the family has one somewhere in the garden named after them. I, of course, am rather partial to this plant here," he said, stopping on the path before a huge, healthy bush loaded with red roses and branches with long, thick spikes. "It's hard to see its deep scarlet color in the moonlight, but this one's called the Mitchell Allen rose."

Gingerly grabbing a branch, he held up a gorgeous fat bloom for her inspection. The bush was a lot like its namesake, she thought, far too conscious of Mitch's gaze on her. A person could get so distracted by its beauty and charm, they'd forget to look out for the thorns.

She leaned over the bloom, becoming instantly lost in its rich, alluring scent. Reaching out impulsively to stroke the crimson petals, she found the rose to be every bit as soft as she'd imagined. She had the sudden, sensuous urge to run its velvety smoothness along her cheek, along her entire body. "Hmm, heaven," she murmured to herself.

Mitch let go of the rose, snapping the branch. Coming out of her daze, Darcy realized he was still watching her closely.

"Actually, Heaven is the name of *that* bush," Mitch said, looking away as he pointed to the left. "Over there, by the fishpond."

"So many roses," she said, happy to switch the attention from herself. "Can you really identify all of them?"

He shook his head. "I know the Mitchell Allen, and of course, the Melissa, Schuyler and Jonathan roses, but after that, you've got to ask Gramps. Especially if you want their true names, or harder yet, their Latin ones. If you have the time, he'll tell you more about roses and their bloodlines than you probably need to hear."

"Bloodlines?"

He smiled. "Gramps says every bush has its own heritage. Most people run down to the local nursery and select a bush for its color or hardiness, but he'll research a particular line for months before choosing one. Over the years, he and Grandma Rose have collected roses from all over the globe, and in the process, they've taken a lot of teasing over this garden. Folks call it 'Rose's folly.'"

"How unfair. It's so beautiful."

"Here's the path to the cottage." Mitch gestured at a stone-lined trail. "As far as unfair, I don't know. I loved my grandmother, but even I must admit she got obsessive about her garden. Each bush had to have the right trellis, the ideal bench or statue to complement it. When I lived in Philadelphia, I used to send money on a weekly basis for food and house repairs, but instead, it always went to paving a new path or installing another fountain. 'A rose for my Rose,' Gramps would tell me with that disarming grin of his. If it made her happy, he had to indulge her. She was his life.''

She was his life. Gazing up at Mitch's strong profile, seeing his mixture of pride and exasperation, she wondered if his grandfather was truly capable of such devotion. In her experience, no one could love another that unselfishly, that deeply, for so long a time.

"Each year on her birthday," Mitch went on, "he'd make a big presentation of the new bush. The planting ceremony became a family event not to be missed. Grandma Rose's job was to come up with a name. Mine was to pick up the shovel."

"Grunt work?"

He laughed. "As corny as it sounds, I always felt a sense of pride when I planted that bush. As Gramps would say, I was adding something beautiful and enduring to the place. I guess I indulged my grandmother, too, but then, I've always been a sucker for family tradition."

Darcy ignored the spike of envy. Who had time to keep up traditions anymore? Or even time for family? Uncomfortable with where the conversation was heading, she tried to change it. "Don't tell me your grandmother's name was actually Rose Rose?"

He grinned. "Actually, she was born Rosemary Lamont, but she took on the family name and traditions as if she'd been born to them, so people got to calling her Miss Rose."

They came to a stop before a cottage straight out of "Hansel and Gretel," lacking only the gingerbread and gumdrops. Two oaks towered over the roof, and predictably, a pair of rosebushes flanked the small porch. To the left, a light beckoned its welcome from inside the bay window.

Leaning an elbow on the white wooden railing, Mitch stared off at the garden beyond. "Grandma Rose was actually born a Yankee, you know. She expected to live and die in Boston, until Gramps talked her into coming down here to meet his family. The moment she set foot on Rose Arbor soil, she claimed, something magical happened to her. She discovered there was another person hiding inside her, waiting all those years up in Boston to burst free. It took mere moments to liberate that inner being, she once told me, and the instant she did, she knew this was where she'd always belonged. She recognized that Rose Arbor was her home."

Darcy watched his face as he spoke, touched by the story far more than she cared to admit.

"So, overnight, Rosemary Lamont became Miss Rose. She and Gramps moved into this cottage," Mitch added, removing his elbow from the railing to gesture behind him. "And here they stayed until she died a few years ago."

"Happily ever after?" Darcy asked in a small voice.

"Pretty much." Mitch smiled at her. "They had their disagreements, like any other couple, but they had Rose Arbor and they had each other, and for them, it was plenty enough."

"Yeah," was all she could say, warmed by the thought that two people had found so much joy together, yet saddened that, for her, such happiness must be so elusive. Nowadays, it seemed life moved too fast to form lasting relationships. People were always moving on and moving out, and anyone who hoped for more was looking to get hurt.

As if sharing her wistfulness, Mitch sighed, drawing her gaze to the play of light on his angled face. The man was a study of contrasts, and she was fascinated by him in spite of herself. Like his features in the lamplight, he seemed to go from bright to shadowed, one moment humorous, the next sad, even bitter. Which was the real Mitch Rose? she wondered. Mr. Pretty-Boy Looks, or Mr. Rock-Solid Stubborn Determination?

As if hearing her question, he turned to her with a teasing smile, a devastating blend of good looks and cheer that made happy endings seem suddenly possible. "Feel it?" he asked quietly, his gaze focusing on her lips. "On nights like this, with the breeze whispering in the oaks, I get to thinking Grandma Rose was right. That there *is* a certain magic to the place."

His words washed over her like a gentle rain, soft, soothing and so inviting. Lifting her face to his, he made it seem the most natural thing in the world to feel his hand on her arm, easing her closer. Gently, but insistently, he pulled her closer until barely a breath stood between them. Staring at his generous lips, reminded of the rose that bore his name, she knew the same, strong urge to feel the softness of his mouth on her cheeks, her entire body.

And hot on the heels of that jolt of desire he leaned down to kiss her.

Magic, her mind echoed as his lips met hers.

She abandoned all logic in the flood of longing his touch unleashed. Conscious only of a deep, throbbing need, she opened her lips to his exploration, savoring the taste of him, craving more. She melted into him, sliding her hands up through his hair to draw his head closer still. She needed to feel the sheer male strength of this man pressed tight against her, his heat fusing with hers. *I want this,* her brain chanted. *I want him.*

"Maybe we should take this inside," Mitch whispered against her lips, softly, reluctantly drawing away.

Lost in the joy of utter sensation, it took Darcy some moments for the words to register. She stared up at him blankly.

"Inside," he repeated with a slow grin. "You know, privacy."

All at once, the magic evaporated. For a moment, she'd forgotten who and where she was, but reality now hit her like a splash of cold water. She was Darcy MacTeague, a woman of practicality and common sense, and there was nothing sensible about going inside that cottage with a virtual stranger. "No," she said, pushing away from his chest.

"No?"

"No inside. No...this." She gestured between them. "I can't. I don't know what came over me."

"Must be the roses," he said with a half grin, reaching out to pull her back into his arms. "Gramps claims that scent can put the strangest notions in your head."

She wished she could blame the roses, that she could give in to this fierce need to pick up where they'd left off, but far too sensible, she stepped away from him abruptly. "Excuse me, but you're blocking the steps."

"Hey, I didn't mean to upset you," Mitch said, plainly bewildered. "It was just a kiss."

Just a kiss? A few minutes more in his arms, and Lord knew what would have happened. "I'm sorry, but it's late and I've got a lot to do in the morning," she said in her most businesslike tone, hoping to reestablish the distance between them. "Calls to make, people to meet."

"Ah, yes, Peter."

Peter. Unnerving, how completely she'd forgotten him. But then, in her own defense, he had never, in all six months of their dating, ever kissed her like that.

"Yes, well, he'll be here tomorrow," she told Mitch, determined to set her life back on its sane, firm footing. "So, if you don't mind, Mr. Rose, I'd like to turn in."

"By all means, Ms. MacTeague." His voice echoed her forced formality as he bowed low, making a sweeping gesture with his arm. "Let me know, though," he muttered as she brushed past up the steps.

She stopped at the door, curious in spite of herself, only to find him already walking off, strolling down the path with his hands in his pockets.

"Let you know what?" she called after him. Though his back remained to her, she could easily picture his grin.

"Why, when the scent of roses gets the best of you again," he called over his shoulder.

In your dreams, she said to herself.

Refusing to watch him walk off, she entered the cottage, muttering about his conceit. The man might be used to women falling all over themselves to jump into his arms, but Darcy MacTeague would never be one of them. She was not about to allow such romantic foolishness to derail her self-designed life-style. She certainly was not going to base a relationship on some hot-blooded groping that could only burn itself out by morning.

Inside, she flopped into the nearest chair. What in blazes had come over her out there on the steps? Never had she responded so vehemently—so instantly—to a man. Not once in her life had she been so tempted to forget caution and succumb to raw desire. Why, even now...

She stood suddenly, denying she felt anything but self-disgust. If she'd been hot for Mitch Rose, blame the soft, seductive breezes, all this heat and humidity. It was the talk about his grandparents, maybe even the scent of roses—not any sense of homecoming. Magic didn't happen to the Darcy MacTeagues of this world, and she'd never belong in the rural South. She'd learned that lesson long ago in Virginia.

She grabbed for her suitcases, set down by the door on a rug of a dark rose color. Glancing around, she realized the entire room comprised a blend of pink shades, from the light-hued cushions of the sofa, to the darker velvet of the wingback chairs before the brick hearth. All that pink should have made the room seem girlish, but it felt cozy and warm instead.

The bedroom was the same, though yellow was the color of choice. Tiny saffron roses had been sewn onto the coverlet of the four-poster bed, as well as on the curtains fluttering in the windows. Darcy tried not to be charmed, but she was finding it easier and easier to understand why Rosemary Rose took one look at this place and refused to leave.

She tossed her overnight bag on the bed and unzipped it. She reached for her nightgown, embarrassed by the skimpy scrap of silk her mother had talked her into buying—what Rita insisted was *de rigueur* for a romantic weekend. A weekend, in truth, that had been more Rita's idea than her own. The woman was convinced that Peter was perfect for Darcy, that she'd never find a man who suited her better, certainly not one with the looks and money to match.

What Rita didn't understand, though, was that romance would never be part of their relationship. Had they both made it to Hilton Head tonight, she and Peter would have devoted the evening to planning the upcoming Tavish presentation, leaving little room for passion. In truth, Darcy probably had more chance of winding up in bed with Mitch Rose.

Struck by how nearly that had happened, and right here in this four-poster, she turned and marched for the shower.

Letting the cool water stream down her body, she told herself she had to get away from this place as soon as possible. Once more, she found herself wishing Peter would come to spirit her away.

Slipping into the scrap of silk, discovering that she'd neglected to pack a robe, she felt suddenly exposed and vulnerable, in less control of everything. This wasn't her, wishing Peter would come rescue her from...

Climbing into bed, she refused to consider who she might need rescuing from. She told herself she had no need of a man to protect her. Darcy MacTeague was perfectly capable of taking care of herself.

All well and good, but as she drifted into sleep, her dreaming had less to do with independence and self-sufficiency, and more with falling into the arms of a tall, blond charmer.

So vivid were those dreams that when she woke to a sharp rapping at the cottage's front door, she was convinced it had to be Mitch.

In a post-sleep daze just after midnight, she leaped from the bed in a mixture of panic and exhilaration. Just thinking about him made her body tingle and her heart flutter. With trembling hands, she reached for her suit jacket, donning it in lieu of a robe, and hurried to answer the insistent knocking.

Flinging open the door, still in the haze of sleep, it took her some moments to register that it wasn't Mitch waiting on the porch. Instead, she found his two sons, J.J. and Ky, their freckled faces beaming with poorly suppressed excitement.

"Hurry," Ky said, already turning down the steps.

"Come on, come quick," J.J. echoed over his shoulder as he danced in his brother's footsteps. "Gramps says she's up pacing the gallery."

Clutching the jacket close to her chest, struggling to make sense of their words, Darcy shut the door behind her to hurry down the steps after them. "What is going on?" she asked. "Who is on the gallery?"

"You know who," they said in unison. "Lady."

Having retreated to his workshop after leaving Darcy, Mitch sanded the Chippendale tabletop with more energy than it required. His efforts were probably doing more harm than good, but he needed an outlet for his frustration.

Thinking again of Darcy, he felt his groin tighten. Too well, he could remember watching her stroke the soft, red rose he held out to her. He'd thought at the time that she was like the bloom itself, so delicate and soft to the touch, and it had seemed inevitable that she would open up to him. Kissing her, he'd expected her to blossom in his arms like an unfurling flower.

Only here he was, rasping sandpaper against wood, feeling more than ever like a teenager chomping at the bit.

Part of him wanted to rush back to the cottage to finish what they'd started, but the sensible part told him to stay put. If he had to spend the night sanding each piece of furniture in the attic, he'd banish his uncontrolled urges. Was he crazy, lusting after Darcy "I-can't-wait-to-get-back-to-the-city" MacTeague? Or was he just looking for trouble?

Hearing her voice outside the workshop, he thought at first that he was imagining her, all part and parcel of his lurid fantasy. But when he heard her companions, he knew his imagination, even at its most fertile, would never dream up his boys. Setting down the sander, he went outside to find out what J.J. and Ky were still doing up at midnight.

"Did you see it?" J.J. was asking eagerly. "That weird light, was that one of those viper trails you talked about?"

"*Vapor,*" Darcy corrected gently. "I saw something, but it might have been a distant headlight."

"Way out here?" Nobody could snort quite like Ky. "I'm telling you, it was Lady."

That last was uttered as Mitch walked up to them, so the "Lady" came out as a squeak, both boys jumping guiltily when they saw him.

"What are you two doing up at this hour?" he asked, doing his best not to look at Darcy.

Typically, she refused to be ignored. "It's my fault. I asked to see their ghost. They were doing their best to be gracious hosts."

"I see. And did you see her?"

"Of course not." Looking at the twins' wounded faces, she smiled tightly. "That is, I, er, got here too late. Lady had already gone, leaving her vi...vapor trail behind her."

"We were late, too," J.J. piped in. "Only Gramps got to see her."

"And just where is your grandfather now?"

The boys exchanged glances, as if debating the wisdom of telling the truth. "Don't get upset," Ky said, sounding more like the parent, "but he went to the garden to talk to Grandma Rose."

Mitch ran a weary hand through his hair, hoping Gramps wasn't heading for one of his episodes again. "Off you go to bed, you two," he told the boys sternly, not wanting to betray his worry. "Ms. MacTeague, I'm told, is anxious to be turning in, herself."

He made the mistake of looking at her, *really* looking, and seeing what Darcy wore. Or more accurately, what she didn't.

His fingers itched to open the hip-length jacket, to see if her silk nightgown was transparent all over. From memory, he knew how it felt to run his hands up her arms, and it left him aching for more. The long expanse of leg, the swells and curves she kept hidden—what he wouldn't give to explore the rest of her.

Not that she had any intention of letting him. Hands clutching the jacket as if her life depended on it, she appeared stiff and closed, nothing at all like the generously blooming rose he'd imagined earlier.

"I'm sorry, I didn't mean to get you in trouble," he heard her tell the twins as she walked with them toward the house.

"Aw, it's not the first time." Trust J.J. to state the obvious.

"We can always try again tomorrow night," Ky added reassuringly.

Shaking her head, Darcy left the boys at the gate to the garden. "I'm afraid not. Remember, I'll be leaving in the morning."

Mitch headed back to his workshop, the image of her half-clad body burned on his brain. Darcy might be taking off tomorrow, but he had a feeling his lust wouldn't vanish so easily.

Lady had nothing on Ms. Darcy MacTeague, he feared, when it came to haunting his mind.

Gramps sat by the *My Fair Lady* rosebush, leaning close so as not to be overheard. "You were right, my dear," he said softly. "She's the one we need."

Glancing furtively over his shoulder, he made certain his grandson wasn't coming along the path. "But it's up to us to get them together. I fear they're both too stubborn to figure it out for themselves."

A faint breeze stirred the leaves with a slight whisper. Gramps nodded with a wistful smile.

"Yes, you're right again. It *is* time to say good-night," he answered. "I suppose I am tired after such a full, exciting day."

With a heavy sigh, he stood stiffly. "Sleep well, my darling. Rest up, for we'll need all our strength and wits about us tomorrow. I could be wrong, Rose, but I have a feeling the excitement has just begun."

Chapter Eight

Darcy opened her eyes slowly, warmed by a sense of peace and well-being. She stretched languidly, relishing the sensation, until she realized that it wasn't warmth, but rather heat and humidity surrounding her. The yellow roses on the curtains, the big, comfortable four-poster—she was in the cottage at Rose Arbor, and as far removed from her normal routine as she was ever liable to get.

A situation she must remedy at once.

Jumping out of bed, she popped into the bathroom to wash. What she needed was coffee, she thought. That was how she usually started her mornings. Sitting in her breakfast nook with lots of hot black coffee, she would take out her Daily Planner and map out her day.

The Daily Planner sat on the front seat of her car, but she could still list today's agenda in her head. First, and most important, obviously, was to take care of the Lexus. Once it was safely off to the shop, she could investigate the most effective means of transportation, then call Peter, find out the arrival time of his flight and arrange her arrival at Hilton Head accordingly.

Satisfied with her game plan, she pulled out her beige linen slacks and brown silk blouse, another outrageously expensive outfit Rita had talked her into buying, insisting Darcy looked "super" in it. Taking extra care in dabbing on makeup, Darcy told herself she wanted to look her best when she finally saw Peter. It had nothing to do with her last encounter with Mitch.

As she thought of his reaction to her flimsy nightgown, more than just makeup pinkened her cheeks. The way his eyes had widened, then narrowed—well, she doubted he'd be letting her join in any more midnight raids with his impressionable young sons.

Not that she meant to stay around, anyway. Clearly, the sooner she left Rose Arbor, the better.

Yet, crossing the living room, she felt the strangest reluctance to leave the cottage. She found herself stroking the pink velvet chairs, memorizing each little knickknack strewn about the room.

Belatedly realizing what she was doing, she marched to the door. Not only had she no real right or need to feel nostalgic, it wasn't on her agenda. Her primary objective, she must remember, was to get to the telephone.

Reaching the main house, she slipped into the phone closet to call the dealership.

This being her first car, she was unprepared for how much it would cost to tow the Lexus. Hearing her gasp, the woman at the dealership recommended that she try a local tow truck, but of course, Darcy knew from her calls yesterday that Jem Marbley would not be available. Having no choice, she made arrangements to meet the dealership's tow truck at the accident site around eleven.

She wasn't as lucky contacting the insurance adjuster. Leaving another message on his machine, asking him to contact her at this number, she moved on to the next item on her imaginary list—transportation to Hilton Head. The bus rolled by around nine, she learned, but a glance at her watch told

her she'd already missed it. To call car rental or taxi com-
panies, she had to find a phone directory, so she decided to
tackle the last item on her agenda, contacting Peter. No sense
arranging a ride, after all, if she still didn't know what time
to meet him.

A quick call to the office provided the unsettling news that
he was again locked in the conference room with orders not
to be disturbed. He'd left a message that Darcy was not to
fret, that as soon as he'd smoothed over these few remaining
minor details, he'd call to make arrangements to meet her. In
the meantime, she was to sit back, relax and enjoy her vacation.

Hanging up, Darcy had the sudden vivid memory of the
sign, telling her to *Stop and Smell the Roses*.

She felt torn. Part of her still worried about the Tavish deal,
and what might have gone wrong with it, but another part felt
a reprieve. Hadn't Peter told her to trust him to take care of
things? And in truth, there was nothing she could do about
anything, anyway, stranded here at Rose Arbor.

Besides, did she truly want to spend her only vacation
hemmed in this cubicle, running up her calling-card bill? If
she wanted a good rental, a decent taxi, she better ask around.
One thing was certain, she didn't want to spend a second
longer than necessary in this claustrophobic closet.

Swinging open the door, she found the Hackett clan again
assembling in the foyer. From what she could gather as she
made her way through the crowd, the men meant to play golf
and the women were off shopping. She dismissed the idea of
begging a ride from them, fearing it might be a case of jumping from the frying pan into the fire. She didn't like to imagine herself stranded on the links—or worse, at a mall.

Besides, she wasn't going anywhere, she decided, until
she'd had her cup of coffee.

Entering the kitchen, she didn't find the coffeepot, but she
did stumble upon Mitch, muttering under his breath as he
vigorously scrubbed the huge, old-fashioned ironclad stove.

"The kitchen is closed," he called over his shoulder. "As

I said earlier, breakfast hours are from six till ten. Oh,'' he said as he spun to face her. "Sorry, thought you were Roy's nephews again.''

She smiled weakly. "Mr. Hackett is in the foyer, marshaling the troops. Someone should give that man a whistle.''

"Heaven forbid," Mitch muttered, turning back to his cleaning and leaving Darcy to stare at his back. Watching the play of muscles in his arms as he worked, she remembered how it felt to have him hold her, how masterfully he'd clasped her against his chest when he'd kissed her...

She felt suddenly foolish, standing there tongue-tied while he seemed determined to act as if last night had never happened. As if *she'd* never happened. "I just wanted coffee,'' she stated to his back.

"There's an urn set up in the dining room," he offered grudgingly. "Might even be a few doughnuts left.''

Realizing she'd been dismissed, Darcy perversely decided not to leave until he acknowledged her. "I know you're busy," she said crisply, stepping into the room, "but I need your help.''

He must have heard, for he paused in his scrubbing, but he offered no encouragement. He didn't even turn to face her.

Irked, she approached the stove, standing beside him and giving him no choice but to notice her. He countered by scrubbing harder.

"Here's the thing," she said to his stony profile. "Peter still can't get away. Business has him tied up at the office.''

"Business? On Saturday?''

The question reeked of innuendo. "Oh, for heaven's sake," she said, truly annoyed. "He's not having an affair, if that's what you're suggesting. He just happens to be a hard worker.''

"Workaholic," Mitch muttered under his breath.

"Working odd hours is vital if you want to get ahead in our business," she told him curtly. "But that's not the point. I need advice. Tell me, is it possible to get a taxi to take me to Hilton Head?''

"Sure, if you own Fort Knox."

She'd been afraid of that. Back in New York, it had seemed wiser to limit the cash she carried, relying on plastic instead. "I don't suppose you have an ATM machine on the premises?"

He looked at her then, plainly exasperated. "No ATM, no computers, not even cable TV. That's the object of the place. Rose Arbor is a retreat from the pressures of the outside world. A haven of peace and quiet, a place where you can figure out who you are and where you are going."

"Some of us find the pressure exhilarating," she said defensively. "Not all of us need to run away from life. I know exactly where I'm going." Even to her own ears, it sounded more a weak boast than true conviction.

His deep blue gaze missed nothing, and revealed even less. Turning to the stove once more, he said only, "Well, if things don't work out, you're welcome to bed down in the cottage another night."

The offer couldn't have been any more grudging. "Thank you, but—"

"All I ask is that you stop encouraging my sons' nonsense," he went on, scrubbing vehemently. "They've been up since dawn, telling everyone who will listen about last night's visitation by Lady. I admit, there's not a whole lot for someone like you to do around here, but my boys don't need any more reasons to be getting into mischief."

"Someone like *me?*" She had to swallow to continue, so outraged did she feel. "Do you really think this ghost stuff is my idea? I was just trying to be polite, since it seemed important to them."

"Really?"

"Really. And since you brought it up, how dare you be so snide? From what I hear, you never bother sitting up with them to watch for their ghost." She poked at the stove with an angry finger. "Seems to me my business isn't the only one that breeds workaholics. Maybe it's time you stopped and smelled some of your roses, yourself."

"I did." He paused, turning to catch her off guard again with his intense blue gaze. "Last night in the garden. Remember?"

Staring at him, it all slammed into her—the need, the wanting. She shook her head, trying to deny her response to him, but it was no use. He need but ask, she feared, and she'd gladly fall back into his arms. "Last night was a mistake," she said sharply, looking away before she could make such a fool of herself. "And we both know it."

"Yeah."

The way he said it, he could be agreeing that the kiss was a mistake, or he could as easily be calling her bluff. He had to guess, staring at her face so intently, what strange yearnings he sent coursing through her body.

But if so, he chose to ignore her reaction, looking back to the stove which once again consumed all his attention.

Which was for the best, Darcy thought as she left him to it. Hurrying to the dining room for her cup of coffee, she knew there was no sense pursuing this. The minute she took care of the Lexus, she'd be leaving and, with any luck, she'd never see the unsettling Mitch Rose again.

Gulping down the first cup of coffee, she took a second with her as she walked out to the accident site to wait for the rental company's tow truck. She had reason to wish she'd grabbed a few doughnuts, as well, for her stomach began growling as her wait extended to one hour, then two. She shouldn't have worn slacks in this heat, she thought, tapping her foot impatiently. They could probably serve *her* for lunch, since she was about to bake in this heat.

It was well past lunch when the truck showed up, kicking up dust and gravel as it backed in behind the Lexus. Waving her empty coffee cup at the driver as he alighted, she demanded to know where he'd been.

"Busy weekend," he said with a lazy shrug as he went about his work, indicating she wasn't the first customer he'd kept waiting—nor likely the last.

Taking his time with the paperwork, he showed undue

pleasure in informing Darcy that they couldn't start work on the car until her insurance adjuster inspected it. Which, this being a holiday and all, might not happen until Tuesday. Even then, he told her with a nasty chuckle, she was looking at a clear-cut case of Humpty Dumpty—it would take all the king's men and a good couple weeks, to put that fancy piece of metal back together again.

Between the leer as he said this, and the cloud of smoke filling his cab, Darcy knew better than to accept his offer to drive her to the dealership. The lure of arranging a rental there—or even finding other accommodations for the night—lost out to her instinct for survival.

Trudging back to the house, she wondered what to do next. Too late, she remembered her Daily Planner, still on the front seat of the Lexus. Let it go, she thought wearily. Her sense of order and efficiency didn't seem to work in this place, anyway.

Besides, she knew what she had to do.

Feeling suddenly rebellious—and loath to go back in that phone closet—she realized she was tired of always being practical and sensible. This was supposed to be her vacation, after all; why couldn't she sample a little of what Mitch said the place offered, see her predicament less as an inconvenience and more an adventure?

Entering the foyer, she found Melissa gathering guests around her for an organized tour of the house. Darcy was about to brush past them, when the irony struck her. The impulse to see Rose Arbor was what had landed her here. Why not take advantage of the opportunity when it presented itself? If she were truly going to adopt this new attitude, if she really meant to have an adventure, she might as well join the tour.

Looking like a blond Scarlett O'Hara with her blue hoop skirt and the despised wig set firmly on her head, Melissa frowned when she saw Darcy in the group, but like an accomplished actress, the girl soon fell into the role of the gracious Southern hostess.

Taking them through the main part of the house, Melissa showed them the parlor and dining areas, describing life in the days of slavery. In the right wing they saw a large ballroom, a gentleman's study and a back parlor. But when a tour member asked about upstairs, Melissa regretfully explained that they wouldn't be going there. The main and right wings contained guest rooms and the left housed the family quarters.

Watching Melissa glide down the halls, her genteel drawl describing the period furnishings as she related historical anecdotes for each room, Darcy found it hard to believe this was the same surly teenager she'd met yesterday. Gone was the bored indifference. Clearly, Melissa loved the place, and she soon had her audience sharing her affection.

Nor did Darcy prove immune. The gleaming hardwood floors, the intricate moldings around the doors and ceilings, the whimsical fire screens guarding the house's many hearths, all underscored Mitch's point. The beauty of Rose Arbor was its ability to portray the slower, quieter pace of a more gracious past. For many, it would be a haven, a sanctuary to retreat to when the cares of the world proved too great. A perfect place to find oneself.

"What's behind that door?" one of the men asked.

"Can't we peek inside?" his wife added.

"It's the lady's morning room," Melissa drawled pleasantly. "I'm afraid it's not scheduled to be renovated until this winter. The furniture still has to be brought down from the attic and restored before we can display it. We do hope y'all will visit us next spring when this room, and a few of the upstairs bedrooms, will be added to the tour. Right now, however, I've a special treat in store for you. Follow me, and I'll show you our world-famous rose garden."

For Darcy, it was a strange feeling, following the paths she and Mitch had wandered the night before. She found it a completely different view with bright sunlight bathing the roses, but she couldn't deny the garden's charm at any time of the day. Listening as Melissa explained the origin of each bush, Darcy heard in the girl's voice the same loving pride her father had displayed.

"And this is our honeymoon cottage." Melissa came to a stop, gesturing proudly at Darcy's current lodgings. "It's known to be a favorite haunt of our ghost."

A murmur went through the crowd. Darcy felt a bit rattled herself. "Lady?" she blurted out.

Melissa grinned at Darcy's reaction. "We Roses have a charming tale about an ancestress, Lady Rose, who fell in love with a Yankee captain during the War between the States. Sadly enough, Lady and her sweetheart were separated by her parents after the war ended and ever since, poor Lady has been waiting for her Captain Allen to return. While roaming the grounds, it's said, she does her best to bring and keep other couples together. I've never seen her myself, but many who have spent the night in this cottage claim to fall deeply in love. Why, one couple returned last month to celebrate their thirtieth anniversary."

Predictably, the crowd oohed and aahed, after which Melissa pronounced the tour at an end. As the group dispersed, Darcy edged closer to the girl. "That was quite a finale," she said dryly. "I thought you didn't believe in ghosts."

Melissa shrugged, once more the obnoxious teenager. "People expect weird stuff in these old houses, so who am I to disappoint them?"

"But a matchmaking ghost? Isn't that taking it a bit far?"

"I get the stuff from Gramps, what can I say?"

"You sounded so convincing," Darcy pressed, not knowing why she did so. "As if you believed Lady is in that cottage, trying to bring people together."

The girl stiffened before recovering her pose of indifference. "It's just stuff to entertain the tourists, okay? Why are you still here, anyway? I thought you were in a hurry to see your boyfriend."

"He's busy." Darcy had meant to be flippant, but the words came out sounding defensive instead. "Besides," she added in an attempt to sound decisive, "I've decided I'd like to spend another night in the cottage."

"You can't!" Melissa's gaze shot back to the gingerbread house. "I'm gonna talk to Dad," she announced, stamping off with her hoop skirt bouncing.

"He's not in the best of moods," Darcy cautioned as she followed the girl. "You might better tell *me* why I can't stay here."

Melissa didn't bother to grace that with a reply, maintaining a collision course with the front porch.

She doesn't know me well enough to dislike me this much, Darcy thought. They reached the front yard at the same time she reached the end of her patience. "For heaven's sake, Melissa, what can it matter if I stay in that cottage?"

"My mom's gonna stay there," Melissa snapped, whirling to face Darcy. "How else is she ever going to realize how wonderful it is here, how wonderful Daddy..."

The girl broke off, lower lip trembling. Darcy saw only too well what the poor kid had been hoping, and she knew how Melissa felt, having gone through divorce after divorce with her own mother. Yet the more Darcy tried keeping Rita married, wanting both a mother *and* father, the faster Rita seemed to get divorced. "Melissa," she said gently, "your parents have gone separate ways. There's nothing you can do to change that."

"Maybe I can't, but there's always Lady."

Darcy realized the girl was banking on the ghost's matchmaking powers. How unnerving, if even this bored, wisecracking teenager believed in Lady.

"Nothing will turn out right if Mom doesn't stay in the cottage," Melissa said fiercely. "She's just got to be here for this weekend. Not you."

Darcy ached for the kid. Melissa needed to talk to someone about this. Once again, Darcy regretted her lack of experience with kids. She sensed anything she might say to the girl would only be resented.

"Lester!" Melissa said suddenly, her blue eyes going wide

with fright. "Those dumb boys. Now they're really gonna get in trouble."

Following her gesture, first Darcy saw the opened gate to the pen, then the runaway goat, charging across the yard in front of them.

Chapter Nine

Melissa glared at the stupid goat, wondering why it had to
choose such an important weekend to act up so bad. Her
dumb brothers had really gone and done it now. If somebody
didn't get Lester back in that pen soon, Daddy was gonna
lose it, big time.

Lifting up her skirts, she started to give chase, but the
woman, that Darcy, reached out to grab her wrist.

"I've got to go get Lester," Melissa snapped. "Daddy's
got enough on his mind without having to worry about paying
for damages to Miss Macon's garden."

"I'll go." Darcy didn't look all that pleased with her offer.

"You? Why?"

"You'll trip and hurt yourself if you go running in that
hoop. I'm at least wearing slacks. I take it Miss Macon's is
across that field?"

Melissa nodded, struck dumb as the woman started running
after Lester.

"You might want to warn your brothers," Darcy said over

her shoulder. "If I don't get back soon with the goat, your dad's going to be none too happy."

Gaping in astonishment, Melissa wanted to hate Darcy MacTeague. She was far too pretty and poised and her dad was far too attracted. The trouble was, the woman didn't act the way she expected—and maybe even wanted—her to. Every time Melissa tried to show her up, to prove how awful she truly was, Darcy turned around and made her seem like the rude, spiteful one.

Darcy could as easily have laughed when Melissa let that stuff about her mom slip out, but instead, she'd looked as if she'd understood what Melissa was feeling instead. She didn't want to think she could be so wrong about the woman, but watching Darcy go tearing off after Lester in her outrageously expensive outfit, all to spare Ky and J.J. the talking-to they deserved, Melissa didn't have much of a choice.

All hopes to the contrary, Darcy wasn't a snob, or some shallow, money-grubbing bimbo, or even a stressed-out grumpy spinster. Feeling suddenly bad for the way she'd been treating their guest, fearing jealousy and insecurity might have a lot to do with it, Melissa conceded that Darcy might actually be...well, nice.

At the least, she could hold off her judgment until Darcy returned with the goat.

No one could have been more surprised by her actions than Darcy herself. She tried to tell herself that she was being practical. After all, she was wearing slacks—albeit expensive ones—and Melissa was wearing that expensive, delicate dress. Yet deep down, she knew her headlong flight had more to do with a need to keep the twins out of trouble. And as Melissa had said, Mitch had enough on his mind without adding Lester's rampages to the list.

She could understand the need to protect two cute little boys, but what was this concern for their father?

Before she could chase that thought, Lester veered off the road, taking off into a thicket of oaks clogged with kudzu.

Cursing under her breath, Darcy tore after him, tripping over a vine and not seeing the puddle until her new leather sandals landed in the middle of it. The groan had barely left her lips when she felt a branch tug her blouse. Her forward momentum tore a gash in the silk.

Clenching her jaw, she plunged on, refusing to think of the cost of replacing the blouse. Fetching Lester had become her mission. Even if it meant sacrificing her entire wardrobe, she was determined to wrestle that errant goat back to its pen.

She had a rough few moments when the road curved and Lester passed out of sight, but she came upon him in a neat, fence-trimmed yard, placidly munching on marigolds in an elaborate country garden.

Horrified, she ran up and snatched at the rope tied around his neck. "That will be enough, Lester," she told the goat. "You're coming with me."

"Indeed? And who might you be?"

The sudden stern voice nearly startled her into dropping the rope. Darcy spun to face a dead ringer for Miss Gulch before she turned into the Wicked Witch. Oh no, she thought—this must be the intimidating Hester Macon.

"I'm Darcy. Darcy MacTeague." She refrained from offering a hand in greeting; the woman's frown indicated the gesture would only be ignored. "I'm a guest at Rose Arbor."

As Miss Macon's sharp gaze went to the goat, a gray eyebrow raised significantly.

"Actually, I crashed my car into their tree," Darcy felt compelled to add, uneasy under such scrutiny. "I'm waiting until the man I'm dating can take me to Hilton Head. He's in advertising in New York—we both are, actually—and the demands of the business can be rather exacting. Not that I mind, of course. I find stress invigorating. Most of the time..." She trailed off, realizing she was babbling in an attempt to justify herself to an absolute stranger. And worse, her defense lacked its customary conviction.

She supposed it didn't matter what she said. She sensed Hester Macon could see right through her, anyway.

"You married?"

"No, not yet, but I've plenty of time for that."

The eyebrow raised higher. "Will you be staying for the party?"

"Party?"

"Melissa turns sixteen tomorrow."

Flustered, not certain what the woman was after, Darcy shook her head. "I expect to be gone first thing in the morning."

"Pity. Mitchell could use the help. Poor boy's got too many demands on his time."

Darcy's grip tightened on Lester's rope. Was Miss Macon suggesting that she should help Mitch?

"That goat's a particular problem," the women went on, glaring at Lester. "I've told Mitchell again and again, I can't have that animal chewing up my flowers. Not with the garden society competition coming up."

Gazing at the yellow and orange dust on Lester's whiskers, Darcy saw she had failed at her mission. Hot and tired, with a ruined blouse and Lord alone knew what damage to her slacks, she still hadn't managed to keep the boys out of trouble. "I'm sorry if Lester ate your marigolds," she told Miss Macon in a pleading tone, pushing her damp hair off her forehead, "but isn't there some way we can work things out? Do we really need to bother Mitch...er, Mr. Rose with all this?"

Miss Macon tilted her head, studying her, before breaking into a dazzling smile. Before Darcy's eyes, she transformed from the stern schoolmarm into a charming grandma. "You're right, of course," she said with a disarming sense of conspiracy. "Don't ever tell Mitchell so, but I actually look forward to that animal's raids."

"You do?" At a loss, Darcy glanced down at Lester.

The woman heaved a sigh. "It's the only time anyone comes calling on me. I see that goat, and I know a Rose is soon on his way."

Darcy felt an unexpected rush of sympathy, imagining this

poor, lonely woman waiting in her tiny home, sitting by the window in hopes of a visitor.

"I once thought my career was all-important," Miss Macon said wistfully. "I gave my all to it, sacrificing friends and family, and look at me now. Here I am, retired and alone, with nothing to fill the day. Be careful you don't end up like me, girl. Don't wind up a cranky, lonely old woman."

Darcy's sympathy faded, went defensive. *You don't know anything about me,* she wanted to protest, but she feared another knowing sigh. Instead, she apologized for the intrusion, bid Miss Macon good day and tugged Lester out of the yard.

"You be there tomorrow," Miss Macon called after her. "Mitchell is going to need you."

Need *me?* Darcy thought. The idea was preposterous.

Dragging Lester home, she tried to tell herself that the woman had probably mistaken her for someone else. Living alone like that, Miss Macon was liable to grow confused.

Yet the closer Darcy came to the house, the more the prospect of being needed grew in appeal.

She indulged herself with visions of how she could help Mitch and his family. She could devise a killer ad campaign for advertising Rose Arbor, perhaps, so that when she left, Mitch would remember her fondly as the city woman who had helped their business. She could come back each year for the rosebush ceremony, and a grateful Mitch would hand her the shovel to help him plant.

So satisfying was the fantasy that when she reached Rose Arbor and found Mitch on the porch, she expected to see him beaming down at her.

Instead, he scowled at his children, gathered below him at the bottom of the steps. Gazing up at their father, J.J. and Ky seemed to shrink in size, while Melissa chewed her gum at ten times the normal speed.

"And just who," Mitch asked, "is responsible this time?"

All three kids turned to her in appeal. No help for it, she thought with a gulp as she found herself stepping forward.

* * *

Mitch listened to the chorus of "No, it was me" from his children, shaking his head. Roy Hackett had been after him since first light, asking for more of everything, from breakfast to towels, and now hot water. With all the teenagers in the clan taking two to three showers a day, the water was bound to run cold eventually, but as Roy constantly reminded, he was a paying customer and Mitch needed his business. Unfortunately, it meant adding the challenge of getting the old auxiliary heater up and running to the ever-expanding list of chores—a hard enough job without all these interruptions.

Especially when one of his distractions showed up wearing a silk blouse, strategically torn to reveal a lacy bra with generous cleavage. Mitch didn't know how Darcy had gotten that mud on her slacks, or her hair so sexily disheveled, nor was he sure he wanted to. He'd already tried going down that path, only to have her stare him in the face and swear their kiss last night shouldn't have happened.

He couldn't believe how much that still rankled. Especially since he'd been within a breath of repeating the same mistake this morning.

"One at a time," he told his kids, putting such thoughts from his mind. "And please, no more elaborate stories. All I'm asking is how that goat got out of the pen."

"Don't blame the boys." Tightening her grasp on the rope tethering Lester, Darcy stiffened her spine and straightened her shoulders. "I'm the one you should be yelling at."

"No one is yelling." He had to force his gaze away from the tear in her blouse, only to lose himself in the melting brown of her eyes. "I'm trying to find out what happened."

Her own gaze slid to the goat. "Well, there I was in the pen, trying to make friends with Lester—"

"Wearing that?"

Smile fixed in place, she faced him squarely. "I didn't realize he'd try to run right past me and down the road. I had to give chase, of course—"

"Of course." That would explain the mud and ruined clothing, but Mitch still didn't understand why she'd go running after Lester, much less get in the pen with the goat. Folding his arms across his chest, he watched the play of emotion across her face. He couldn't tell if he saw guilt or defiance, or if that fleeting grin meant she was merely amused by herself.

"By the time I could catch up with Lester," she went on determinedly, "he'd already reached Miss Macon's marigold bed."

"Oh, no," Mel blurted out. "She didn't yell at you, did she?"

Mitch eyed his daughter, who seemed genuinely concerned about Darcy. Mel's outburst surprised him, since up until now, she'd barely managed to be civil to their guest.

"I managed to corral Lester before he could cause much damage, so Miss Macon agreed there was no real harm done." Darcy smiled a bit too brightly at each of the kids. "As long as all's well that ends well, what do you say we just put Lester back in his pen, secure the gate and pretend this whole incident never happened?"

All three kids nodded enthusiastically, exchanging glances with Darcy that screamed *conspiracy*. Mitch was left feeling that he'd missed something important.

"Are we forgetting the *whole* incident?" he asked Darcy. "Or will I be getting a dry-cleaning bill?"

She looked down as if noticing the condition of her clothes for the first time. "Oh my, I look a wreck, don't I?"

No, she did not, which was precisely the problem. She looked young and vulnerable and completely approachable. He wanted to brush the smudge of mud off her cheeks, to kiss the lips she now nibbled. Which was exactly why he kept his arms folded across his chest.

"Get Lester in the pen where he belongs," he grumbled at the kids, "and for Pete's sake, keep him out of trouble until I can get the old water heater hooked up. The Hacketts will be back soon, all of them looking to take showers. They've got some party in town tonight."

"Hallelujah," Mel muttered. "A whole night we don't

need to hear the Fast-Food King rave about the virtues of Happy Burgers.''

"That will be enough of that, young lady,'' Mitch told her with a frown. "Don't forget, those Happy Burgers are paying the bills.''

"Sorry, Daddy. You look a little stressed-out. Can I help?''

Mel's sudden concern made him feel like a bear. Sometimes it was easy to forget they were only kids, trying their best. Just because an unwilling houseguest went around in flimsy nightgowns and torn silk blouses, he didn't have to take out his frustrations on his children.

He forced a smile. "Thanks, Mel. Actually, if you could take fresh towels to the bathrooms, you'd be saving me the trip. Not to mention the inevitable complaint from Mr. Hackett.''

"Sure thing, Daddy.''

Nodding at Mel, he turned to the boys. "I imagine the less said about Lester the better. But as I recall, I asked you boys a week ago to fix that old water pump. You took it apart, now put it back together. Just as soon as you've got that goat squared away.''

Recognizing a reprieve when they saw one, the twins fell all over themselves to bring Lester back to his pen.

That left Darcy.

"You'll probably be wanting to take a shower, too, huh?'' Mel asked their guest, getting to Darcy before him. "If you want, I can bring fresh towels to the cottage.''

"I can't stay—''

"Yeah, you can.'' Mel smiled at her disarmingly. "After braving Miss Macon, you deserve the best Rose Arbor has to offer.''

Watching them exchange reluctant grins, Mitch again felt as if he'd missed something vital.

"I need to go inside and check for messages,'' Darcy told Mel. "I might as well come with you and get the towels myself.''

They walked past him into the house, leaving Mitch feeling

slightly off-kilter. Ever since the woman had crashed into his tree, his life had definitely shifted balance. It was vital to get that old water heater up and running, but here he stood, staring after her, wishing he could...

That was the trouble, he realized. He didn't know what he wanted from Darcy. He just wished she wasn't always running away from him.

"Wasn't necessary, what she did," Gramps said, materializing on the porch behind him.

Mitch spun, embarrassed by his thoughts. "I beg your pardon?"

"I think that Darcy has a heart bigger than she wants us to see. Imagine, her stepping up to take the blame to spare those boys a yelling."

Yeah, imagine. The woman was entirely too unpredictable, Mitch decided. Every time he thought he had her pegged, she came at him from a different angle.

"Nice girl, I'm thinking."

Mitch eyed his grandfather suspiciously. "I'm not sure *nice* is the word I'd use."

"Poor Mitch." Gramps chuckled. "Got you going, doesn't she?"

It annoyed Mitch that his grandfather could read him so accurately. "What's got me going is Roy Hackett and his demands for hot water."

"Your grandmother and I think she could be good for you."

Mitch wanted to groan. Maybe he could overlook Gramps "talking" to his dead wife, but he wasn't about to let the old man start meddling in his private life. "She's too much like Beth," he said with forced patience. "Darcy's a big-city businesswoman. We have nothing in common."

"Me and Rose thought we didn't suit, either, when we first met. Don't go dismissing the opportunity out of hand."

"I can't afford to take time to work on a relationship."

"Maybe you can't afford *not* to. Your grandmother is worried about you, son. She thinks you're hiding from life, letting your first marriage keep you from finding real, lasting magic.''

''*Magic!*''

''Don't you sneer until you've felt it, son. You can't know what you're missing.'' Gramps studied him carefully, his concern plain. ''And while you're at it, stop comparing Darcy to Beth. They're not the same woman, you know, except maybe on the surface. Dig deeper, and you'll find there's more to that girl than meets the eye. And a whole lot more between you than you care to admit.''

Unwillingly, Mitch thought of the scene with the kids, of how even Mel had responded to her. ''Sorry to disappoint you, Gramps, but the only thing Darcy and I have going between us is a good dose of lust.''

The old man merely laughed. ''So? That's as good a place as any to start. Go on, go exploring, son. You owe it to yourself.''

If only it were that easy. Mitch could well imagine tearing the rest of her blouse off her, leaving her velvety flesh open to his touch and taste, but where would they go from there? ''I've got three kids to look after, and this latest incident proves that I can't take my eye off them for an instant.''

''As the kids would say, lighten up.'' Grinning, Gramps turned back for the house. ''The boys weren't to blame for Lester escaping his pen, you know.''

''Just a minute.'' Mitch wasn't about to let him waltz off so casually. ''If the boys weren't responsible, who was?''

''Ah, Mitch.'' Gramps chuckled again as he went inside. ''Open your ears and eyes. Who else could it have been but Lady?''

Chapter Ten

Waking into a pitch-black room, Darcy rubbed her eyes, trying to focus on where she was and why she was there. She'd flopped down on the four-poster after her shower, she remembered slowly. She must have dozed off. Odd, how she seemed to fall asleep here easier than in her own bed.

And no wonder, she thought as she listened to the night noises. She heard the crickets chirping, the distant hoot of an owl—unfamiliar sounds to someone accustomed to the discordant rhythms of city streets, yet she found it somehow soothing. A person could get used to this.

But not Darcy. Sitting up as reality slammed into her, she remembered the phone calls she had yet to make.

She had to get in touch with the insurance adjuster, and of course, Peter. At the least, she had to find out what was happening with the Tavish account.

Something must be wrong. Surely the ever-efficient Peter Arlington shouldn't need two full days to iron out mere details. What if there had been some serious oversight on her part? If the firm lost the account, it could mean more than her promotion. She could lose her job.

She hesitated, sitting on the edge of the bed. For a moment, with the balmy, scented breeze caressing her face, she had to remind herself why keeping her job was so important. The busy, bustling world of Manhattan seemed so far away.

The condo, she chanted as she went into the bathroom to splash cold water on her face. Having spent her childhood flitting from place to place with her undependable mother, Darcy was determined to have a home that was hers, and hers alone.

Enough shirking—she had to go to the house, face that phone closet and make those calls. She snatched a pair of denim shorts and a hot-pink T-shirt out of her suitcase and dressed quickly.

Slipping into her sandals, she headed for the living room, catching a whiff of delicate spices as she clicked on the lamp. Immediately, her stomach started growling, and she realized how long it had been since she'd eaten. Noticing the tray on the coffee table piled high with fried chicken and vegetables, with a basket of buttered biscuits sitting on the side, she truly thought she had died and gone to heaven.

Sitting on the couch, saying a happy goodbye to her waist-line, she dug into the food with gluttonous delight. The meal tasted even better than it smelled, and she ate more than she should have.

Lifting the tray, she decided to work off the calories she'd just consumed by taking the tray to the house and washing the dishes.

Melissa was already at the sink when Darcy got to the kitchen. "I see you found your supper," the girl said with a wary smile, her gaze going to the nearly empty tray. "I hope you don't mind my barging into the cottage while you were sleeping. I figured you'd be hungry when you woke."

"I was starving. Thanks, Melissa, dinner was delicious."

"Really? I know it's not fancy food, but it's all I know how to cook."

"You're way ahead of me. I can't even boil water. And frankly, it's a good thing I can't. If I ate this well back home, I'd soon be as big as a house."

"Well, I'm glad you enjoyed it." Melissa's sudden smile faded, leaving an awkward moment of silence. She opened her mouth as if she was about to say something but closed it again with a frown.

"Here, let me finish those," Darcy said, approaching the sink. "The least I can do is help clean up after myself."

"But you're a guest."

"A nonpaying, unexpected one. If I'm going to keep using your cottage, it's time to start earning my keep." Taking the sponge from Melissa's hands, Darcy plunged her hands into the dishwater.

Melissa continued to stand there, awkward, stiff and looking torn. Darcy decided to try for a truce. "I've been thinking that we got off to a bad start yesterday. Tell you what. Why don't I just forget I wrecked my car and you forget, well, whatever it is about me that annoys you? We can act like we're meeting for the first time." She held out a soapy hand. "Hi, I'm Darcy."

With a reluctant grin, the girl took her hand and shook it. "I'm Melissa. Or better yet, just call me Mel, like my dad does."

Darcy turned back to the sink, trying not to smile at the teenager's disgusted expression. "You don't like the nickname?"

Mel shrugged as she picked up a towel to dry. "It's okay, I guess. It's just, well, sometimes I can't help wishing Dad would notice I'm growing up. He treats me like I'm still his baby. I'll be sixteen tomorrow, not six."

"That's how dads are, I'm told." Not that Darcy would know from experience. None of Rita's husbands had stayed around long enough to even notice her growing up.

Frowning, Melissa took the plate from her. "The thing is, I could be a help to Daddy, if he'd just let me. I know he's got money troubles, so why doesn't he ever discuss them with me? All I get is rules and regulations.''

Money troubles? Looking around, she realized this big old house must be a sinkhole of financial demands.

"Maybe I should just go live with Mom, like she asked."

Darcy felt a sudden, unexplained sense of alarm. "But your dad. How would he feel if you left?"

Melissa's expression hardened. "I'm tired of being treated like a baby. Do you know I'm the only girl in my class who's not allowed to go on a date?"

Ah, so this was about boys—that age-old battle between father and daughter. "Have you ever tried talking to him about how you feel? It could be that he just needs to see that you're mature enough to handle dating."

There was another moment of silence in which Darcy feared she had pushed too hard. She was about to apologize and say it was none of her business, when Mel spoke out. "I guess I haven't exactly been acting my age lately. It's just, well, I'm sore at my mom for not showing up for my birthday, and I'm taking it out on everyone else."

Darcy felt a pang of empathy. She could relate, having been in the same situation too often herself.

"I know she's busy and all," Mel went on. "I wouldn't have expected her if she hadn't promised me she'd come. Don't tell Dad, but she said she wanted to come take me to live in Philadelphia with her and Tom."

"Tom?"

"Her husband. He's really rich, but kind of old."

So the wife had wasted little time in remarrying, Darcy thought. She wondered if that was why Mitch had gotten custody of the kids.

"Mom said she'd take me shopping, have my hair done and have all kinds of parties so I could meet the right kind of boys. She said it would be so much fun now that she has all that money and I'm old enough to take care of myself."

What a lousy position to put your kid in, Darcy thought, dangling the fantasy life every teenager dreamed of before her, tempting Mel to abandon the father who had always stuck by her. "So," Darcy asked, trying to sound noncommittal, "you planning on going with her?"

Mel shrugged. "Part of me wants to, but I can't help wondering if going to Philadelphia will be all that great. I mean, if she's too busy to remember my birthday, will she make time for me once I'm living in her house?"

"Having a busy mother is tough," Darcy commiserated, reminded too strongly of her own teenage years. "Rita—that's what my mom insisted I call her—was always on the go. If she wasn't out dating, or honeymooning, she was off somewhere recovering from a divorce. I don't think she ever remembered my birthday."

"Never?"

She'd thrown that information out to show Mel they might have something in common, but the sudden pang proved how much the old hurts had festered. "My own sixteenth birthday was the worst, actually. I spent the week before anticipating the surprise party I thought for sure Rita was planning for me. She'd been so busy, whispering on the phone, running off to here and Lord-knew-where, I was convinced this time my birthday would be special. I told her I just wanted earrings, something with diamonds since that was my birthstone, but all I really wanted was that party. I was so excited thinking about it, I could hardly sleep. Silly me."

"It was a real dud, huh? No boys, or kids your age?"

Darcy shook her head. "Worse. All those secretive whispers, I later learned, were only Rita making plans to go away with her newest boyfriend. I spent my birthday sitting alone in our empty apartment, waiting hour after hour, hoping against hope that Rita hadn't forgotten again."

"That stinks."

"Yeah, well, it was the last time I ever sat around waiting. From that night on, I made sure I was always too busy myself."

The words seemed to echo across the kitchen, the admission surprising even Darcy. How much of her hectic life-style, she wondered, was in defense of those old hurts?

"And I thought I had it bad," Mel said after a time. "At least I have my dad."

Darcy almost envied her, but that was the past and she'd done what she could to compensate for the lack of a loving, caring father. "In the end, I went out and bought my own diamond earrings," she said proudly, leaning over to show the studs in her ears. "I've been wearing them ever since."

"I noticed them, first thing. I'd just about kill for earrings like those, but my poor dad will never be able to afford diamonds."

"If you really want them, do what I did. Work and scrimp and save."

"It must have taken forever. They're gorgeous, Darcy. I bet they're real valuable, too."

"They are to me." Darcy reached up with a wet hand to touch the diamond in her earlobe. "It's a comfort, knowing they're there. It proves I don't have to sit around wallowing in self-pity when things don't work out the way I hope. If I want something bad enough, I can go out and get it myself."

Taking the last dish from Darcy, Mel nodded thoughtfully. "I guess you're right about that. I suppose I was looking for too much from my mom's visit."

Hearing the hurt in her voice, Darcy ached for her. "We can't change who our parents are," she said as she drained the water from the sink. "They split up for reasons that have nothing to do with us, and we can't make those reasons go away just because we wish it." Even as she said the words, she realized she was saying them by rote, having been told them so often.

And they lost her credibility. "Now you sound like Dad," Mel snapped, tossing her towel on the counter.

"Hey, you're not the only one caught up in divorce, you know. I know exactly how you feel. I had the same feelings of helplessness and guilt with my own mother."

"Your folks split up, too?"

Handing Mel the last plate, Darcy drained the water from the sink, taking the time to choose her words. "My dad died before I knew him. Went to Vietnam and never came back. Maybe that's why Rita flaked out. I don't know, since she won't ever talk to me about him. All I know is that she's been married six times already and she's out there now looking for number seven. If I let myself get hurt each time she left a husband, there wouldn't be much left of my heart."

The kitchen fell silent again as Mel looked at her, then around the room. "I guess I should stop complaining," she said. "I really don't have it that bad. I mean, Ky and J.J. are here, and Gramps. And there's something about Rose Arbor, you know?"

Darcy did, but it scared her more than she cared to admit. "You know what they say," she said flippantly, embarrassed at having revealed so much of herself to this teenager. "It's a nice place to visit, but I wouldn't want to live here."

Melissa gave her a funny look. "Why not?"

"Because I belong in the city," Darcy said firmly. "I have a life there. A good, solid life."

Mel continued to study her.

"Look at the time," Darcy said suddenly, uneasy under the girl's scrutiny. "Considering tomorrow's your birthday, you probably should be turning in."

"Now you really sound like my dad."

She heard an added note in Mel's voice, an accusing tone, as if Darcy had somehow let the girl down. But what could Mel expect from her? They both knew she'd be leaving in the morning.

"Sleep tight." Even to her own ears, the words sounded lame. "If I don't see you tomorrow, have a great birthday."

"Yeah." Mel faced the counter, staring off into space. "I'll try."

Darcy left the kitchen, haunted by the girl's lonely stance. It struck her that they did have a lot in common, she and Melissa Rose. Darcy, more than anyone, knew how the teenager must be feeling tonight.

The question was, what was she going to do about it?

No, that was crazy. She had nothing to do with this family. She'd be leaving tomorrow, and would never see them again. Just because some sad little teenager had touched her heartstrings, made her feel things she'd buried long ago, it didn't mean Darcy had to act thoroughly out of character. What did she plan to do, throw Mel the party she herself had never had?

Wandering into the garden, letting the roses work their magic, she found she was tempted by the prospect. In her mind, she could see the great big smile of happiness spreading across Mel's face as she realized how much trouble her family had gone through to make her birthday special. Facing her father, her brothers and grandfather, Mel might even find it impossible to leave Rose Arbor to live with her mother.

Darcy was smiling, already planning arrangements in her mind, when she heard a murmuring on the path ahead. She paused, recognizing the bushy white beard in the moonlight. Just as she raised a hand in greeting, she heard Gramps call out a name. Rose, she remembered from her conversation with Mitch, was the name of his dead wife.

Sensing Gramps wouldn't want to be caught in such a private moment, she lowered her hand and stepped into the shadows. From her new position, she not only heard every word he uttered, she could see the old man, as well.

"You did a splendid job this afternoon, my dear," he was saying, bending low over a rosebush. "Opening that gate was a masterful stroke. She leaped right to the rescue, just as you predicted."

Had Gramps opened that gate? Talking to plants, plotting with his wife's imaginary ghost—maybe he was more senile than she'd thought.

After a moment of quiet, Gramps shook his head. "Trouble is, Mitch isn't being very nice to her. Right now, he's out stewing in his workshop behind the barn, no doubt planning out more nasty things to say to her."

Well, at least the old man had that right.

Gramps paused again, this time nodding his head. "I know, my dear. It's up to us to help her see through his gruffness to the man underneath. He's lonely and hurting and doesn't know how to deal with it."

It made her uneasy, thinking of Mitch being lonely. She didn't want to consider his feelings. He was dangerous enough to her peace of mind, as it was.

After another pause, Gramps began to chuckle. "Ah, Rose, as usual, you hit the nail on the head. I guess Mitch is just like all us men. He needs the right woman to make him happy again. Then maybe he won't spend so many hours by himself in his workshop."

Darcy found it a poignant picture, Mitch alone with his tools, working through his pain. It couldn't be easy for him, facing such awesome responsibility on a daily basis—three lively kids, a struggling bed-and-breakfast, an eccentric grandfather, and let's not forget the wayward goat.

"You're right again," Gramps said suddenly with a heavy sigh. "It's getting late. You take care, my love, and take my love with you to keep you warm and safe."

The gentle blessing tugged at Darcy's heart long after Gramps shuffled past on the path. In his soft words, she'd heard both his devotion and his loneliness, too. Was everybody in this family hurt and alone?

It gave new meaning to the *Help us*, she'd heard before the accident.

Once again, she felt a desire to help them. No one was better than Darcy MacTeague at arranging things and she already had ideas for beefing up Mel's party. If she could show Mitch how to impress his daughter, how to use the party to show Mel he loved her, then maybe neither one would need to be lonely and Darcy could leave this place with everyone smiling.

Only one problem with that idea. Before she could begin, she'd have to talk to Mitch.

Mitch entered his workshop, trying to shake free of this unsettled mood. Breathing in the comforting scents of solvents and wood, he went straight to his bench, anxious to get back to work on the Chippendale table. He knew no better way to relieve his restlessness and frustration.

He'd just come from the pantry. He'd been working on the water heater when Darcy had entered the kitchen. He'd meant to let her and Mel know he was there, but after his daughter started talking, he'd decided he better listen. A good thing he had, too, for he'd learned more about Mel in that ten minutes than he had in years.

How could he not have known his daughter had been considering moving in with Beth?

It had come, the situation he'd dreaded most, and he didn't know how to prevent it from getting worse. Beth and her rich new husband had so much to offer a teenager, while all Mitch had was Rose Arbor. And for Mel, unfortunately, it was no longer enough.

Nor could he blame her. These past few years, he'd been so caught up in his own pain and bitterness, he hadn't stopped to notice how his behavior affected his kids. Listening to Mel talk to Darcy, he'd seen how the girl needed a woman to confide in, to discuss all the difficult business of growing up.

Yet he knew Beth, and he feared she would only end up disappointing her daughter. Should he put his foot down in an attempt to protect Mel, or let her go and learn her own painful lessons?

Darcy seemed to have survived her own mother's neglect, he thought. In some ways, she'd grown stronger because of it. He had to admire the way she'd bought herself those earrings. She hadn't sat around whining, expecting others to take care of things for her.

Unnerved to find himself thinking about his far-too-attractive guest again, he grabbed the sander. He'd come out here for the express purpose of putting her out of his mind. The same independence that had her taking care of herself, he must remember, would be taking her back to New York. And the last thing Mitch wanted, or needed, was a long-term commitment with any female. Whatever he might feel for Darcy was just physical, a need easily appeased by a good long roll in the hay.

Yet, sanding the wood, sliding his hands over the smoothed surface, he was reminded of how he'd rubbed her arms with that same fluid motion, how he'd ached to stroke her legs, her entire body. The thought of Darcy beneath him, eager and willing, began to consume him. He could almost smell her sweet scent, hear her soft, measured breathing.

More than almost. Looking up, he found her watching him from the doorway.

Chapter Eleven

Entering Mitch's workshop, Darcy felt as if she'd drifted back in time. She could be twelve again, lured in by the scent of turpentine and sawdust, drawn by the fascination of watching Simon work with his hands. Each night, she'd wander down after the other kids had gone to sleep, taking care not to disturb her stepfather's concentration until he glanced up to acknowledge her with a wide, welcoming smile.

The man working on this drop-leaf table wasn't smiling. With an expression just short of a scowl, Mitch glanced up to eye her warily.

"That's a beautiful piece," she said, stepping up to the table he was sanding. "How will you cover the stain? Varnish or tung oil?"

He tilted his head, studying her as she slid her hand over the polished surface. "You know something about refinishing furniture?"

"A little. One of my stepfathers used to go to estate sales and auctions, hunting up battered pieces. He liked to 'bring them back to life,' as he put it. I used to help him, when he'd let me. Simon claimed that working with wood brought him an inner peace. He made it sound so attractive, I wanted that feeling myself."

"Did you find it?"

"Yeah, I guess I did. I didn't realize until walking in right now how much I'd missed it. I don't suppose you need a hand?"

He could be no more surprised by her offer than she was. She hadn't come here to help Mitch, but now that she thought about it, maybe working as they talked wasn't such a bad idea. It might be easier to say what she wanted if his attention wasn't focused so intently on her face.

She smiled winningly. "I really do know what I'm doing. And this time, at least I'm appropriately dressed."

He eyed the shorts and T-shirt, his assessment making her belatedly aware of how much of her was uncovered. Tingling as his gaze traveled down her legs, she fought the urge to pull at the hem of her shorts.

"If you don't mind sanding by hand," he said, gesturing at the Queen Anne desk in the corner, "that needs to be done next. You'll find the block and paper on the workbench next to it. Use the medium grit to start."

Setting up her sanding block, Darcy gazed at the many pieces of furniture in varying stages of refinishing. "I took Mel's tour of the house today," she told him as she began to work. "All that wood, those beautiful armoires and period pieces. Did you restore all of it?"

He shrugged. "Like your stepfather, I find it satisfying work."

"You're very good at it. If you ever give up on the bed-and-breakfast thing, you could always try your hand at restoring antiques."

He stiffened. "It's not exactly the safest way to support three kids."

"That never stopped Simon," she said, and instantly regretted her words. She hadn't meant to vent her bitterness like that.

Looking up from his sanding, he eyed her curiously. "Yeah, well, the 'bed-and-breakfast thing' seems to be keeping us afloat, so maybe I'd just better stick with that for a while."

He didn't say, "And you can stick to your own business," but Darcy nonetheless knew she should.

"You should know," Mitch said hesitantly, "that I was in the pantry fixing the water heater when you and Mel were talking before. I heard what you said about your mother and the series of divorces you went through."

"You make it sound like an obstacle course from which I emerged victorious."

"Didn't you?"

Funny, but considering it now, she supposed she had. "It made me older and wiser, if that's what you mean. And, I guess, less apt to make my mother's mistakes. I figure she's been married enough for the both of us."

"So you steer clear of wedded bliss. Smart girl."

Ordinarily, she'd have agreed with him, but his cavalier dismissal of the institution made her suddenly want to defend it. "I'll get married someday, but I intend to be careful before I make a commitment."

He stared at her for a moment, as if she puzzled him, before, with a slight shrug, he returned his attention to the table he was sanding.

Watching him work, Darcy was filled with a strange yearning. The tanned, muscular arms revealed by the rolled-up sleeves of his blue chambray shirt moved with grace and efficiency, gliding over the wood with a deft touch. Hard not to make the comparison, impossible to stop thinking how those strong, capable hands would feel sliding over her body...

"What about you?" she asked shakily, determined to nip such thoughts in the bud. "Surely you intend to remarry eventually."

"No, ma'am, I don't." He gave a mock shudder. "You know what they say. Get burned once, and you don't stick your hand back in the fire."

Darcy couldn't help wondering about his ex-wife, and why they'd split up.

"Besides," he added with a frown, "with this house, the kids and my grandfather, I haven't time or energy to put into a full-time relationship."

"Who does anymore?" she offered flippantly. If he'd meant the words as a warning, it was a good one. He might as well be wearing a sign that read, "Don't get involved with this one."

"What about Peter?" Mitch asked, catching her off guard.

"Peter?" Staring into the electric-blue eyes, she couldn't immediately place the face with the name.

"Yeah, Peter. Isn't he the man you're in such a rush to see in Hilton Head? I just assumed that you might be planning to *eventually* marry him."

She looked away, disconcerted. In her mind, she supposed she'd thought of one day becoming Mrs. Peter Arlington, but the prospect now seemed less like marriage and more like a merger. "I suppose I will," she told Mitch, feeling defensive. "Peter and I have a lot in common, after all. Our jobs, our life-styles, our ambition to get ahead."

"Sounds like a marriage made in heaven."

No, it did not, and she resented his pointing it out. "Peter offers everything I need. Intellectual stimulation, stability, security."

"Hey, maybe I'm old-fashioned, but what about love, and caring? Doesn't it bother you that he hasn't shown up to help you?"

"No. Why should it?" Not for anything would she admit to that brief pang of disappointment. "He'll be here as soon as he can get away."

There was a moment of silence, the rasp of sand against wood making the only sound in the room. "Does he do this often?'' Mitch asked quietly. ''Make plans, then cancel them at the last minute?''

Darcy began to sand harder. ''In his place, I'd do the same. You have to, to make it in our business.''

''As long as you're comfortable with that.''

''I am,'' she told him defiantly, making the mistake of again meeting his clear blue gaze. In that instant, her pose fell apart and she knew he could see all her confusion, her yearning, as if it were written on her face.

To her further dismay, he suddenly grinned, a knowing smile that should enrage her but didn't. There was a sense of conspiracy about it, the message, *We're more alike than you might think.*

''Maybe you're comfortable,'' he said, nodding at her hands, working furiously at the desktop. ''But my poor furniture isn't.'' Setting down his sander, he strode over to stand behind her. ''The object is to smooth out the surface, not carve out ruts.''

She held her breath as he took her hands, guiding them over the wood. Too intimately, she could feel his nearness, his heat, the power in his strong, capable hands.

''Here, like this,'' he said soothingly in her ear. ''Nice gentle strokes. Now, what were you saying? Something about being comfortable?''

Comfort had to be the last thing on her mind at the moment. Intensely aware of Mitch behind her, his body pressed against hers, their hands joined and working together, she could think only of the kiss they had shared last night, and the unappeased need that had haunted her all day.

Had she truly only known this man for thirty-six hours? It seemed as if they'd been grappling to understand each other for a lifetime, and somewhere along the line, their arguing had gotten mixed up with desire. What would happen, she wondered, if she turned to face him now, offering not words of protest, but her lips instead?

Silly question, Darcy. You know exactly what would happen.

Yet, she turned, drawn against her will.

Mitch was no longer smiling. Every inch of him stood tensed and primed for action, his eyes searching hers, testing the waters before he plunged in. Irrationally, she wanted him to sweep her into his arms, brushing away her fears, and taking the decision out of her hands.

But he was Mitch Rose, every inch the gentleman, and he'd clearly seen the hesitation in her eyes. "It's late," he said gruffly, moving away to gather up his tools. "I'll walk you to the cottage."

Darcy took a deep breath to steady herself. What had come over her? Now that he'd moved off, she could see how kissing this man was far from a good idea.

Too bad her body still ached for it.

"I don't need an escort," she said abruptly, working to regain her composure. "I know the way to the cottage by now."

"Just consider it part of the Rose family hospitality." Standing at the workshop door, he gestured outside. "The package includes protection from lions and tigers and bears."

She was amazed at how adroitly he could change the tone of their conversation, sliding easily from the deeply personal to this light banter. Amazed, but grateful, and she decided to take his cue. "Protection, huh? Where were you this afternoon when I had to face Miss Gulch?"

"Miss..." His expression clouded, then broke into a grin. "Oh, you mean Miss Macon. I guess the old gal can be somewhat intimidating."

"Somewhat? I kept waiting for her to say, 'I'm going to get you, and your little goat, too.'"

Mitch laughed at her imitation. "You should have seen her at work in the classroom. Hester has a way of saying 'Mitchell Allen Rose' that makes Miss Gulch seem like a guardian angel. It still has me cringing."

"I can well imagine," she said as she fell into step beside him, though she found it hard to picture anyone intimidating Mitch Rose. "She sure put me through my paces."

"She'll do that, but in all fairness, the woman is really more like Toto—all bark and no bite. She just tends to lose it when it comes to Lester eating her precious flowers. Two visits in as many days. You must bring out the worst in him."

"Me?" She thought of what Gramps had said earlier about opening the pen gate deliberately, but she refrained from repeating the old man's words. She couldn't see how it would reassure Mitch. "Why keep Lester around if he's so much trouble?" she asked instead.

"Got no choice." He shrugged, sliding his hands into his pockets. "Lester's been part of the family ever since the day he strolled into my grandmother's garden. He must have wandered into her heart, as well, she never found it in her to shoo him away. Grandma Rose used to brag to Hester that the goat never so much as touched a petal off her blooms. She claimed it was gratitude and loyalty that kept him from eating her roses, and maybe she was right. They had this competition over their gardens, she and Hester, and darned if that goat doesn't head straight for the Macon place whenever he gets a hankering to forage. It's enough to leave you wondering if Lester truly does have an ulterior purpose in mind."

"Are you saying Lester eats Miss Macon's marigolds to keep Rose Arbor ahead in the competition?"

"Stranger things have happened," he said with another grin. "Especially here at Rose Arbor."

Amen to that.

Strolling into the garden beside Mitch, Darcy realized how much the atmosphere of the place must have affected her that she could actually be considering a goat capable of sabotage. Was it mere coincidence that Lester always managed to escape the instant she decided to leave?

"Besides," Mitch went on, "the boys love that stupid goat. I don't have the heart to take him away from them."

"Lucky kids," Darcy said wistfully. "I wish I'd had a father who let me keep a pet."

He looked at her, his gaze softening, and she remembered

he'd overheard her complaining about her revolving door of stepfathers.

"Listen," he said with a grin, "if you're still looking for a pet, you're more than welcome to share Lester."

"Thanks." She grinned, grateful for the lighthearted talk. "I hope this doesn't mean I'll have to be visiting Hester Macon more often."

"No, once is more than enough." He sobered suddenly. "Am I really such a bear that you felt you had to spare the twins from my temper?"

She nearly passed off his question with a polite, no, not really, but with this man, she sensed, honesty would always be best. "I figured you had enough on your mind, and those two, well, they're really cute kids, you know."

"And really forgetful ones."

"They swear they latched that gate. Maybe…"

He shook his head in exasperation. "Let me guess. You've been talking to Gramps."

No, she'd been listening—Gramps was talking to the rosebush, plotting to find Mitch a wife.

Aloud, she merely said, "I have to admit, I'm confused. I thought the ghost was an ancestress named Lady. Gramps always refers to her as if she's his wife."

Mitch sighed. "He took losing Grandma Rose pretty hard. It was after she died that Gramps started having his…episodes. Forgetting to eat, wandering outside at night, talking to the air. That's why I moved my family down here, to look after him."

"You *moved* here?" She paused, then said, "That's right, you lived in Philadelphia."

"I did my stint in the city, working my butt off running a fairly successful construction firm. I hated it, though. The long hours, the constant demands, losing one opportunity after another to watch my kids grow up. After twelve years, I was happy to return home to this quiet little corner of the world."

"You had a successful business and you just walked away

from it?'' Hard to keep the dismay from her tone. Harder yet not to liken Mitch to her stepfather, Simon Conners.

"I walked with a sizable profit,'' he said dryly. "Trouble was, I wanted to use it to restore Rose Arbor and my wife wanted to tour Europe. Beth begrudged every cent I ever put into the place. She saw the house as a mausoleum, and shuddered at the thought of running a bed-and-breakfast out in the country. She wanted the fast track of high society.''

"That's why you split up?'' Darcy encouraged, wanting to hear why they'd divorced.

"I guess it was the proverbial straw on the camel's back. We married too young, before we knew ourselves, much less each other. We never did have an ideal relationship, but this situation with Gramps brought our differences into focus. Beth wanted to lock him away in a nursing home, but I couldn't do that. It would break his heart to leave Rose Arbor, and where was the harm in letting Gramps talk to statues or rosebushes, or anything else that brought my grandmother back into his life? Still, I suppose you could say I put the last nail in the marriage coffin by insisting we come here to live.''

He gestured around him. "All the space here, the fresh air and quiet—it turned out to be a perfect fit for me and the kids, but Beth was miserable, and determined to make everyone miserable with her. For two hellish years, we were either at each other's throats, or she was running off to her folks in Philadelphia. I tried to keep the marriage going for the kids, but it actually came as a relief when Beth announced she'd found someone else.''

So the woman had left *him?* It shouldn't make a difference, since his marriage had still failed, but for some reason, Darcy felt better knowing Mitch hadn't walked out on his wife.

"The thing of it was,'' he went on, "I always thought I'd be like my grandparents, married to one person for all of my life, but the differences between us were too fundamental. Beth never could fathom what this place meant to me.''

Looking up at his profile, seeing the clean, firm line of his jaw, Darcy realized that Mitch was as much a part of Rose

Arbor as its columns and rambling fields. His wife must have been blind to consider uprooting him from his home, yet she really couldn't blame Beth for trying. Whatever the problems between them, it must have been hard to leave this man behind.

Mitch stopped suddenly, and with a start, she realized they'd reached the cottage. "I didn't mean to ramble on," he said. "I guess I'm just trying to explain why I've been such a grump. There's no excuse for rudeness, I know, but I've been under a lot of pressure to make the place work, to prove it's the ideal environment for my kids. It certainly doesn't help knowing Beth's been after Mel to come live with her."

He grimaced and Darcy's heart went out to him. "If she left them, how can she can get custody if the kids want to stay with you?"

"There's the rub. Mel is more than a little tempted by the fast life she knows she can live in the city."

Now Darcy remembered why she'd gone to the workshop in the first place. "Maybe Mel wouldn't feel so tempted if she had more of a social life here. Instead of a small, family gathering, why not give her a real sweet-sixteen party, with kids from her school?"

His eyebrows raised. "How? Her birthday's tomorrow."

"I could help. I'm very good at arranging things."

He stared at her, as if trying to figure her out. "I don't doubt it, but why would you want to?"

Why indeed?

"The last I heard," Mitch went on, "you were on your way to Hilton Head. To meet Peter."

"The way you say his name, you'd think it was a dirty word."

He kept his gaze trained on her. "I just can't have much respect for a man who would leave his woman alone, stranded with strangers."

"Peter knows I can take care of myself," she said with forced bravado.

"But why should you have to? You totaled that car. I

would think the least you could expect is the support and comfort of your lover.''

"He's not my lover!" she snapped, running out of excuses.

Mitch smiled. "Ah, so the plot thickens."

"He isn't my lover, *yet*," she amended. "I took time to think, to be sure, but if you must know, this was going to be *the* weekend."

"He knows this and he's still not here? Lady, maybe you should think some more."

Staring into his eyes, feeling the heat building in the core of her body, she feared he might be right. "I don't see how it's any of your business," she said stiffly, trying to hide how his sheer physical presence had her tingling.

"No, it isn't." He gazed down at her ruefully. "But I still say Peter's a fool."

Cursing under his breath, he reached for her, burying his hands in her hair as he pulled her against him. There was no asking this time—only taking. Holding her face in his hands, he gave her a kiss that was a slow, drugging assault of the senses, a powerful meeting of the lips meant to last a good, long time.

A wise woman would have pulled away, run away, while she still had her wits intact, but Darcy was lost the moment he touched her. With a small, smothered moan of protest she surrendered to the sweet, melting warmth of his mouth.

Kissing Mitch was all she remembered, and more. That honeyed sense of urgency, the need to give of herself—to take in return—jumbled itself into a rolling snowball of emotion. She arched into him, reveling in the sensation. She felt so alive, so strong when Mitch held her. Heaven help her but she had to have more.

Yet even as she reached up to pull him closer, he broke away roughly. "If you were my woman," he said, breathing hard and fast, "I'd be on the next plane."

Shaking his head, he strode off, leaving her standing there still trembling with need. How male of him, she thought, hugging herself with her arms. Drop the bombshell, and then saunter off without looking back at the damage.

If you were mine, he'd said, his voice as soft and beguiling as the petal of a rose.

Enough nonsense, she thought as she entered the cottage. Dangerous nonsense, considering how very nearly she'd succumbed to it. She and Peter had a perfectly satisfactory relationship. They shared a wonderfully ordered existence in New York, the ideal life for her—even if she found it hard to remember its appeal on a moonlit Southern night.

Yet, as she undressed and slid into bed, she kept thinking about Mitch and her reaction to him. The man was utterly unsuitable, a divorced father of three with no dependable income, yet all he had to do was pull her into his arms and she was happy to forget the rest of the world existed.

So much so, she realized suddenly, she'd again forgotten to call Peter.

She knew she should get up and phone him now. She needed to hear his voice, to let Peter's calm, efficient tone anchor her back to her life in the city.

But it would mean getting dressed, and trudging all the way to the house, a good million miles in the distance. Besides, it was too late to be calling anyone.

Peter could wait, she decided drowsily. She'd call him first thing tomorrow.

Gramps stood in the shadows outside the cottage, quietly chuckling over what he'd just witnessed. That had been quite a kiss Mitch and Darcy had shared. Too bad they had to ruin it by parting so abruptly.

Shaking his head, he crumpled the paper in his hand. It was late and Darcy was clearly upset, so he saw no reason to bother her with the message. All things considered, he'd be wiser to wait before telling her that her boyfriend had called, and that he expected—no, demanded—that she call him back.

In truth, Gramps hadn't particularly liked the man's tone.

This Peter Arlington seemed a bit too haughty for his taste, and far too complacent about Darcy.

Stuffing the note under the porch, he decided to wait and tell her in the morning.

If he remembered.

Chapter Twelve

Scrubbing the iron stove after breakfast the next day, Mitch counted off the thousand things he had to do. Roy had already submitted his daily lists of demands, which ranged from delivering breakfast in bed to his wife, to supplying the Hackett teenagers with lawn games, the idea being that Mitch would keep them busy while the rest of the clan went sight-seeing. Bad enough having to put off his other chores to go rustle up the games, but the Hackett teens—Harley and Danny in particular—were going to require constant supervision. Add Roy's additions to the routine maintenance chores, throw in this worry about a possible hurricane, and how was Mitch to get ready for Mel's birthday?

Though to be honest, it wasn't the day-to-day stress that had him on edge. If he felt restless and distracted, once again, blame Darcy.

It was driving him crazy, the way she drifted into his thoughts. Try as he might to banish her from his mind, he kept seeing her face as she parted her lips, kept smelling her delicate perfume, feeling her soft, warm flesh beneath his hands.

Disgusted with himself, he threw the dirty sponge into the sink with more force than necessary. What was it about that woman that wouldn't let go of him? Was it the lure of the forbidden, the unattainable, that had him acting like a caged bull? Shoving the breakfast pots and pans into cabinets, he told himself it was no wonder he was in a bad mood. Walking around in a nightie, wearing those skimpy shorts, she was constantly titillating and tantalizing him with visions of what he was missing. It was the combination of denial and frustration that drove him, fanning a simple physical attraction into raging lust.

Maybe he should just bed the woman and end the mystique.

He paused, wondering if maybe it wasn't that bad a solution. After all, they were both mature, experienced adults. Indulge themselves, and they could scratch the itch right out of their systems. A quick seduction, a meeting between the sheets satisfactory to them both, and they could go on with their lives from there.

He stood, frowning, resting his hands on the counter as he stared out the window at the garden. After talking with her last night, after kissing her and holding her in his arms, he knew it wouldn't be that easy. Nothing about Darcy Mac-Teague would ever be simple. Take this woman to bed, and the least she'd expect—and deserve—was commitment.

She was right—she probably was better off with Peter.

It made Mitch angry, though, and frustrated beyond belief. The prospect of being near her, of being able to look but not touch, was liable to drive him nuts.

Muttering an oath, he pushed off from the counter. The smart thing to do—the only thing to do—would be to put distance between them. If he had any smarts, he'd drive Darcy to Hilton Head himself.

That's what he'd do, he decided as he marched from the room. Not today, of course, since he had to deal with the

Hacketts and Mel's birthday, but first thing tomorrow, he and Ms. Darcy MacTeague would set out for the coast.

And in the meantime, he'd do his best to avoid her.

Determined to find her own mode of transportation, Darcy was heading across the front lawn to the phone, when Gramps came walking toward her. "Ah, Darcy," he called out, "I was just coming to ask for your help. I seem to be in a bit of a dilemma."

"I have to make some calls. Are you in a hurry, or can it wait?"

Gramps shook his head. "At my age, I try to avoid any situation that requires me to hurry, but this is quite urgent. It concerns poor Mel."

Poor Mel? Darcy felt a spurt of alarm. "Her mother didn't call, did she?"

"No, no. It's about her party. Or more accurately, the cake. I don't know what's the matter with me lately. I know Mel's favorite is chocolate mousse, yet somewhere between last Tuesday when I ordered it, and this morning when I brought it home, it became plain white on white instead."

Seeing his bewildered expression, Darcy tried to console him. "I doubt the mix-up was your fault. The bakery must have been a zoo, with this being a holiday. I'm sure if you explain things to them, they'll replace the cake and give you the one you ordered."

He shook his head. "It closed early for the holiday and now we're stuck with that ugly sheet cake. I can scrape together a decent meal for the kids, but I've never been much of a baker. I was wondering—hoping—perhaps you could try?"

He looked at her with such appeal, Darcy hated to deny him, but she was a disaster-on-legs in the kitchen, and besides, she'd waited too long already to contact Peter. Every moment she spent at Rose Arbor, her life in New York faded more out of focus. She needed to find out about the Tavish account, to remember what was truly important, before the charm of this place led her into acting as impulsively as her mother.

Yet before she could try to explain this to Gramps, she saw Lester barreling across the yard in front of them. And close on his heels came the boys, shouting and screaming at the goat.

Déjà vu, she thought.

Gramps was grinning ear to ear, Darcy noticed when she turned back to him. "That's my Rose," she thought she heard him mutter.

"Gramps, Darcy, help us!" both boys shouted as they scrambled past, their words reminding Darcy of the plea that had first landed her here.

Still, whether it was a ghost or sheer misfortune that set the goat free, Lester needed to be corraled before he got to Hester Macon's marigolds. Reasoning that she could run faster than the boys, especially now that she knew the route, Darcy made the split-second decision to go after the animal herself.

Fortunately, she was wearing denim shorts and sneakers today, as well as a red tank top more durable than the poor silk blouse. As such, she managed to reach Hester Macon's in relatively good shape, mere moments behind Lester. "No, you don't," she told the goat angrily. "Get out of that garden and come with me."

Lester looked up with soulful eyes, then trotted over happily as if glad to see her. Darcy found herself reaching out to pet his neck, feeling an unlikely affection toward the silly goat. He was, she supposed, the closest she'd ever come to having a pet.

"Go on, scat! Get out of here!" Miss Macon shouted behind her.

Darcy whirled, stunned to find the old woman brandishing a broom.

"Oh, it's you, Miss MacTeague. I thought you'd left Seven Corners."

"I'm trying to."

"Well, you go on and take that dreadful creature away from here. Nobody's wrecking my flowers." Snarling, Miss Macon poked the broom in Lester's direction. With her gray hair in disarray and dark eyes glittering, she seemed a far cry from the poor, lonely old woman Darcy had left in this spot yesterday. "This year, I'm going to win the Seven Corners Garden Society award, and there's nothing the Roses can do to stop me."

"Lester escaped by accident, Miss Macon. Surely you can't think Mitch would stoop to sabotage."

Hester waved the broom with less enthusiasm. "Not normally, I suppose." She glared at Lester. "But three times in one week goes beyond coincidence. Maybe Mitchell isn't at fault, but I wouldn't put it past Edgar."

Considering his grin as she left him, Darcy couldn't exactly vouch for Gramps. Nor was she about to offer an explanation, when the culprit seemed to be his wife's ghost. "I, er, think there's something wrong with the latch to the pen's gate," Darcy offered. "With the Hacketts demanding his time, Mitch hasn't been able to fix it yet."

"Hmmph." Setting the broom down, Hester leaned her weight on it. "Well, just see that you keep that goat on Rose property. The next time I find it in my garden, I'll be pulling out the shotgun, not this old broom."

Darcy moved protectively in front of the goat. "Surely it's not necessary to shoot Lester."

Miss Macon raised a steel-gray eyebrow. "I have neither the patience nor the time to be dealing with that stray at the moment. I have a good dozen cakes to finish baking for tomorrow."

Darcy now noticed the woman's apron and the smudges of flour on her face. "A dozen?" she asked, wondering for whom this self-proclaimed recluse could be baking all those cakes.

Hester looked at her as if Darcy were a simpleton. "I always supply goods for the garden society bake sale at the

Labor Day picnic. The more I bake, the more cash we can raise for the beautification of Seven Corners.''

"I don't suppose you could put together a chocolate mousse cake?''

"Why? You looking to buy a cake?'' Hester now eyed her with speculation, as if she'd found a live one.

This is ridiculous, Darcy thought. As Mitch suggested, she had other, more important items on her agenda. She meant to leave Rose Arbor as soon as humanly possible.

Still, she couldn't deny that this was the perfect solution for the problem with Mel's cake, and by supplying it, maybe Miss Macon would feel needed and useful. "Can you have it ready by late this evening?'' she asked. "I'd be happy to pay for the extra trouble.''

As it had yesterday, Hester's stern expression transformed with a sudden, dazzling smile. "Is this for Melissa's birthday?''

"There seems to have been a mix-up at the bakery,'' Darcy explained. "We'd be ever so grateful if you could help us out of a jam.''

Hester's eyebrow raised again at the "us,'' but she directed her scowl at Lester. "You keep that creature out of my garden, and I'll not only decorate that cake up special, I'll hand-deliver it myself tonight.''

The poor soul was angling for an invitation, Darcy realized. "The party is at eight,'' she said, not finding the heart to deny her. "I'm sure the Roses will be delighted to hear you'll be a part of their celebration.''

"You just make sure to keep that goat where it belongs,'' Hester said firmly, marching back to her kitchen.

"I promise,'' Darcy told her, but all the way to Rose Arbor, she wondered how on earth she would keep her word. Short of setting up an armed guard at the gate, she knew of no way to prevent Lester's escape.

Unless, she thought, there was somewhere inside the barn where she could lock him in for the time being.

Dragging the goat behind her into the barn, she discovered

that while the structure must once have housed cattle, the stalls were now empty and clean. "You should be happy here," she told Lester as she herded him into the nearest stall and shut the gate across it. "Don't worry, I'll get you plenty to eat."

Going out to the pen to gather Lester's feed and water, she made a side trip to the porch for a potted marigold. "That ought to keep you content for a while," she told the goat as she set it down in front of him.

She was leaving the barn, feeling fairly pleased with herself, when the boys came running up with wide, worried faces.

"We looked everywhere but couldn't find Lester," Ky said breathlessly, his serious face clouded with worry.

Even J.J.'s exuberance was subdued. "Dad's gonna kill us," he panted beside his brother.

"Don't worry, Lester's inside," Darcy assured them, resisting the urge to hug them both. Being boys, they'd be embarrassed, and besides, they were covered in mud. "I found him at Miss Macon's. *Before* he could eat her marigolds."

J.J. beamed at her. "Wow, Darcy, you're the best."

"Yeah." Even Ky was emphatic. "Lady sure was right about you."

"Oh, boys." Sighing, Darcy squatted between them, wanting to be at eye level. "You've got to stop talking as if the ghost were real. People are going to think she's part of the family."

"But she is." Ky's steady clear blue gaze reminded her of his father. "She's part Lady, and part Grandma Rose, too."

J.J. patted her shoulder consolingly. "Don't feel bad if you can't see her, Darcy. Gramps says only the young and the old get to spot Lady, because everyone else is too busy. Their lives are too cluttered to notice anything they can't see with their eyes."

"It's Lady who lets Lester out of the pen, you know," Ky added solemnly. "We think she does it to keep you here."

Darcy didn't enjoy hearing her own suspicions echoed by

the twins. "Don't be silly," she told them. "Why on earth would your ghost want *me* to stay?"

"To help us," J.J. stated simply.

Awkwardly, Ky reached out to touch her arm. "She's worried about us 'cause we don't really have a mom anymore."

Gazing at their young, trusting faces, Darcy felt an ache deep in her gut. She should tell them to abandon such fantasy, that she wasn't cut out to act like anyone's mother, but a small, buried voice inside her urged her to gather these two kids close and protect them from all the ills of the world.

"What are you boys doing here?" Gramps asked, suddenly coming up behind her. "Shouldn't you be out back getting that pump put together? Your father is fast losing patience and I can't say I blame him."

Darcy rose to her feet. Two seconds more and she'd have embarrassed them all by giving this pair a big sloppy hug.

Instead, she stepped forward, unconsciously shielding them. "It's my fault, Gramps. They were helping me get Lester settled in the barn. After all, we can't have Lady letting him out of the pen again."

The old man's frown eased into a smile, lending support to the theory of his guilt. Exasperated, Darcy explained her deal with Hester Macon. "So, you see, we've got to keep Lester locked up in the barn, or Miss Macon won't bake the chocolate mousse cake for Mel's party."

The boys nodded with a marked lack of enthusiasm. "That was nice of you, Darcy," Ky said, ever the diplomat. "But I don't think it's gonna make Mel any happier."

"She's says she's a grown-up now, and cake and ice cream is for little kids like us," J.J. added in a perfect imitation of Mel's preening. "She doesn't care about the party 'cause it's just gonna be boring anyway."

"She says everything about Seven Corners is boring," Ky added. "Compared to Philadelphia."

Gramps sighed. "Take it easy on your sister, boys. Mel's suffering growing pains. The real reason she wants to go live with your mother is that she thinks it's the only way she can go on dates and wear makeup.''

The boys looked from their grandfather to Darcy, clearly confused. "If that's the problem," Ky asked with his knack for logic, "why doesn't Dad let her do that stuff?"

"Yeah," J.J. seconded. "He could give her a party with boys and dancing. Then Mel would want to stay here with us."

"I don't understand you two," Gramps said. "The way you're always scrapping with your sister, I'd think you'd jump at the opportunity to get Mel out of the house."

They looked at their great-grandfather as if he'd spoken in a different language. "She's our sister," J.J. said as if that explained everything.

And perhaps it did. In their minds, Darcy realized, they were family and therefore inseparable. They might tease and argue among themselves, but they would fight tooth and nail to stay together.

Listening to them, Darcy felt a deep envy, wishing just once she too could experience such a tight bond. "You know," she found herself suggesting, "I don't think it would be hard to throw together the kind of party Mel wants."

All three Roses turned to her with surprise.

"All you'd need is a decent stereo. Have you got one in the house?"

The boys nodded eagerly. "We don't have a lot of tapes and CDs," J.J. told her, "but we can always borrow them from our friends."

"Yeah," Ky piped in, "but where are we gonna get boys?"

Again, all three turned to Darcy.

"I imagine Melissa has a best friend, doesn't she?"

"Yeah, Joan." J.J. looked more puzzled than ever.

"Well, get me Joan's phone number," Darcy said with a smile. "Who better than a best friend to help us contact the boys Melissa would want invited to her party?"

"The number's in the address book at the front desk,"

Gramps volunteered, his expression quizzical. "Under H, for Holleran."

"While I'm at it," Darcy said, thinking aloud, "maybe I could ask Joan to spirit Melissa away for the afternoon so we can decorate the ballroom."

"Wow," J.J. said, blue eyes widening. "Decorations. This is gonna be great."

"Yeah!" Even Ky grinned ear to ear. "We can blow up balloons, and we've got those leftover streamers from our Power Ranger party."

Darcy tried not to wince. "Actually, we could try something more feminine for your sister. I thought we might use flowers from the garden."

The boys whooped and cheered, but Gramps merely gaped at her, obviously appalled. "But tomorrow is the garden society competition. How can we win with the flowers wilting in the house?"

"I'm sorry, I forgot about the competition." Caught up in the boys' enthusiasm, she hadn't stopped to consider the rivalry with Hester Macon.

"That garden means everything to my Rose," Gramps said wistfully. "She worked like a dog every year to win that trophy."

"Forget I mentioned it," Darcy told him, patting his arm. "We can use the streamers. I know how important the competition is to you."

Smiling, Gramps reached down to cover her hand. "No, you're right. Our flowers will add the perfect touch to Mel's party, and I know this is one tradition my Rose won't mind me breaking. Better to use those roses for love, she'll say, than for garnering yet another trophy we have to dust. She'd be the first to tell you that family always comes first."

Family comes first. The words caused a strange, building warmth in her chest.

"Besides," Gramps added, his eyes twinkling as he glanced back at the barn, "it might be good politics to let Hester win once in a while."

Darcy returned his grin. "Yes, there is that."

"Only thing is," Ky said ominously, "what about Dad?"

J.J. shook his head sadly. "Yeah, he'll never let you invite boys to Mel's party."

With a sigh, Gramps let go of Darcy's hand. "I'm afraid they might be right. Mitch tends to be a tad overprotective when it comes to his little girl. Considering everything else going on around here, I doubt he'll want the extra worry of playing chaperon to a bunch of teenage boys tonight."

"You're worrying needlessly," she assured them, caught up in her enthusiasm. "Actually, I've already brought up this subject to your father."

"And he said yes?"

The boys spoke in unison, and with such disbelief Darcy had to backtrack. "Well, not exactly, but he didn't say no, either." And Mitch hadn't, though, thinking back, she realized he hadn't let her get very far in relating her plans.

The three Roses exchanged worried glances.

"You guys just concern yourselves with setting up the stereo and gathering flowers," she told them with far more confidence than she felt. "Leave your father to me. I can handle Mitch."

Brave words, but as she marched to the house, she took care to make sure no one noticed she'd crossed her fingers behind her back.

Chapter Thirteen

Mitch stormed through the house, calling for his kids and receiving no answer. He needed help setting up the games on the front lawn, but his family seemed to have vanished. Worse, the boys had left the old pump in even more of a mess, with mud and puddles all over the backyard. "J.J., Ky," he shouted. "Where the devil is everyone?"

He heard a faint "In here" from the ballroom.

He should have known it wouldn't be his children he'd find when he paused in the doorway, but Darcy MacTeague, looking like the May queen, surrounded by baskets of flowers.

Darcy, who he wanted to drive away from here at the first possible moment, who he meant to avoid at all costs.

The trouble was, she looked like an enchantress amongst all those flowers. Gazing at her, it was all he could do not to sweep the baskets aside, lay her down in a bed of those sweet-scented flowers and make hot, glorious love to her for the rest of the afternoon.

But that would be madness, and he knew it.

"Where's my family?" he barked, feeling as if he'd been thrown another curveball. "And what the devil are you doing in here?"

Smiling tightly, she returned her attention to her work. She was snipping the thorns off the roses, Mitch noticed, before twining their stems into a string of leaves.

"Gramps is out in the garden," she told him calmly. "The boys have gone to...I believe they said the Femmers' house?"

"What are they doing way out there? They know they're not allowed to play until they put that pump back together."

"They're not playing. They're on an errand for me."

"For you?" Mitch didn't know which annoyed him more, his boys' disobedience, or the way Darcy was ignoring him. "What errand can be so important they feel justified in disobeying my orders?"

"Sinatra." Shrugging, she reached into a basket for another garland of greenery. "They've already tried the Ryans and most of the closer neighbors but no one seems to have the right cassette or CD. Your grandfather insists you haven't danced until you've waltzed to 'Strangers In The Night.'" Lifting a fat yellow rose, she snipped off the thorns, then poked the stem into the garland before reaching for another bloom.

Determined to capture her full attention, Mitch strode into the room, coming to a stop before her. "Would you please explain what's going on? Why I suddenly feel like a stranger in my own house?"

She glanced up, meeting his gaze squarely. "I'm sorry. I assumed you'd know we were getting ready for Melissa's party. We did talk about this last night."

"I remember what happened last night," he began, then paused at the sudden flush that rushed to her cheeks. No wonder he could never get his bearings around her; the mixture of city sophistication and little-girl naïveté always caught him off guard.

He picked up a soft yellow rose, staring at it rather than

letting himself be distracted again by her full pouting lips. "I don't recall ever agreeing to Sinatra and roses. Or turning ice cream and cake into such a big production."

"Don't worry, we have everything under control."

"We?"

"Me, Gramps and the boys. You don't have to do a thing except show up at eight sharp."

"Really? And what about the houseful of Hacketts I have to deal with?"

"Actually," she said with a tight smile, "I invited them, too."

"I beg your pardon?"

"Well, they do have seven male teenagers, and poor Joan was having trouble rustling up enough boys at this late date—"

"Boys?"

"Boys," she said more firmly. "That's who young ladies dance with. I'm sure you must remember, having once been sixteen yourself."

Mitch tossed the rose into the basket. "All right, you've made your point. Maybe I should have invited a few boys from her class, but I draw the line at mingling socially with the guests. I want my daughter's birthday to be a private, family affair," he said, determined not to let her get to him. "Not some three-ring circus."

"But it's not *your* birthday," she said gently. "Isn't it more important to have the party Melissa wants?"

"And you're the expert? Can you be so certain that you're not putting together the sweet-sixteen party *you* wanted?"

It was a rotten thing to say—he knew it the minute he saw the hurt flash across her face.

"I admit, I'd have loved to have a party like this," she told him evenly enough, "but I also know it's too late to relive the past. I'm not doing this for me. I just hate to see Mel suffer."

She laid down the rose, leaning forward, her eyes sincere and pleading. "A girl is her most insecure at sixteen. Not a child anymore, yet not quite a woman, so she's left feeling like she doesn't fit in anywhere. What Mel needs right now is to see that she's important to you and the boys. Give her this party, Mitch. Treat her like the young woman she wants to be.''

Deep down, he knew it would be the perfect touch, and he wished he had thought of it himself. But it had been Darcy's idea, this unpredictable female who was determined to leave them without looking back. ''Mel's not mature enough to be dating,'' he said stubbornly.

Darcy sat back, sighing as she picked up her shears. ''I guess you'll have to work that out between you, but what can it hurt to have boys in for supervised dancing, especially the Hacketts who will be gone tomorrow? At the least, it will show Mel that you're willing to compromise, that you love and trust her. Can that be a bad thing?''

Mitch knew she was right, but he still felt guilty that a stranger should have to tell him this about his own daughter. ''I guess that depends on how much all this is going to cost me.''

''Not much. Gramps is whipping up his lemonade punch, and Mr. Hackett agreed that we should avoid serving alcohol because of the teenagers, so he has offered to supply soda and chips from the local Happy Burger stand. Gramps is working on some finger foods, and we have lots of cake. The rest is just a matter of pitching in to do the work.''

''Well, I can't pitch in,'' Mitch said gruffly. ''I've got to run over to Sunnybrook Inn to pick up horseshoes and badminton rackets to keep the Hackett kids occupied, and I still have to load up the hay wagon for the picnic tomorrow. You'll have to do this on your own.''

If he'd hoped his words would discourage her, he was doomed to disappointment. ''All right,'' she said cheerfully. ''As long as we have your okay.''

Mitch hadn't meant to give his approval, but looking at all the flowers, realizing how much she and Gramps had already done, he couldn't say no. It struck him that Darcy had gone to far more trouble than Mel's own mother had ever done.

It touched a chord inside him, a spot he'd kept shielded for years. It unnerved him, how deeply Darcy probed with her soft, melting gazes, and made him all the more determined to avoid her at all costs.

"Sure, whatever," he said over his shoulder, anxious to get away from Darcy and the uncomfortable yearnings she aroused in him. "Just don't break the bank."

Darcy let out her breath, feeling as if she'd just gone ten rounds with the champ. What was it about that man that always got her adrenaline going?

Adrenaline? a tiny voice asked. *Or was it another set of hormones?*

She rubbed her arms, reluctant to admit how just being near him could make her tingle. So much for handling Mitch. She'd gotten permission, but at what cost? Standing before him, explaining why the party was so important, she'd felt as if she'd been baring her soul to him.

Is that such a bad thing? the tiny voice again prompted.

She had to admit there was something nice about talking to Mitch Rose. Even when they were arguing, even as gruff and ill-tempered as he tried to act, she could sense he was listening, really listening to what she had to say.

Smiling at the thought, she looked up to find Gramps stumbling in with the stereo. She jumped up to help him, and as they set up the system on the oak banquet table, Gramps entertained her with tales about past competitions with Hester Macon. He was telling her about the year she had tried painting the leaves of some of her plants a deeper green, only to have them wilt and die in the sun, when the boys bounded in. Ky lugged the heavy bag of cassettes behind him, while J.J. held up the elusive Sinatra CD with ill-disguised triumph.

Snapping it out of his hands and slipping it in the player, the old man let a slow, pleased smile cover his face. "Now *that's* music," he said, a faraway look glazing his eyes as the strains of "Strangers In The Night" filled the room. "That's the kind of tune a man can romance his lady to."

The boys made faces, insisting that music was for listening to, not dancing—and certainly not for something as silly as romancing.

"Don't be so close-minded," Darcy told them with a grin. "There's all kinds of music, for all kinds of occasions, and judging by the size of that bag, we'll probably have opportunity to hear most of it. I hope you've marked which tape goes where so we can return them tomorrow." At their stricken looks, she added, "Do it now, before you forget."

They darted from the room, Ky still dragging the bag behind him.

Chuckling, Gramps came over to stand behind her. "It's amazing, but our roses have never looked lovelier. I must say, I'm impressed by how much you've been able to accomplish in such a short time, Darcy. You do this often?"

"Arranging things is one of my few talents." She sighed. "But I don't know how I'd have managed without you and the boys. I only hope it turns out the way we want."

"You worried about what Mitch will do?"

"Yeah, I suppose I am."

"Don't you fret over Mitch." He patted her shoulder. "He's a tad grumpy, what with all his worries, but deep down, he wants what's best for Mel. Trust me, this party is important to him. He's just afraid to show it."

She nodded, letting that revelation sift in. Mitch always seemed so strong, so capable, it was hard to remember he must be suffering doubts too. After all, he stood to lose the most, if after all this, Mel still chose to go off with her mother.

"It hurts to love," she said, thinking out loud.

"Maybe, but I'm thinking it hurts more not to."

She turned around, looking at him. "Are you trying to tell me it's better to have loved and lost?"

Gramps grinned. "Something like that." He moved away to take the CD off the player.

Watching him, she sensed that he had a point to make and she wouldn't escape without hearing it. "Go on," she said impatiently. "I know you have some pearl of wisdom you want to add."

He faced her with grandfatherly concern. "I worry about you, my dear. All those emotions, bottled up inside, they're gonna start choking you if they don't soon find an outlet. You'll feel much better if you give of yourself, Darcy. You need to love."

I give plenty, she thought defensively. In her own way, she loved her mother—maybe even Peter.

Yeah, a tiny voice inside her nagged, *then why haven't you called him?*

She was spared answering by a sudden chime of the front doorbell. "That must be Frank's Deli with the sandwiches we ordered," Gramps said, clearly happy to exit now that he'd said what he wanted. "I'll go take them to the kitchen."

Watching him retreat, Darcy swore that she'd show Gramps how much she cared about Peter. She'd make that call to New York, just as soon as she could manage a short break.

Unfortunately, first she had to finish these garlands, then drape them strategically around the room. She needed to set up tables for food and drink, hopefully with tablecloths, and she hadn't even begun to figure out how to decorate the veranda. She knew Mitch was busy, and doing his best to avoid her, but she couldn't help wishing he would spare a few minutes to help.

Glancing up, she saw Mitch in the doorway, his arms loaded down with strings of tiny lights. "These were up in the attic," he muttered as he entered the room. "I thought, well, as long as we're going to do this, we might as well do it up right."

A soft, warm glow spread through her at the sight of him marching across the ballroom to the French doors. She needed help and here he was, Mitchell Allen Rose, once again coming to the rescue. Gramps was right, she thought. This man might grumble and complain, but he would always do what was best for his family.

Hearing him curse as he tried unsuccessfully to open the doors with his hands full, she set down the flowers. "Lights, huh?" she said as she hurried over to open the door for him. "Twinkling or steady?"

"Both. I figured I'd put the blinkers in the bushes and decorate the balustrade with the others. It makes for a, well, a kind of magical effect."

She nodded at the semitangled strands. "Need help?"

His was a reluctant smile, but a genuine one nonetheless. "I came down here to help *you*," he told her, setting down the pile to untangle the lights. "And I guess to apologize. All evidence to the contrary, I really do appreciate what you're doing for Mel. I guess I've been pretty dense, not realizing she might prefer a party with boys and dancing."

"It's a girl thing," she said, more than happy to let him off the hook after that disarming speech. "Most dads would overlook it. I mean, did you want to dance at your sixteenth birthday?"

"No, but I did, anyway." With a wry grin, he handed her a finished string of lights and set to work on another. "My grandmother decided it was time to show me there was more to life than fishing and tinkering with broken cars. I couldn't have been more embarrassed, since none of my friends would even consider having a dress-up ball for their birthdays. But once I saw how good the girls looked in their dresses, and how they all loved the dancing, well, I was a convert. It turned out to be the best party of my young life."

"Let's hope it's the same for Melissa."

"We can give it our best shot." He frowned, handing her a second string. "I hope it's enough, showing her we care, that we want her staying at Rose Arbor with us and not going off to Philadelphia with her mother."

Laying the separated strings over the balustrade, Darcy chose her words with care. "Whether or not the party is wonderful, she might still choose to leave. She's at that age where she needs to have a woman around.''

"All well and good if the mother's dependable." He tugged at a string with more force than necessary. "What Mel needs now is to put down roots. After going through our divorce, the kids all need stability and discipline. They shouldn't have their lives constantly disrupted.''

Putting down roots, she thought with strange yearning, was something she herself had never managed to do.

"Beth could have had joint custody of the kids," he went on bitterly, "but she didn't want it. Not then, when they needed her most. Now that Mel is old enough to take care of herself, it's suddenly attractive to have a daughter, but what happens when Beth discovers there's more to raising a teenager than dressing her up and showing her off? It'll break Mel's heart if her mother walks out on her again.''

"Then refuse to let Melissa go.''

"I can try. But Beth's new husband has the hard cold cash to slug it out in court. I don't. As much as I love Rose Arbor, it isn't exactly a money-making machine.''

"Oh, but it could be." The ad executive in her burst to life. "You've got a ready-made market just waiting to be tapped. City people all over the country are aching to escape to such peace and quiet. You've got the gimmick, that Come-Smell-the-Roses thing. Just surround it with a campaign—some billboards, ads in the papers, a few auto-club ratings—and you can turn this place into a highly profitable venture. Maybe even expand into...''

Too late she realized she had impulsively put her hand on his arm. He was staring at it as if it was about to bite him.

"Haven't you been listening?" he asked, pointedly pulling away. "Ad campaigns, expansion, I left all that behind in Philadelphia. I brought my family here to escape the rat race, not to create another one.''

He turned away to string the lights through the hedges, leaving an awkward silence between them. At first, Darcy thought of apologizing, fearing she'd been butting in, but the more she considered it, the more she found Mitch to be a proud, stubborn fool. He'd said he needed money and she'd tried to help. A mistake she'd never make again.

Annoyed, she went back to arranging flowers, work she obviously shouldn't have left.

When he was done with the lights, Mitch walked over to her, pausing before her chair. For an instant, she thought *he* meant to apologize, but glancing up hopefully, she found his expression far too cool and guarded.

"Listen, I'm tied up right now keeping the Hackett kids busy, and later, we have this party," he said with a marked lack of enthusiasm, "but if you still need that ride to Hilton Head in the morning, I have an old pickup that can take you where you want to go."

How like a man, she thought. Talking about everything *except* what was really bothering him. "I don't think that will be necessary. I expect to hear from Peter soon."

The wariness became a scowl. "Whatever. The offer still stands, though, if you need a ride."

He sauntered off, no doubt feeling better now that he'd thrown her that bone, but Darcy merely felt saddened. She wondered if she could ever have a conversation with him that didn't turn into an argument.

She was still stewing over Mitch when three of the Hackett teenagers raced through the ballroom, Harley and Danny chasing a squealing Merry Sue. They came to an abrupt stop when they saw Darcy's frown.

When they professed to be bored with the lawn games, she saw the chance to help both Mitch and herself by asking for their assistance with the decorating. Though at first surprised by the request, they fell into the spirit of things eagerly, completing each task she assigned and calling for their cousins to come in and join in on the fun. As such, Darcy spent the next two hours supervising their efforts and answering endless questions.

And when they were done, every post had a garland of roses, and the throne they'd devised for the birthday queen was a snowfall of gardenias. She thanked her helpers and told them the ballroom looked like a dream come true.

Hurrying through the garden, Darcy mentally crossed the to-do items off her list. The decorations were done, the sandwiches were arranged on platters, the soda was on ice and the music was set up and ready, with Harley and Danny Hackett volunteering to take turns playing deejay. She'd taken care of everything except maybe...

A gift!

Glancing at her watch as she entered the cottage, seeing it was already seven, she knew she'd never have time to reach a store—even if she could get a taxi—and return in time for the party. Still, she wanted to give something to the girl, some little token that said it didn't matter if her mom wasn't here, Mel was still pretty special. Something that Darcy herself would have wanted at that age.

Automatically, her hands went to her ears.

Diamonds were far from *some little token*, she thought, yet the more she considered it, the more she liked the idea of giving her earrings to Mel. All they'd ever been was a symbol, a statement of her worth. She liked to think that by passing them down, she might help give Mel the confidence she needed to make her own way in the world.

What was it Gramps had said? That Darcy would feel better if she gave of herself? Smiling as she removed the studs from her earlobes, she realized she felt pretty darned good, at that.

Digging through her suitcase for the little jeweler's box in which she sometimes kept the earrings, she remembered the call she'd never put through to Peter. She toyed with the idea of returning to the house to phone him now, but another glance at her watch warned that she barely had time for a quick shower.

She wasn't stalling, she told the tiny voice nagging her. Racing into the bathroom, she decided she would shower and change, and then she could phone Peter. She swore it.

Chapter Fourteen

Mitch swore softly as he added another tie to the pile on the bed, unhappy with them all. Where was his blue-striped silk, anyway?

"What are you growling about?" Gramps stood at the door, eyeing Mitch humorously, as if he knew the exact reason his grandson was grumbling.

"I can't find my lucky tie. I bet Beth threw it away before she walked out on me. She always said she hated it." Just one more reason that a man should never get married, Mitch thought irritably.

"And just what do you need luck for, son? It's just a simple birthday party, isn't it?"

"A *simple* birthday? Try explaining that to *Ms*. Mac-Teague. Do you know she took it upon herself to invite Roy Hackett and his entire clan?"

"Now I wonder why she'd do that?"

"Because the businesswoman never sleeps, that's why. She saw an opportunity for me to wheel and deal. She probably expects me to set Roy up as an investor in *Rose Arbor, Incorporated,* so we can have one of his Happy Hamburger stands in the dining room, or better yet, the garden.''

Chuckling, Gramps strolled over to the bed. ''I'd have thought by now she'd realize you aren't interested in that kind of thing,'' he said offhandedly as he sifted through the pile of ties.

Mitch would have thought so, too, which was what made him so angry. He wanted Rose Arbor to stay what it was, peaceful and serene. Darcy and her insatiable ambition could see only killer ad campaigns that would turn his simple, family-run business into some huge, ever-expanding conglomerate to chew up his life. He'd had his taste of her dog-eat-dog world; he was done with sacrificing time with his family in the interest of getting ahead. If that's what Darcy wanted, then good luck to her, but in that case, she should leave him and his kids alone.

''She knows I'm not interested,'' he told Gramps, ''but like Beth, she can't be content with the little successes. Always pushing, trying to achieve more. Why can't Darcy see that Rose Arbor is just what it should be, that commercialism would only ruin the place?''

''Why are you asking me? Shouldn't you be telling her this?''

No, Mitch thought vehemently. He should just stay as far away from that female as was humanly possible. Only, look how angry—and frustrated—he'd been this afternoon.

Gramps held out the tie Mitch usually wore with this suit. ''Maybe Darcy *is* ambitious, but she's put her energy to good use. Look how hard she's worked to make this party special for Mel. Beth would never have spent hours breaking her back to decorate the ballroom.''

Against his will, Mitch pictured Darcy as she'd been earlier, surrounded by flowers, beaming up at him as he entered with the lights. No one should be allowed to run around in shorts that revealing, he thought as he snatched the tie from his grandfather and yanked it around his neck. Standing next to her, Mitch had been so distracted by the prospect of running his hands up and down those bare, shapely legs, he hadn't been able to think straight.

"Stop riding her so hard, Mitch, and try understanding her instead."

"What are you up to?" he asked, narrowing his gaze.

Gramps refused to look at him. "Maybe I can't see any sense in you both being lonely, not when there's no need. Just try getting to know Darcy better, son, and letting her see the real you. What can it hurt?"

"Not *what*, Gramps, *who*." Turning back to his closet, Mitch slammed the door shut, hoping to close the conversation, as well. "I tried making a relationship work once before, remember, and none of us enjoyed the results. I see no reason to let another female put this family through that emotional wringer again."

"No relationship is ever easy." His grandfather said it as if he was agreeing, perhaps even consoling him, but being Gramps, there was inevitably more. "The trick is not to give up. As long as you and Darcy keep working at it, love will find a way."

"Love? Gramps, please. I've known the woman all of three days."

The old man gave his secretive smile, the one that drove Mitch crazy. "Yeah, funny how that works sometimes, isn't it?"

"Funny? I'm not laughing."

"Come now, Mitch, why get in a such a stew about everything? Just relax, and trust in fate, and one way or another, things will work out as they should."

Watching Gramps amble from the room, Mitch fought the urge to throttle him. The old man was forever tossing out cryptic messages, then sauntering off without bothering to explain what they meant. Did Gramps truly believe that he need merely trust in fate, and a willing, loving Darcy would be served up to him on a silver platter?

Yeah, right. Nothing was that easy.

Annoyed that he nonetheless found the prospect appealing, he told himself he had work to do, arrangements to oversee. Hurrying out of his room, he insisted that was all that concerned him.

That and his missing blue-striped tie.

Dressed and ready for the party, Darcy was crossing the foyer and heading for the dreaded phone closet, when she heard a strange thumping noise, then muffled whispers. Frowning, she glanced over her shoulder and realized the sounds must be coming from the porch.

She eyed the phone hesitantly. She knew she should make the call, now while she had the chance, but curiosity got the best of her and drew her out the front door.

Ky and J.J. squatted on the porch with a patently unhappy Lester caught between them. While the goat struggled to get his head through the slats in the railing, no doubt to consume the pots of marigolds lined up on the lip, the boys stubbornly attempted to capture that same head and slip over it what seemed to be a blue-striped tie.

"Boys, what are you doing?" she asked, stepping out to join them.

They stood immediately, moving in front of Lester as if to hide him.

"Why, hello, Darcy," Ky said conversationally, as if it were perfectly normal to be wrestling with a goat on the porch. "We were just getting Lester ready for the party."

"Goats don't go to parties," she said, trying not to laugh. "They don't know how to dance."

"But we feel bad for Lester. He's lonely, way out there in the barn." Frowning, J.J. leaned down to hug the goat. "It's not fair. He's part of the family. He loves Mel, too."

"I'm sure he does, but does Mel return the feeling?"

Ky knelt down beside his brother, on the other side of the goat. "She just gets that way to hide her true feelings. Lady calls it being prickly."

Such astuteness made it hard to remember that these twins

were only ten years old. "Still," Ky added, "even Mel knows how important Lester is."

"Yeah," J.J. echoed. "Lester is what Dad calls our roots. With him around, it's like we never have to miss Grandma Rose, because we always have a bit of her here in Lester."

Ky nodded earnestly. "Yeah, and it's not so bad anymore that Mom left us."

Darcy gazed at the scrawny animal, understanding somehow, how Lester might fill the void their mother had left behind. How could she possibly laugh, or dismiss the goat's importance, when these two looked up with such pleading expressions? "You're right," she told them. "Lester *is* part of the family, and it's not fair that he can't come to the party, but don't you think he'll be miserable in the ballroom with all those people dancing around, pushing him here and there, stepping on his toes? Why, think about it. He'd have to listen to your grandfather's music."

The boys glanced at each other and made a face.

"Maybe we can take turns, coming out to the barn to visit Lester," she suggested gently. "Then he won't be lonely and he won't have to wear that tie, either. I hope it isn't one of your father's."

They popped up, looking guilty as sin. "Not one of his good ones," J.J. hurried to explain.

Maybe not, Darcy thought, but considering that the pump still wasn't put back together, these two were in enough trouble without adding theft to their crimes. "I'm not sure it's fair to take something from your dad without asking," she felt compelled to point out. "Tell you what. Ky, you can run upstairs and return the tie while J.J. settles Lester back in the barn. Do it quickly, please. You two need to get into your dress clothes, not Lester. It's already time for your sister to be getting home."

Reminded of how near it was to eight, Darcy began to fiddle with the box in her hands.

"Is that a present for Mel?" Ky asked, eyeing the tiny box, his brother adding, "What is it?"

Darcy shook her head. "I'm not telling, not until you guys are dressed and ready to dance. I took extra care with my appearance tonight so I wouldn't embarrass you when we take our turns on the dance floor."

"You could never embarrass us, Darcy," Ky said with touching sincerity. "You're always pretty, but you sure look special nice tonight."

"Yeah, and you smell real good, too," his brother added.

Their compliments went right to her heart—and confidence. She'd had her misgivings when she bought the dress, fearing Peter might consider it too flashy. Normally, she stuck to conservative styles and colors, but she'd wanted something special for this weekend, a knockout of a gown for when they went dancing, and the shimmering blue silk fit the bill. Hugging her hips and twirling around her knees, it was the kind of dress that made a girl feel feminine and delicate, like a lady, yet its low neckline and bare back let her feel deliciously wicked at the same time. A perfect dress to be kissed in.

And wouldn't you know, Mitch would pick just that moment to stroll up the driveway.

She felt a sudden panic, not ready to test his reaction to her dress. "Quick, take Lester to the barn," she told the boys, hoping to stall the confrontation with their father until she felt more poised and in control. "Here, I'll take care of the tie."

Snatching it from Ky's hands, she shooed the pair down the steps and hurried into the house. Behind her, she could hear Mitch greet his sons, then the boys' animated chatter, and for an instant, she wished she'd stayed to join them.

She hesitated, looking at the tiny box in one hand, the tie in the other. Eyeing the winding staircase, weighing her chances of sneaking upstairs to find both Mitch's and Melissa's bedrooms—then delivering both items unnoticed—she knew she would have to hurry.

At the top of the staircase, she turned left, knowing from Melissa's tour that the rooms in the main hall and right wing would be guest rooms. Not that she would have had trouble identifying them, with the laughter and chatter coming from behind each door. The Hacketts were rarely a quiet group, but they seemed doubly excited tonight as they dressed for Mel's party.

Darcy continued toward the family quarters. As she pushed through the heavy oak door separating the private area from the other wings, she felt as if she'd entered a different world. Slightly shabby, without the fresh paint and plush carpeting of the public rooms, this area felt far more homey.

Most of the doors stood open, as if the family was accustomed to slipping in and out of each other's bedrooms whenever the need, or urge, arose. Inside the first door, she found what seemed to be a family room, complete with television, telephone and other modern conveniences Mitch supposedly held in disdain. The next room, she decided, must belong to Gramps. On every bureau and tabletop, she saw pictures of a woman at all stages of life—no doubt his beloved Rose.

The third revealed what had to be J.J. and Ky's room, with its bunk beds and cartoon-character curtains at the window. Staring at the clutter covering the floor, she saw the pair hadn't gotten to tidying up their room, either. Knowing their father would soon see this mess, Darcy found it all the more imperative that she get his tie back to where it belonged.

She marched to the door at the end of the hall. Unlike the others, it stood closed, seeming isolated and cut off from the flow of things. She assumed it was Mitch's, who, as a father of three, must value privacy.

As she held the tie in her hand, debating whether to invade his domain or to play coward and slip it under the door, her gaze slid to the open doorway to her right.

Obviously a man's room, dark and functional, it held a total lack of feminine frills. This, then, must be where Mitch slept. Any doubts that it could belong to anyone else disappeared the moment she crossed the threshold.

Just like him, the room was simple and unpretentious, furnished with a plain pine dresser and matching armoire. The only real decoration was an elaborate starburst quilt on the simple pine bed.

In contrast to his sons, he kept the bedroom clean and neat, except for the collection of ties strewn across the quilt. She pictured him, irritably rummaging through them before deciding which to wear. Staring at the tie in her hand, she hoped for the boys' sake that he hadn't been looking for this one. The question was, should she toss it on the bed with the others, or seek out the spot where Mitch hung his ties? It would be best to put it where the boys had taken it from, she knew, but she had no way of knowing where that could be.

Unable to make up her mind, she found herself wandering over to the bed, running a hand over the headboard, the pillows. As she did, she caught a whiff of his aftershave. The scent conjured up his image in her mind. Mitch, lying there in the bed, smiling as he reached up to...

She yanked her hand back, disturbed by how easily she'd slipped her own face into the imagined scene. Her pulse was still throbbing, as if she'd actually been in the bed with him. Her heart raced like a marathon runner's.

But it stopped cold when she heard the door slam at the end of the hall.

Panicking, she thought of hiding in the closet, or under the bed, before realizing it would only make things worse. This was no slapstick comedy; she had a perfectly legitimate reason for being in Mitch's room.

That reason, though, had her instinctively hiding the tie behind her back. Explaining, she realized, would only get the boys into further trouble. The urge to hide hit her again.

Before she could move, Mel hurried past the door. "Darcy?" she asked, doing a double take, clearly shocked to find their houseguest in her father's room.

Darcy's initial relief at not seeing Mitch turned into embarrassment. "I, er, came to deliver your present," she tried to explain as she crossed the room, grateful that at least she hadn't been caught with her hands on his pillow. "I wandered in here, thinking it might be your room."

"Present?" Trust the teenager to zero in on what concerned her most. "You got something for me?"

Anxious to herd them both from the room, Darcy didn't at first realize why it should seem odd to the girl, having momentarily forgotten the party was to be a surprise. "I hope you don't mind, but your dad invited me for some ice cream and cake," she hedged when she joined Mel in the hall.

"Dressed like that?"

All Darcy's insecurities rose to the surface. "It's a bit too much, huh? I kind of knew when I brought the dress home from the store that it was all wrong, that I'd look like I'm trying to be something I'm not."

Mel shook her head. "Heavens, no. You look gorgeous. A bit too gorgeous for cake and ice cream. I thought maybe you had a date."

"Hey, a sixteenth birthday is a special occasion. In fact, I talked your dad and brothers into getting dressed up, too. Here," she said, holding out the box. "Happy birthday."

Mel eyed the tie with confusion.

"Not that," Darcy groaned, wishing she'd just flung the stupid thing on Mitch's bed. "That's a whole other story. Your present is in the box."

With a delighted smile, Melissa took the box from her hands and slowly opened it, as if afraid of what she would find. "Wow! Diamonds!" she breathed, before looking up quickly to Darcy's empty earlobes. "Oh, Darcy, I can't take these. They're special to you."

Darcy pushed the box back at her, shaking her head. "Which is why I want you to have them. Every time you wear them, just remember that you're special, too."

"I don't know what to say." Blinking, Mel looked up at Darcy with a troubled expression. "I don't get it. I was so nasty to you."

"I was far from a saint, myself." Darcy smiled. "Let's just say you remind me a lot of myself at your age. It seemed fitting that you should have my earrings now. Consider them a token of friendship. I think we have too much in common not to be friends."

"Yeah, maybe we do." Mel returned the smile tentatively.

"Oh, Darcy, these are incredible." Lifting the earrings out of the box, she held one up to her ear. "Joan will have an absolute cow when she sees I've got diamonds. Can I wear them tonight?"

"They're yours now. You can wear them whenever you want. But they'll need the right kind of dress to set them off."

Melissa glanced over her shoulder to her door. "I have a closet of stuff my mom bought me, but I don't have the slightest idea what looks good. You wouldn't happen to have a few minutes to help me?"

Darcy knew Mitch was waiting downstairs with a room full of guests, but she was so touched by the request, she'd have stalled the president himself. "Are you kidding? There's nothing I like better than poking through another woman's closet."

Melissa went to the door. "My room's not exactly the neatest."

"Don't worry, I saw the boys' room when I was passing by."

With a grin, Mel opened the door and gestured Darcy inside. "I hate all this heavy old furniture, but Daddy says I'm stuck with it until I show I'm responsible enough to take care of the antiques from the attic. I've been trying to keep the place clean, but every so often..." She dashed across the room to toss a pair of shorts into a wicker hamper. "I guess I was in too much of a hurry to go off to the lake with Joan. Here's the closet," she said, flinging open the doors.

Darcy found a treasure trove of dresses. "They look brand-new," she said, running her hands appreciatively over the expensive material. "Don't you ever wear any of these?" She thought of what Mitch said about his wife playing dress-up with their daughter and wondered if these clothes were a case of Beth trying to buy Melissa's love.

"There's not much need for dressing up around here, not when I'm not allowed to date." Melissa faced Darcy, hands on hips. "What do you think? Any chance you can make me look gorgeous?"

Darcy reached for a toffee-colored silk creation and held it up to Mel's chin. "Most definitely," she told her. "Just give me a half hour."

Thirty minutes later, Mitch climbed the winding stairway, wondering what was keeping his daughter. Everyone else had been assembled in the ballroom for twenty minutes and he couldn't contain them much longer. Roy Hackett and Hester Macon under one roof made a volatile combination, as potentially destructive as the hurricane the weather service warned was heading their way.

So much for Roy's conviction that it would veer out to sea.

Making his way to the family wing, Mitch hoped the storm would wait until the Hacketts were gone and he had time to secure the shutters and store the lawn furniture. At least he need no longer worry about the hay wagon. By tomorrow, the last thing folks would concern themselves with was the Labor Day picnic.

Uneasily, he remembered offering to drive Darcy to Hilton Head. He'd be obliged to take her there if the as-yet-to-be-seen Peter again failed to show, but he wasn't looking forward to it. Avoiding the effect she had on him would be harder than ever cooped up in the front of his pickup. He'd be wanting to touch her, hold her, beg her to stay—a dangerous prospect.

Dangerous? Hell, it was insanity.

Distracted by the noise coming from the end of the hallway, he wondered why Mel's door stood open, when as a rule she militantly guarded her privacy. Judging from her easy laughter, she certainly seemed happy enough.

Striding to her room, he froze in the doorway when he saw Darcy.

She was looking over her shoulder, chatting to someone in the closet. Watching the soft blue silk dance around her shapely legs, he felt his groin tighten. What he wouldn't give to run his hands along the silk, her flesh, savoring each soft, curving line...

She turned then, and for an instant, he was lost in her soft brown gaze. He wanted to drink her in, get intoxicated on the promise he saw there, but Melissa spoke up behind her, drawing his attention. With a jolt, Mitch remembered where he was.

"Oh, Daddy, just in time. What do you think? How do I look?"

He barely recognized his daughter. He remembered the short, strapless dress; he'd objected strenuously when Beth bought it, insisting Mel was too young to go strutting about in such a thing.

Yet, watching his daughter parade before him, her hair piled on her head and her bare shoulders thrown back, he saw a young woman, poised and confident, eager to take the world by storm. Part of him was still afraid, wanting to shield and protect her, but a large part burst with pride.

She looked at him, biting her lip, and he realized how much she relied on what he said next. "Wow, you look incredible, kiddo. I'll be beating the boys off with a stick."

"Some boys," she muttered to cover her obvious pleasure. "There won't be a male at my birthday who isn't old enough to be my father."

"Sorry about that," he told her. "I guess I'm just selfish, wanting you all to myself for a little while longer."

He was far too aware of Darcy, beaming behind Mel. He wondered how she'd done it, gotten in to Mel's inner sanctum. For that matter, he wondered why she would bother. Once again, here was Darcy, doing the unexpected.

"Well, you're a real pig then," Melissa teased, "because you'll have two gorgeous females to surround you. Doesn't Darcy look terrific?"

Mitch didn't dare glance at the woman, knowing precisely how good she looked. "Yeah, terrific," he said noncommittally. "If you two are done making a mess up here, what say we get downstairs? Aunt Emily and Uncle George have been sitting in the parlor for over an hour."

Darcy's voice seemed strained. "You two go on down to your company and I'll tidy up a little."

"Darcy, no," Mel protested. "I'll get it later."

"I made most of this mess." Darcy leaned down to lift the unwanted dresses off the bed. If Mitch hadn't been eyeing her legs, he might not have noticed the thin strip of striped blue silk that slipped to the floor.

"Here, let me get it," Mel said suddenly, running over to grab the clothes away, taking care to kick the strip under the bed. "We want you coming downstairs with us, don't we, Daddy?"

He saw the look of gratitude Darcy gave Mel, the sense of conspiracy the two shared. That was his lucky tie they were hiding, Mitch thought, stiff with resentment. Maybe it wasn't the greatest tie in the world, but his wearing it should be his choice, not his daughter's, and certainly not some stranger's. "Let's go," he said abruptly to Mel. "I'm sure Darcy will do what she wants anyway."

"Daddy!" Mel looked at him with confusion. "Come on, both of you," she said, forcing a smile as she reached out to tug their hands. "I'm starving and I want my cake."

Mitch led his daughter from the room, taking great care not to look at Darcy. He knew he'd been rude, but how could he not resent how she'd taken control of everything, from his daughter's party to his choice of attire? The woman even controlled his thoughts.

He was angry about the tie, but deep down he knew he was blowing things out of proportion, using rage as a self-protection mechanism to save him from temptation. Couldn't the woman see how much he wanted to say the hell with it all, to slowly unwrap her from that sexy blue creation and make love to her all night long? How rapidly he was losing the will to resist?

He had to hold tight to his anger, or he'd never make it through the night.

Chapter Fifteen

Darcy was also wondering how she would get through the night if Mitch was bent on being so miserable. Grimacing as she stared at his stiff, retreating back, she knew he must be angry about his stupid tie.

Trailing behind him and Mel down the hall to the grand staircase, she tried to think of a way to explain that wouldn't involve the boys. Too bad her mind had gone blank the minute Mitch entered Mel's room.

Standing there, facing his scrutiny, it had dawned on her why she'd worn this dress and taken extra care with her hair and makeup. She'd been picturing herself gliding down this staircase, an absolute vision in blue, while Mitch waited at the bottom, watching enthralled, unable to take his eyes off her.

Instead, he'd taken one glance and looked right through her, his swift dismissal cutting her to the bone.

It shouldn't matter this much, she knew, nor should it hurt that he continued to ignore her. Staring at his back as she followed him to the ballroom, she told herself that this was his daughter's big night, that it was only natural for his attention to be focused on Mel.

Darcy's should be, too, for that matter. A few moments more, when Mitch flung open the doors to the ballroom, she should be wearing her biggest, happiest smile.

Raising her chin, she managed that smile, shouting, "Surprise!" with the fifty or so people waiting inside the ballroom. And it grew easier to smile, watching Mel's face as the girl took it all in—the garlands of flowers, the soft music in the background, the twinkling lights on the veranda. Mel looked like a little girl on Christmas morning, facing a glittering tree with a mountain of unexpected presents beneath.

"Happy birthday, kiddo," Mitch said quietly.

"Oh, Daddy." Mel fell into his arms, hugging him fiercely, as her friends rushed forward to surround them.

Squeezing her, Mitch stepped back with a smile of regret, gesturing at the teenagers around them. "Looks like you'll be too busy for your poor old dad tonight."

Mel shook her head fiercely.

"Yeah?" He flashed her a boyish grin. "Then do you think you can spare the first dance?"

Melissa nodded eagerly. Happy tears glistened in the girl's eyes as she waltzed off with her father.

"Kinda nice, isn't it, seeing those two getting along instead of arguing?" Gramps said, stepping up beside Darcy.

Darcy had been so caught up watching father and daughter, she hadn't realized anyone else was there. "Real nice," was all she could manage to say lost in a mass of conflicting emotions. Watching the two blond heads so close together, Darcy felt a combination of satisfaction and melancholy. She'd done it, pulled the party together. But now that the arranging was done and her part was over, she should probably just steal away. She was no longer needed here. She wasn't family.

"I'd best be getting over there myself, if I want my chance to dance with that girl," Gramps went on. "I wonder where those two young scamps have gotten off to. Mitch will be wanting them to dance with their sister.''

"I'll go get the twins," Darcy volunteered. "They're probably out in the barn with Lester."

She hurried off before Gramps could argue, grateful for the excuse. Out in the barn maybe she could get better control of her emotions. At the least, she could do her part in entertaining Lester.

Stepping onto the front porch, she noticed the flowerpots lining its lip and thought instantly of the goat. What better way to keep him happy? Impulsively snatching up two plants, she hoped Mitch wouldn't get angry about this, too, but hey, it was a party, wasn't it?

As the twins would say, Lester was family. The least he deserved was his marigolds.

Mitch danced with his daughter, unaware that his gaze searched the ballroom.

"Looking for Darcy?" Mel asked, causing him to start.

"Of course not. I'm just checking things out. It's my job to make sure everyone is having a good time."

"Yeah, sure." Mel grinned up at him.

"Mind letting me know what's so amusing?"

"You." She tilted her head, studying him. "It won't work, you know. Being so rude, pretending that you're angry at her."

"Pretending?"

She shrugged, as if losing interest. "This party was her idea, wasn't it? She wanted to make sure my sixteenth birthday was better than hers."

Listening to his daughter, Mitch was stunned by her grasp of everything. It struck him that it was time to start looking at her as an adult, and not as his baby girl.

Mel was right. His anger was unjustified. Looking around the ballroom, gazing at his daughter's glowing face, he had to give Darcy the credit she richly deserved. "Yeah, it was her idea. She made me see what a pigheaded jerk I've been, trying to pretend you're not growing up. Sorry, but I guess I feel like I've missed too much of your growing-up years. I suppose I was trying to extend them.''

"You're cute, you know that?''

He laughed. "Yeah, that's me. Cute as a bug.'' He sobered, deciding to ask the question hovering between them. "I hear you're thinking about going to live with your mom.''

"Darcy tell you that, too?'' Mel asked, suddenly wary.

He shook his head. "I overheard you two talking. This isn't easy for me to say. You know how I feel about your mom—''

"Daddy, try to understand—''

"I am trying, Mel.'' He took a deep breath, praying he'd find the right words. "The thing is, I want the best for you, and if you feel the best is up there in Philadelphia, then I won't stand in your way. Whatever you decide, I'm still going to love you. We all will. The doors will always stay open here at Rose Arbor.''

"Oh, Daddy.''

"I know, kiddo,'' he said, rubbing her back. "I know.''

She clung to him as they circled the dance floor, his baby girl again, if only for a few precious moments.

Mitch savored that time, knowing that his emotions were being tweaked by the music they danced to, the corny strains of "Daddy's Little Girl.'' Moving around the dance floor, he grew conscious of her girlfriends waiting to talk to her, the boys eager to ask her to dance, a whole outside world calling her away. It hurt, thinking that all too soon Mel would be flying off to live her own life, leaving a big, empty hole in the family nest.

Lord help him, but he was feeling maudlin tonight.

Noticing Gramps cross the floor toward them as the song came to an end, Mitch sighed heavily. It was time to start letting go.

"Look,'' he told Mel, keeping his voice light. "They're already lining up to dance with you.''

She glanced up, then grinned ruefully. "Can Gramps actually dance, or do I need to watch my feet?''

"Just the left one. But please, don't tell him I told you so. He thinks he's a regular Fred Astaire."

"Who?"

Laughing at her confusion, Mitch knew there were some areas in which they'd never communicate. "Never mind. Just be nice."

"I'm always nice. It's you I'm worried about. Make sure you don't bite off Darcy's head when you ask her to dance."

"I'm not planning to ask her."

"And why not?" Mel eyed him sternly, suddenly looking far older than her sixteen years. "What is it Gramps always says? Bite off your nose to spite your face? Go on and ask her, Daddy. You know you want to."

"Listen, young lady—"

"No, you listen. Stop being so protective. We're big kids now, all three of us, and we like Darcy. We think, well, when you two are together, it's good somehow. Like all is right with the world."

Mitch stopped dancing to look at his daughter. "Melissa Ann Rose, are you trying your hand at matchmaking?"

"A right fine idea, if you ask me," Gramps said, taking Mel's hand. "I sent Darcy out to the barn to fetch the boys. Go get her, and leave me to dance with my great-granddaughter." Both of them grinning at Mitch, Gramps and Mel waltzed off.

Mitch was suddenly conscious of standing in a roomful of people, surrounded by music and flowers and bright twinkling lights, and still feeling terribly lonely. Part of it was the thought of losing his daughter, perhaps, but Mel had been dead right when she'd accused him of looking for Darcy. Darcy, who was so noticeably missing from the room.

Jamming his hands into his pockets, Mitch left the dance floor shaking his head. He didn't know what those two thought they were up to, but he wasn't buying into it. He had no time to dash off to the barn. He had at least a dozen duty dances ahead with the Hackett females, and conversations he owed Aunt Emily and Hester Macon.

Still, he found himself veering toward the front porch. He had to find out what his sons were up to, now, didn't he? With a houseful of company, he couldn't afford to let that pair get into mischief.

Great motivation, if it were true, but the fallacy exploded in his face the moment he stepped inside the barn.

Darcy stood between the boys, feeding his grandfather's prized marigolds to the ornery old goat. Framed in the lamplight, her hair like a soft cloud around her golden face, she looked like an angel with her flock gathered around her. It must be his night to be corny, he thought. She looked so incredibly lovely, she took his breath away.

He watched her, fascinated, reluctant to stop her as she reached for the second pot. He hoped Gramps knew he hadn't a prayer in this year's garden society competition, the way Darcy was going through his flowers. Still, knowing his grandfather, he'd probably let her get away with murder.

And hearing her laugh with his boys, Mitch found it harder and harder to convict her himself. *We like her,* Mel had told him, and the way Ky and J.J. now beamed at Darcy lent credence to the claim.

Glancing up, they noticed him in the doorway, all three looking guilty as sin. Mitch couldn't help chuckle. "Let me guess. Lester make another jailbreak?"

"Darcy had to make a deal with Miss Macon." Ky took a step forward, as if unconsciously shielding Darcy.

J.J. grinned sheepishly. "Yeah. We just had to keep Lester out of her garden and she made Mel's cake."

Mitch turned to Darcy, waiting for her contribution. She tried a half smile. "It seemed a good idea at the time. I'm afraid the deal also included inviting Miss Macon to the party. I know you didn't want a circus, but she was angling for an invitation and she's such a lonely old woman and...what? What are you grinning about?"

"That supposedly lonely old woman scammed you. I don't know what she was up to, but she already had an invitation.

No one hereabouts would dare consider *not* inviting Hester to a party. She's something of a neighborhood matriarch.''

"That devil. She made me feel bad for her. She said...'' She gave him an adorable grin. "Never mind. As you said, I got scammed.''

"Just how do you succeed in business with such a soft heart?'' He threw that out as a tease, but her fierce blush gave him pause. Darcy might like to act tough, he realized, but it was all a facade to protect a heart too easily broken. All along, she'd merely been scamming herself.

Give me your heart, he found himself thinking. *I'll make sure it's always protected.*

In the back of his mind, Mitch could hear the boys chattering, but the world had faded into the backdrop, overshadowed by the glow of this woman. Watching her, he was filled with such a sense of yearning, of tenderness, he wanted to take her in his arms there and then. It was only the conviction that he'd shock the daylights out of her that stopped him, forcing him to jam his hands back into his pockets.

"And that's why we took your tie,'' he heard Ky say as if from a long way off. "We wanted Lester to look good for the party.''

"Darcy said we should have asked first,'' J.J. added, "but we figured it was such an old tie, you wouldn't care if we used it.''

"Are you talking about my blue-striped silk?'' Mitch asked, the pieces slipping into place. "That happens to be my lucky tie.'' He watched the boys grimace. "Want to tell me how it got to be on Mel's bedroom floor?''

"That would be me,'' Darcy said, raising a tentative hand. "I was trying to put it back, but I got waylaid, delivering Mel's present.''

"Darcy was trying to help us.'' Again, Ky moved in front of her.

So did J.J. "Yeah, Dad, don't get angry at her. It's not her fault.''

The last thing Mitch felt was anger. He missed it, though.

This fresh, new tenderness left him feeling a bit too raw and vulnerable.

"Come on, boys," Darcy said suddenly. "We'd better get back inside. I promised Gramps I'd bring you in to dance with your sister."

Both boys looked as if they'd rather be shot. "Yeah, but what about Lester?" Ky protested.

"Yeah, we can't just leave him here all alone in the barn," J.J. said.

"You only have to dance for a few minutes," Mitch told them with a chuckle. "Just enough to show Mel we love her, okay? And don't worry about Lester. Now that we have the cake, I think he can go back out in the pen. I'll put him there myself and make sure the gate is securely latched."

"Won't do any good," Ky said.

"Not if Lady's around," J.J. added.

Mitch was about to chide them on their superstitions, when Darcy spoke up. "Don't worry," she said to the boys. "Lady only does that when she thinks I'm leaving, and I'm not going anywhere tonight."

Grinning at her, they both dashed off to the house, clearly satisfied with what she'd told them.

Mitch wasn't nearly as comfortable. "You believe that?" he asked as they led the goat out of the barn. "You really think a ghost is keeping you here?"

"No!" She frowned, looking at him with a troubled expression. "Well, I have to admit, it is weird, all these coincidences. Frankly, I don't know what to believe anymore."

"Coincidences?"

"You said yourself that Lester's escapes were unusually frequent. I know it sounds crazy, and a few days ago I would have laughed at the idea, but I don't know, there's something about this place..." Her voice trailed off with a sigh as she glanced back at the garden. "I keep thinking about the legend concerning the cottage."

Leading Lester to the gate, Mitch shook his head. "If you're talking about the place's ability to bring people together, it's just something my grandmother concocted. She fell so in love with this place, she couldn't see why everyone else wouldn't, too."

"What's not to love?" Darcy leaned against the pen railing, looking over at the garden once more. "Just look around. Spanish moss and bougainvillea. Moonlight and all those gorgeous roses."

"Remember, folks call it Rose's folly."

She smiled. "It's all in the perspective, I suppose. My own grandmother would have sided with her. Gran would have called this dying and going to heaven."

Watching her sigh, seeing her sudden sadness, he again had the urge to gather her in his arms and protect her.

"Unfortunately, she had this dreary apartment in Brooklyn," Darcy went on wistfully. "Its only saving grace was a tiny balcony with room enough for two lawn chairs and her buckets of roses. Oh, how she babied those bushes, watering them, feeding them, even speaking to them, but each summer, she'd have fewer and fewer blooms. I once asked what was wrong, and she turned to me with the saddest expression. 'Some of us get planted in the wrong places,' she told me. 'We survive and grow, but we never fully blossom.'"

"Was she talking about the roses, or herself?" From her startled expression, Mitch realized he'd hit a nerve. He might as well have added, *Or are you talking about you?*

She looked away, hugging herself. "I asked her why she didn't move to the country. She said she'd been in the city so long, she'd gotten used to it. There's a danger in transplanting. The abrupt change can sometimes kill a plant faster. It's not easy to uproot and start over and I guess she didn't have the heart for it."

"Was it the heart she lacked?" he asked, once again sensing that it wasn't just her grandmother she meant. "Or was it the courage?"

"Does it matter which? The older you get, the deeper you dig your roots. Look at your own grandmother. Do you honestly think you could have ever convinced her to leave this place?"

Herding Lester over to his feed and water, Mitch shook his head. "No, but then, Grandma Rose saw this place as her mission in life. She had this notion that she'd been hand-picked by our resident ghost to watch over things here. Every other generation, she claimed, Lady chose one special female to act as caretaker. My grandmother was convinced that she was that person and no amount of logic could talk her out of it."

Sighing, Darcy gazed around them. "I can't say I blame her. It would be quite an honor to be the woman chosen to serve as guardian of Rose Arbor."

Mitch hadn't meant to tell that story, fearing it made his grandmother sound slightly unbalanced, yet Darcy's reaction left him wondering if maybe she understood his grandmother better than Mitch had himself.

"Yeah, well, the concept could get to be a bit much," he said dryly. "She insisted I had to marry well, in case my wife was her successor. I sometimes fear it was defiance that had me marrying so young, but let me tell you, I learned my lesson. I'm not about to repeat that mistake."

"Never?" she asked in a small voice. "Not even if you find the right woman?"

The right woman. Feeling as if his heart were stuck in his throat, he stood there staring at her incredibly lovely face, wanting to sweep her into his arms and kiss her silly.

Caution held him back, and perhaps hard experience, and Darcy saw this. "You're a wise man, Mitch Rose," she said, straightening as she pushed off from the fence. "As you said, marriage is not for the faint of heart."

She did a complete personality shift, the soft, gentle angel transforming into the brittle city woman before his eyes. To Mitch, the gap between them seemed wider than ever. "Darcy," he said anyway.

"Will you look at the time?" she said in a rush, glancing at her watch. "The night will soon be over if I sit out here chatting, and I promised the boys I'd dance with them. I really should get back.''

She turned, hurrying off, suddenly acting as if she couldn't put enough distance between them.

He slammed the gate shut, latching it with a low, muttered oath. What was the sense in calling for her to stop, chasing after her? No matter what he did, he seemed destined to drive the woman away.

Looking up to the house, watching her race in the front door, his grandfather's words came back to haunt him. *Just relax,* Gramps had told him, *and let things work out as they should.*

"Sorry," he told Lester, "but I'm wasting time stewing about this out here with you. I might better go argue with the woman herself."

Chapter Sixteen

Dancing with Gramps, Darcy found herself looking for Mitch, just as she'd been doing for the hour or so since they'd returned from the barn. Invariably, she found him running to and from the back of the house with ice and more soda—Mr. Hackett dogging his heels—or circling the dance floor with every other female in the ballroom.

She had to face facts; the man was trying to avoid her.

Nor could she blame him. Mitch must have felt the awareness sparking between them, sensed the softening in her. Any hope she might have had that he would pursue things further should have been cut dead with that comment about marriage.

He needn't have bothered with the warning. She could see why, with his responsibilities to his kids and Rose Arbor, the man would be leery of making commitments, of starting something he could never finish. After all, she felt the same reluctance herself.

Yet she kept watching for Mitch, half hoping they'd collide when she went to the kitchen to add to the sandwich tray or refill the bowls with chips. She didn't know what she expected from the encounter, but she had a vague sense of longing, of time running out, and Mitch Rose seemed to be at the source of it.

"Penny for your thoughts," Gramps said gently. "It's not altogether flattering to discover your dance partner's attention is miles away."

Darcy snapped back to the here and now, forcing a smile. "Sorry, I was just thinking about the food. Hoping there's enough. I forgot to take into account that we'd be feeding teenage boys."

"Relax," he said, laughing. "There's always Hester's cake."

Darcy laughed with him. Miss Macon had outdone herself, creating a cake large enough to feed a small army. "She knew more about the size of this party than I did."

"We're a close-knit community here in Seven Corners, all of us look out for one another. Hereabouts, folks tend to know each other's business, and at the center of all that knowing, you'll generally find Hester Macon. I bet she's busy planning Becky Holleran's wedding right now."

Glancing where Gramps pointed, Darcy saw Hester in a crowd of women, holding court. "So the old fraud *was* scamming me. She told me not to be so absorbed by my career, or I'd wind up like her, a lonely old woman."

Gramps chuckled. "Let me guess. She was trying to convince you to settle down and get married."

"I take it she does this often?"

"Actually, she doesn't bother meddling unless she thinks you're worth the effort. She must like you."

Darcy shook her head. "I can't see how. She doesn't even know me. I met the woman twice, briefly, with Lester in tow."

"She's a quick study, that Hester. She and my Rose used to have a game between them, to see who could sum up a person's character the fastest. Hester generally won, but Rose was the first to figure out which people went together. A pair of regular matchmakers, those two. Half the couples in Seven Corners owe their happy marriages to Hester and my wife. You could probably do worse than to listen to their advice.''

A few days ago, Darcy would have pointed out that neither woman could be much of an expert if one was a spinster and the other a ghost, but somehow she'd lost the ability to scoff. ''I'm sure they could find all sorts of wonderful men,'' she told Gramps. ''But I'd rather do my own choosing.''

''Peter,'' he muttered unflatteringly.

She didn't want to know how Gramps knew Peter's name, or why he held such a poor opinion of him. ''Tell me,'' she said, preferring to change the subject, ''when did Hester and your wife have the chance to play Cupid together? I thought they were too busy feuding.''

''They got along fine, except for the week of the garden society competition...'' Gramps stopped dancing, his face clouding. ''Why, I nearly forgot Mel's present. I've got to give it to her. I do hope you'll excuse me.''

''Of course.'' Puzzled by his sudden urgency, Darcy stepped aside. ''I really should put out more sandwiches, anyway.''

Though clearly distracted, Gramps took time to pat her arm. ''Don't you be spending your time in the kitchen, my dear, or folks will be calling you Cinderella. How are you going to find your Prince Charming if you don't mingle and do some dancing? That's how I found my Rose, you know. One magical dance and we fell instantly and permanently in love.''

Smiling, he strolled off, leaving Darcy to stare after him in exasperation. She knew where he was going with that Cinderella and Prince Charming nonsense. Gramps must fancy himself a matchmaker, too.

Give it up, she wanted to tell the old man. If Mitch meant to ask her to dance, he'd have done so by now.

Yet she found herself searching the room for him again.

She spotted Mitch in the middle of four elderly females.

He wasn't talking, or showing much animation, but his timely nods and generous smiles made him seem properly enthralled.

He was a genuinely nice guy, Darcy thought, unable to take her eyes off his handsome features.

He looked at her then, focused on her, his sudden intensity dispelling any warm, cozy feelings she might have entertained. Nice, maybe, but Mitch was no tame and biddable boy-next-door. Behind that laid-back manner and good-old-boy charm hid raw, demanding desire, and it burned in the gaze he directed her way.

Half exhilarated, half scared to death, she watched him mutter something to the ladies, though he kept his gaze fixed on hers, locking her in place. Mitch smiled, an expression laden with so much promise, her heart beat at three times its normal speed. This is it, she thought in a panic, the moment she'd been waiting for unconsciously. The thinking part of her all but screamed for her to flee, to run away, but the feeling part wanted to fling herself into his arms.

Before she could do either, Gramps stepped up to block Mitch's path, gesturing urgently toward the garden. Darcy felt a sky-dive jolt in the stomach as the link between them snapped and Mitch focused his attention on his grandfather.

Look at me, she thought frantically.

Mitch did glance up, but this time she saw only regret in his gaze as he turned to follow his grandfather to the veranda doors.

She felt as if Mitch's compelling gaze had stripped her down to her soul, forced her to admit her raging demons and desires, only to leave her, trembling and aching, and alone. He had warned her, hadn't he? This was how it always would be, lots of promise, but no commitment.

Watching him march off with Gramps, hearing them invite the crowd to join them in the garden while Gramps presented Mel's gift, Darcy fought to pull herself together. It was for the best, she insisted. Mitch belonged with his family, while she had her own life to be getting back to now.

Mentally shaking herself, she went to the kitchen for sandwiches. Her yearnings were useless, ridiculous, and based on illusion. Gramps and his reference to fairy tales had her acting out of character, grasping at make-believe straws. What did she think, that Prince Charming would see her across a crowded room and fall so madly in love he'd forget his mistrust of the entire female species and vow to adore her forever?

She paused at the ballroom doors, glancing over her shoulder at the tall, blond head vanishing past the veranda. She had places to go and things to do in the morning, so if this particular Prince Charming meant to make good on the hot, throbbing invitation she'd seen in his eyes, he had only until the stroke of twelve to do so.

She glanced at her watch, noticing with a spike of alarm that it was already eleven. Only one more hour to midnight.

In the confusion of following Gramps outside, Mitch lost sight of Darcy, a far too common occurrence throughout the evening. He'd been trying to track her down since coming in from the barn, but Roy Hackett seemed determined to get in his way. Between requests for more ice, and the various *eligible* women Roy had put in his path, Mitch barely had time to catch his breath.

Impatiently, he scanned the crowd gathering in the garden, unable to find Darcy among them. He wanted to gesture her over to stand by the family, knowing she'd enjoy seeing the expression on Mel's face when Gramps presented his gift. Unfortunately, the woman seemed to have vanished.

Ever the showman, Gramps cleared his throat and gestured with his arms. "Most of you folks know me well enough by now to understand how much I miss having my wife around. She had a rare smile, my Rose, and it's never quite seemed the same without her here beaming up at me."

A rare smile, Mitch thought, thinking instantly of Darcy.

"But recently," Gramps went on, "I've come to realize that Rose would want me smiling, too. She wouldn't want me grieving, turning our garden into a grim shrine to the past.

When she was still with us, she liked to call each new bush our tribute to the future. That's what life is about, she'd tell me, people carrying on and making new beginnings.''

New beginnings, Mitch thought, liking the concept.

Gramps turned to Mel. ''I was sitting at the supper table the other day with my great-grandchildren, when Melissa turned to gaze at me with her Grandma Rose's smile. I saw it so clearly then, how the past rolls into the future, one generation taking up where the other leaves off.''

Sighing, Gramps reached down to lift up this year's acquisition, a coral tea rose from Spain, its roots still wrapped in its packing. ''Happy birthday, child,'' he said to Mel as he handed her the rosebush. ''Let this be our new beginning.''

''You're presenting the rosebush to *me?*'' Mel looked ready to cry.

''You're the lady of the house, aren't you?''

''This is...this is...I don't know what to say.''

Gramps wrapped an arm around her shoulders. ''For starters, honey, just tell us where you want the bush planted. Then you can come up with a name for it.''

Mel blinked, looking around the garden. ''How about over there?'' she said, pointing to the marble statue of Apollo. ''Then I can make sure I'll see it every day from my bedroom window.''

Taking the shovel, Gramps walked over to the statue and dug up the first, ground-breaking clod. ''I now proclaim this year's site open,'' he said theatrically, passing the shovel to Mitch. Completing his ceremonial dig, Mitch handed the shovel to J.J. and Ky, who in turn gave it to Roy Hackett.

Surprised, yet obviously pleased, Roy hefted his share of dirt before giving it over, the process continuing until everyone had played a small part in the ceremony, and Mitch was left with a far too large hole in the garden. He'd do the actual planting and watering tomorrow, he decided, when all these people would be less likely to trample the poor bush in the mud.

Clearing his throat, Gramps announced it was time for Mel to come up with a name.

She milked the moment, pretending to weigh the decision in her mind. Scanning the crowd, she broke into a wide, beaming smile. "I know, I'll call it the Darcy Rose."

Mitch followed his daughter's gaze and saw Darcy hovering by the kitchen door. She was shaking her head, as if to protest the decision, while Mel pointed to the diamonds now sparkling in her ears. "This way, we can both always know that we're special," the girl added solemnly.

Mitch watched Darcy visibly melt.

"And maybe," Mel said with a grin, "it will give her a reason to come back and visit us."

The smile Darcy exchanged with his daughter spoke of both understanding and acceptance. What could have happened between them, Mitch wondered, for his daughter to have so quickly lost that chip on her shoulder?

"What was all that about?" he asked Mel, stepping up to her as Gramps was announcing the ceremony concluded. "And what are you doing with Darcy's earrings?"

Listening as Mel explained the significance of the gift, Mitch did some melting of his own. He found he was perfectly content to let Darcy throw out his blue tie if she wanted; hell, she could throw out all his ties if she could work such magic with his children.

"Anyway, I just wanted to let her know she's welcome here," Mel concluded. "Like you said to me. You know, about the doors of Rose Arbor always staying open."

"You did a good job, kiddo," he told her, not knowing when he'd ever been prouder of his daughter. "Every bit the lady of the house."

She preened. "Yeah, well, at least one of us is doing our duty."

"And what's that supposed to mean?"

"C'mon, Daddy, you're supposed to be the host of this party. Don't you think Darcy has noticed you've asked everyone to dance but her?"

"Blame Roy Hackett for that, not me. I can't believe one family can have so many unmarried females."

Mel giggled. "Poor Daddy. Tell you what. If you go now, I'll run interference for you. I still haven't thanked Mr. Hackett for the Happy Burger gift certificates he gave me. But you'd better hurry. I'll never forgive you if I have to dance with him."

"Fair enough." Patting her on the shoulder, Mitch slipped to the edge of the dispersing crowd. Though he headed straight for the kitchen, he found the room empty. That was one fast exit, he thought, frustrated. If he didn't know better, he'd think Darcy was trying to elude him.

But he did know better. A man knew when a woman was interested, and the look she'd given him had been pure invitation. He'd just keep searching until he caught up with her.

Returning to the ballroom, he was waylaid three times, then forced to wait through the cake-lighting ceremony, and still found no sign of Darcy. Cursing softly, afraid that she'd worn herself out and retired for the night, he strode out to the veranda, determined to march to the cottage to get her.

Planning what he would say, he was caught up short at the sight of Darcy leaning against the balustrade, gazing out over the garden, her thoughts a million miles away.

For a long moment, he stood watching her, relief and pleasure coursing through him—and a good measure of excitement. He had her, a captive audience, and nothing was going to stop him from claiming her.

Come hell or high water, the next dance was his.

Darcy glanced at her watch for the tenth time, seeing the hands creeping inexorably to twelve. Only three minutes to midnight. It looked as if Prince Charming wasn't going to show.

She was embarrassed, actually, to catch herself spinning such silly, useless fantasies. Enough was enough. She was going inside to wish Mel a final happy birthday, and then she would call it a night. In more ways than one.

Fighting regret, she turned to find Mitch striding toward her.

She stood still, unable to move, even to breathe as he closed the distance between them. His measured pace, the intensity of his gaze, all made it clear that he was a man with a purpose.

In the distance, she could hear the mellow strains of Sinatra. Gramps was playing matchmaker, she thought as she recognized his infamous "Strangers In The Night."

"Forgive me for such a blatant line," Mitch said as he reached for her, "but I do believe they're playing our song."

Taking her in his arms, he left her no time to think—only feel—and she very much felt like dancing with him.

Swept off around the veranda, she was amazed at how snugly she fit in his grasp, how perfectly her steps matched his own. With the lights twinkling around them, the moon bathing them in its golden glow, it seemed perfectly logical to believe in fairy tales.

He came for me, she thought in wonder. *And just in the nick of time.*

As they moved in perfect harmony, she grew steadily aware of his physical presence, the strong arms enfolding her, his warm, firm body pressed against hers. Laying her head on his shoulder, she breathed in his enticing scent, letting her hands stray up to encircle his neck. His own grasp tightened considerably.

She had sudden, urgent, wicked thoughts. She wanted to slip her hands inside his shirt, ripping open the buttons, leaving his chest bare to her touch, her taste. It was a frightening hunger, this need to reveal all of him, to touch and possess him, a greed she had never known with anyone else.

Too soon, the music ended, and so did their dance. Mitch pulled away slightly to gaze at her. "Have you any idea how beautiful you are?" he said softly, brushing her cheek with the back of his hand. "Ah Darcy, I think I have to kiss you."

He leaned down, his lips taking hers, their tongues joining in a slow, pulsing dance of their own. For Darcy, the world disappeared. Her entire universe focused on the hands caressing her sides, the thigh wedged in between her legs, this dear precious face so near her own.

All until she heard the forced cough behind them.

Breaking apart, breathing heavily, they looked with wonder at each other before turning to face Gramps.

"Sorry to, er, disturb you, but Roy Hackett is combing the halls for you, Mitch. Says he needs to talk to you right away."

Mitch moved closer, his arms sliding around her waist protectively. "Let him look," he growled. "Tell him I'm busy."

"I think he's anxious to settle up his bill. He says they want to leave at the crack of dawn, what with the hurricane and all. You better go deal with him, because he's about bursting at the seams with praise. This party was such a wonderful idea, he's been telling everyone they have to come back next year for the rose-planting ceremony."

"But isn't that good news?" Darcy asked when she saw Mitch's frown.

"Yeah. Super."

"Roy has also been telling whoever will listen that he's recommending the place to his business associates, too," Gramps added.

Glancing from Darcy to the ballroom, Mitch looked torn. "Listen, can you wait here while I go deal with him?" he asked her. "You and I have unfinished business."

As she nodded, she couldn't deny the thrill of pleasure, nor the unsettling feeling as he left, taking his calm, assuring presence with him.

Hugging herself, she gazed up at the sky, the twinkling stars slowly covered by clouds moving across the sky. "Oh, Gramps," she said, conscious of the old man hovering beside her. "Wasn't this a wonderful night?"

"Maybe," he said cryptically. "But then again, it could be just the calm before the storm."

She looked over at him, surprised. "Storm? Oh, you mean the hurricane."

He shook his head sadly. "No, I meant the telephone. You have a call from New York."

"Peter?" she asked in a rush of guilt, realizing that she never had tried to call him.

"Peter. And I guess I should warn you—" Gramps sucked in a breath "—he doesn't sound all too happy."

Chapter Seventeen

Shutting the phone-closet door behind her, Darcy struggled
to control her emotions. Of all the times for Peter to finally
call, did it have to be while she was kissing Mitch?

Picking up the phone, appalled to find her hands trembling,
she realized she was thinking more about what Mitch had
termed their "unfinished business" than what she would say
to Peter.

"Finally!" he barked, his voice squawking from the receiver. "I'd begun to think I'd never hear from you again.
What *is* that ungodly racket?"

His tone annoyed her. She didn't bother to lighten her own
as she explained, "I guess the party is winding down and
everyone's wandering out to the foyer."

"You've been partying? That's why you've been too busy
to return my calls?"

"What calls?" As far as Darcy could remember, Peter had
been keeping himself incommunicado.

"I've been trying since yesterday afternoon to get through

to you, but some old man keeps telling me you can't come to the phone. What is going on down there?''

Gramps, she thought. *Playing matchmaker again.*

"You had me concerned," Peter continued, not waiting for an answer. "It's a good thing I reached you. I was just about to hop in a car and race down there."

Mitch would have, she knew. And a long time ago, too. "What stopped you?"

"I beg your pardon?"

She realized that there was no sense in pursuing this. Peter would never see any value in simple "hand-holding," not when there was work to be done. Nor would he understand why she suddenly felt the need for it. "I imagine you had a reason for this phone call?" she asked, unable to hide her exasperation. "Other than chastising me?"

"What is the matter with you?" He paused, as if recognizing he'd betrayed his own ill humor, then tried again in a calmer tone. "Babe, what's wrong? Why so peevish?"

Peevish? Even his choice of words irritated her, but he was right; she was acting peevishly. It wasn't fair to direct her anger at Peter when all he'd done was interrupt...

No, she mustn't take that train of thought. This was Peter, she reminded herself. Wealthy, ambitious Peter Arlington, the man she'd planned to spend the weekend with, the one she'd been waiting to hear from for days. "I'm sorry if I'm cranky," she apologized. "It's just late and I've had a long day. Let's forget I said anything, and bring me up to date on the Tavish account. What exactly is wrong?"

"Nothing's wrong," he said glibly. "Things couldn't be better."

"Then why has it taken—"

"C'mon, babe, didn't I tell you to trust me? Actually, that's why I called, to let you know we wrapped things up. I'm taking the first flight down there in the morning so you and I can start celebrating."

Darcy thought Peter sounded almost too jovial, his enthusiasm forced. "Isn't it a tad premature to be celebrating?"

she asked, not wanting to think he might be hiding something from her. "We still have to get through the presentation on Tuesday."

"Maybe you've been down there too long, babe. You're starting to talk like the natives. What's with this *tad?*"

Again, his light tone seemed forced, leaving her to wonder if the change of subject had been deliberate. "All I meant was that we might better spend our time going over our notes."

"That's my Darcy. Always the workhorse."

His chuckle annoyed her. It reminded her of cocktail-party laughter, the kind found in boardrooms and at business meetings, with rarely a trace of genuine humor in it. "The Tavish account is important to me," she pressed, needing to reach Peter on a more honest level. "You know I need that commission to close the deal on my condo."

"Didn't I say everything's under control? Listen, I should be landing about noon tomorrow. Just give me time to pick up a car and I'll be swinging by no later than two. Be packed and ready, babe. I'm looking forward to getting to the beach for some R and R."

Peter, here at Rose Arbor? She tried to picture him in the rose garden, with the boys—or good heavens, chasing Lester—but all she could envision was his aristocratic nose, raised in the air. "I'm not sure that's such a good idea," she said. "Just arrange the rental for me and I'll come pick you up at the airport."

There was a moment of silence before Peter spoke in his stern, fatherly tone, "You just had an accident. You shouldn't be driving around on those back country roads."

"I would think that should be my decision," she said stiffly.

"It was your decision to drive down there in the first place, and look what happened."

She began to see red. "I've been driving for twenty years without even a speeding ticket. Just because of one little mishap..."

"You totaled the car. A very expensive car, at that."

"No injuries to me, but thanks for asking."

"What's with you tonight?" Peter sounded genuinely puzzled. "You act as if you're itching for a fight. I've never known you to be so unreasonable, so illogical. Can't you see I'm trying to do what's best?"

Best for whom? she nearly demanded, but deep down she saw Peter was right. She wasn't acting herself. At least not the self he knew.

Perhaps it wasn't so much a matter of Peter acting strangely, she decided, but of her perception altering. Somewhere along the line, she had let herself become so enmeshed in Mitch's world here at Rose Arbor, it was as if she were dreaming, and Peter was her alarm clock, urging her to wake. She might know she should heed his discordant ringing, but she felt a desperate need to cling to the dream, to see it out to its conclusion, and she chose to shut out his noise instead. There would be plenty of time to face reality and all its problems in the morning.

Apologizing again, telling Peter she was too tired to discuss this tonight, she put him off by promising to be at the phone waiting for his call in the morning. To her relief, Peter seemed happy enough to comply.

Hanging up the phone, she tried to picture his face, his form, but all she could see in her mind was Mitch, smiling down at her as their dance ended. She had a sudden strong need to see him, to touch him, to test what was real and what was not.

Heading back to the ballroom, she found the party had disbanded, but Mitch wasn't among the few who'd remained to tidy up. She did her best to hide her disappointment, since the cleaning crew consisted of Gramps, Mel, Dex Bradley and the matchmaking Hester Macon.

Obviously, Darcy wasn't wearing her poker face, for Gramps came over to pat her on the back. "Mitch is still with Roy, hashing over the bill."

"No, he isn't." Ky bounded into the room, J.J. at his heels, both boys going straight to the food table to finish what little remained of the cake.

"He's on the phone," J.J. mumbled, his mouth full. "Mom called."

"She's back from Europe?" Mel squealed. "Is she coming here? Maybe I should go talk to her."

J.J. shook his head, giving them a big chocolate grin. "Don't bother, she's still in France."

"If I were you, I wouldn't go near the phone," Ky cautioned grimly. "They're fighting again, big time. Dad's gonna be in a rotten mood."

So much for their unfinished business, Darcy thought with a pang of disappointment.

Still, she stayed in the ballroom as long as she could, hoping that international rates, if nothing else, would get Mitch off the phone with his ex-wife. But after an hour passed, and the place was straightened up, she had to accept the fact that for her, the night was over.

Time to wake up, she told herself as she walked through the garden to the cottage. She was only kidding herself if she thought tonight would go anywhere. What had sprung up between her and Mitch was one of those wonderful holiday romances, glorious while they lasted, but destined to end with the vacation. Thinking differently had always been Rita's mistake and look at the disasters that created.

Normally, just the thought of her mother's many divorces would be enough to snap her into focus, but tonight Darcy kept thinking about what Gramps had said, that it was better to love and lose than never experience emotion at all. Just once, couldn't she give in to the yearnings swelling within her and let herself be swept away by passion? Her holiday romance might inevitably end, but oh, what memories she could take with her.

Dangerous thinking, she tried to tell herself. She'd worked too hard to get where she was to give in to such weakness now. This place was seducing her, lulling her into thinking nothing else mattered but the warm, balmy breeze, that soft floral scent...

Must be the roses.

Leaning down to sniff the sole bloom on the My Fair Lady bush, one of the few remaining roses in the garden, she conceded Mitch's point, that there must be something about their fragrance that clouded one's judgment. Too bad he wasn't around, she thought ruefully. As she recalled, he'd wanted to know when the scent of roses got to her again.

She should be glad he wasn't here, she told herself as she hurried to the cottage. During the day, she could still manage to keep her head and remain sensible, but the soft evening air brought an assault to her senses, beguiling her, seducing her, until she lost sight of the path she'd mapped out for her life. After dark, she became her most vulnerable to honest laughter and smooth-talking Southern charm. Every night, she seemed to grow more relaxed, letting go, being herself.

Only, which herself was that? she thought with a start. The one her mother and Peter recognized, or the strange, new creature she'd discovered here at Rose Arbor?

Some of us get planted in the wrong places.

She didn't like how Gran's words kept coming back to haunt her. *I belong in the city,* she thought stubbornly. And even if that wasn't so, as with her grandmother, it was too late to be transplanting herself now. Wasn't it?

A disturbing question, and one that sat at the root of her restlessness.

But perhaps that assessment wasn't quite accurate. Reaching the cottage, she saw there might be another, more vital source disrupting her peace of mind.

Mitch Rose stood on the porch, watching her walk toward him, his dazzling smile broadening with every step. Part of her knew she could be making the mistake of her life, that at best she was acting in completely illogical fashion, yet she continued toward Mitch, unable to turn away from his beckoning smile. It seemed suddenly a bright, shining light in an otherwise hostile world, a precious beacon lit to welcome her home.

"I was waiting for you," he said quietly.

Watching her walk toward him, Mitch knew he'd been right to come to the cottage. Only Darcy, with her rare, comforting smile, could help him forget the ugliness of his long-distance conversation.

Typically, Beth hadn't thought of the time difference or how she might have woken them up. Her sole reaction to learning she'd forgotten her daughter's birthday had been to lash out, accusing Mitch of deliberately not reminding her. No apologies, no attempts to come home and make it right— Beth had ended the call with the threat that if Mel wasn't waiting at her parents' house in Philadelphia when she returned from Europe, she and her new husband would take Mitch to court for custody of all three children.

In contrast, there was Darcy, making light of her efforts all night while doing her best to spare Mel from the same miserable birthday she'd had. Gramps had been right and so had Mel. Mitch was wasting his time trying to fight this woman's effect on him. He might as well give in to the attraction and see where it led them.

He need only look at Darcy to strip away the effects of his run-in with Beth. Watching her approach, he felt calmed and ready to start over.

New beginnings.

Hesitantly, she stopped on the step below him, so incredibly lovely with the moonlight glinting in her hair. Mitch was filled with a sense of rightness, of inevitability. The link was there between them, waiting to be forged.

Reaching for her, he saw her fear and confusion, but refused to allow it to affect him. He crushed her against his chest, kissing her fiercely, possessively, showing her his certainty with his lips, his heart, his entire being.

She responded as he'd hoped she would, as she had the night before, clinging to him with a soft little moan. Feeling her hands slide up his neck and dig deep in his hair, Mitch released a more guttural moan. If he didn't watch out, he'd be taking her here on the porch.

Tonight, he wasn't risking any interruptions.

Sweeping her into his arms, he carried her over the threshold into the cottage, fully aware of the implications of that little ritual. If the woman wanted commitment, he figured it was a darned fine place to start.

He carried her into the bedroom, setting her down in front of the bed. Even in the semidark, he could see her eyes widen with alarm. "Oh, Mitch," she said, even her voice trembling. "We shouldn't—"

He put a finger over her lips. "Don't fight me," he said hoarsely. "Not now, not tonight. Just let it happen, Darce. Let's find out what there is between us."

Once again, he gave her no chance to protest. Covering her mouth with his, he let his hunger do the talking.

He couldn't get enough of her. He didn't have enough hands to undress and caress each part of her as he revealed it, to treasure her bare, sensitized skin. It didn't help that she proved as eager as he, grabbing at his shirt, his pants, tugging and yanking them from his body. They were like two young kids, discovering lust for the very first time.

And in many ways, it was a first for Mitch. Never before had he felt so sure, so determined, as if making love to this woman was what he'd always been meant to do. Lowering them both to the bed, he explored every inch of her, marking her with his touch, his mouth. Tomorrow might come and still she would leave him, but he meant to make certain she took a powerful memory along. No one else would make her feel such joy, such exultation. No other man would ever love her as he did tonight.

With all his willpower, he took his time pleasuring her, forcing them both to wait, to let the sweet tension build between them. He could feel her trembling beneath him, could hear her groaning deep in her throat each time his tongue traced over her nipple. He licked and laved it until she thrust the breast up, inviting him to take it into his mouth, but instead he used his tongue to painstakingly seduce her, swirling around the base of her breast, then sliding up, up, to encircle the peak. He pulled it into his mouth, suckling gently, then harder, more urgently.

Hands digging deep in his hair, she offered both breasts with a languid arching of her back.

His control slipping, Mitch lavished them with all his pent-up emotion, lapping, suckling, as if he could draw the very essence of Darcy into his mouth, keep her there to stay with him forever.

Yet he gave as well as he got, sliding his hand down her belly between her thighs, offering his touch deep inside her. "Oh, Mitch," she cried as his fingers delved into her secret warmth. Going half-mad at the sound of his name on her lips, he kissed that mouth, her face, her ears, then her breasts all over again as she twisted and pressed herself against him.

"Darcy," he muttered over and over again in her hair, telling her how sweet she smelled, how lovely she was, how desperately he wanted to know all of her.

Then, with a startled, "Oh, Mitch," she began to shudder beneath his touch and he could feel her slow, building orgasm erupt around them.

Mitch watched her eyes close as she writhed with pleasure, certain he'd never seen anything so satisfying, so beautiful. He wanted to spend a lifetime putting such an expression on her face. He longed to make love to her forever.

Slowly withdrawing his finger, he reached down to his pants pocket for the protection. No more waiting, he decided as he slipped it on. He had to take her, and take her now, when she was still soft and warm with desire.

Her eyes flicked open as he parted her thighs, but the momentary surprise turned into immediate welcome. Opening her legs to him, she reached up to draw his head down to her own. "You're a magician, Mitch Rose," she told him huskily. "I never knew it could be like this."

"I know, sweetheart," he whispered, holding her head between his hands. "And we've only just started."

This time when he kissed her, he did so slowly, and deeply, wanting to forge the link between them as he eased inside her. Welcoming him into her sweet, liquid warmth, she slipped her legs around his thighs and her arms up around his neck, binding them together as they embarked on the ride of their lives.

It was sheer magic, the way they moved together. She met his gentle thrusts with her own, eased back with his every withdrawal, in an ebb and flow of rhythmic sensation. He watched her face as their movements intensified and grew more urgent. Mirrored in her eyes, he could see the same aching torture that compelled him as he pulled himself to the very brink, the same utter joy as he drove deeper and deeper inside her.

Clinging to him, uttering his name over and over, she kissed his arms, his neck, his chest, until all at once, what slim control he had left slipped out of his grasp. He plunged into her, driving his every emotion into her core, filling her with every last part of him, forcing his name from her lips. She cried it out once, then again, as almost a plea, and by the third, "Mitch!" she was shuddering all around him, urging him to spill his every last ounce of love into her in a wild, frenzied release of passion.

And even then he continued to move inside her, trying to defy nature and go on forever.

"God, Darcy," he said, holding her face in his hands. "That was incredible. You are incredible."

She looked up at him, blinking away the moisture glistening in her eyes. "Oh, Mitch, can we do that again?"

Rolling her over on top of him, he laughed with all the joy in him. "That we can, darlin'. That we most definitely can."

Chapter Eighteen

Nestled against Mitch's warm, wonderful body, Darcy marveled at how good the man could make her feel. Incredible, he'd said, and that had been just the beginning. Hours later, here she was, still tingling and aching for more. Holding him close, hearing his heart beat so steadily near her own, she felt more alive than she ever had in her life.

Yet deep down, she knew that nothing this good could last forever.

So she clung to him, making the most of this one night together, painfully aware that come morning, reality would be knocking at the door.

She stared up at his profile, wanting to take in every last detail, awed by the sheer strength and beauty of him. Smiling at the stubble sprouting on his chin, she imagined herself watching Mitch shave, him standing by the sink with a towel wrapped around his waist, and his hair still wet from the shower. A sweet, intimate moment they could never actually share.

Not when she'd be leaving in the morning.

He gazed down at her then, smiling with such tenderness she melted on the spot. Tomorrow they could talk and face all the reasons they could never share a future together, but tonight, as his arms tightened around her once more, all she could think of was returning his kiss.

One more time, she promised, molding herself against his body. Tomorrow would come soon enough.

Prophetic words, for when Darcy opened her eyes the next morning, she found the other side of the bed empty.

She'd fallen asleep with Mitch's arms around her waist— "sleeping like spoons," he'd called it—and she'd truly expected to wake in the same comforting position. That she did not, that she awoke patting the bed in a groggy attempt to find him, reminded her forcefully that last night had been a fantasy. Clearly, she'd made a mistake.

Jumping out of bed to dress in slacks and a blouse, she berated herself for being caught unaware. She should have known Mitch would see the absurdity in pursuing a relationship, the futility. And being male, he'd taken the easy way out. Just disappear, leaving nothing behind. No gentle words, no kiss—just an indentation on the pillow next to hers.

Brushing it with her fingers, she remembered the pillow in his bedroom, how she'd imagined Mitch upon it, smiling up at her. And that she'd played out the fantasy to its inevitable conclusion.

She yanked her hand back, moving away from the bed, disturbed to discover that she was still lingering in that dreamworld. Soon Peter would arrive and she'd need to plan for the most important business meeting of her career, yet here she was, overcome by an insane need to fondle a pillow.

A mistake, she chanted as she tugged the brush through her hair and jammed her belongings into her suitcases. A big, never-again-to-be-repeated error in judgment. As a businesswoman, she knew when to cut her losses. Making love to

Mitch had been great—all right, incredible—but as his hasty exit had made crystal clear, it was time to forget and go on.

Snapping her suitcases shut and setting them by the front door, she turned to face the cottage. Amazing, how hard it was to leave it. Her hands had to pat the cushions of the couch, glide over the smooth oak tables. Why did she suddenly feel as if she were pulling up roots?

Forcing herself to leave, she pushed open the front door. A gust of wind all but yanked it from her hands. A storm, how appropriate.

Grimacing, she gazed up at the heavy clouds rolling and boiling across the darkening sky. The light filtering down from the sun glinted an ominous gray. Unless she was mistaken, it would seem the hurricane had definitely veered inland and was heading straight for Seven Corners.

Deciding to return for her things later, she shut the door and hurried through the garden. All along the path, dead leaves skittered past her feet, scratching out protests to the unheeding breeze. Looking at the bare bushes, Darcy realized that it was just as well they'd picked most of the blooms since there wouldn't be much left for the competition, anyway.

Poor Hester Macon. For the first time in years, the woman had her one real shot at winning, and a hurricane showed up to ruin her garden.

Then again, Darcy thought as she reached the house, there probably wouldn't be a contest, nor much of a Labor Day celebration. All those plans to be canceled, those vacations cut short...

It dawned on her that the seashore would not be the ideal place to visit right now. In all likelihood, Hilton Head would be evacuated. Come to think of it, she realized simultaneously, what if Peter wasn't able to catch a flight down here?

Was it with dread, or excitement, that she faced the prospect of being stranded again at Rose Arbor?

Not that she was given much opportunity for thought. Inside the house, she found utter chaos. It was like entering the evacuation center in a battle zone—Hacketts everywhere, shouting and scurrying about with luggage, their faces taut and desperate, clearly afraid they'd never get out in time.

A harried Mel sat behind the desk processing each individual release with all the precision—and lack of patience—of a drill sergeant. Gramps stood beside her, doing his best to help, and to smooth down ruffled feathers, while the twins ran errands and helped carry baggage to waiting cars.

Hearing the telltale ring of a phone, Darcy went to the closet, figuring it was the least she could do to help out in the confusion. "Rose Arbor," she said into the receiver.

"Darcy, honey, is that actually you?" Rita asked with a girlish giggle.

"Where are you?" was all she could think to ask, thrown off balance. The last voice she'd expected to hear this morning was her mother's.

"I told you Tuesday I was going to the Hamptons with Dave. It's not like you to forget, those people must really have you rattled. How come they have you answering the phone?"

Listening to the scatterbrained Rita, Darcy again had the disorienting sense of straddling two worlds. "With a hurricane threatening, it's total confusion here," she tried to explain, even while doubting her mother would understand any better than Peter. "I'm just trying to help out."

"For heaven's sake, I hope you don't feel you owe anything to those people? Not after they caused you to crash your car."

Darcy wanted to protest, but she could imagine Rita's reaction to hearing that a ghost was to blame for the accident. Besides, her mother was typically off on a tangent, too engrossed in her own train of thought.

"Just goes to show we were right," Rita was rambling on. "We tried to talk you out of it, Peter and I, but no, you had to go driving down there on your own. Do you have any idea what worry you've put us through? I don't think we've had a wink of sleep between us."

From experience, Darcy knew better than to take that claim

seriously. Extravagance was Rita's middle name; she always exaggerated. More likely, she'd slept like a baby. "I doubt you listened to your messages," Darcy said dryly, "so can I assume Peter called you about my accident?"

Hearing Rita confirm her suspicion annoyed Darcy no end. What had he hoped to accomplish by calling her mother to tattle on her?

"He's a bit miffed, you know. He's got this idea that you're fooling around on him."

Darcy went beet red. "Peter has no claim on me," she snapped, justifying her actions to herself as much as to her mother. "How I spend my vacation is my own affair."

Hearing the silence on the other end of the line, she realized too late how much she'd actually admitted to her mother. "I hope you're not judging me," she lashed out defensively, knowing she was making a bad situation worse but unable to stop herself.

"As long as you know what you're doing," Rita said stiffly.

She didn't, but was there any sense in taking advice from a woman who knew less than she how to slip safely through the minefields of romance? "Tell me, just for the record," Darcy found herself asking. "All those husbands, do you still love any of them? Steve, Chuck...Simon?"

"What kind of question—"

"What about my real dad? Do you still have any feelings for him?"

"Really, Darcy, I called to see if you were all right. I don't know why you're giving me the third degree."

Nor did Darcy. When had Rita ever confided in her, or shared anything of a personal nature? Why, she knew more about Mitch and his family than she would probably ever know about her own. "I'm just confused, I guess," she offered, knowing it wasn't much of an explanation.

Not that Rita needed or wanted one. Clearly, she had her own agenda. "Peter wants to marry you, you know."

If Darcy hadn't been sitting, it would have knocked the

legs right out from under her. Days ago, she might have been
thrilled to hear such news, but the timing couldn't be worse.
"That's funny," she said, though she wasn't amused at all.
"He never mentioned marriage to me."

"He's waiting for the right moment. Oh, dear, I hope I
haven't spoiled his surprise. It's just, well, he's just such a
catch. And I'd hate to see you let this one get away."

Rita was right, despite the corny metaphor. Peter was everything she could ask for in a husband—solid, dependable,
predictable. No demands, no disappointments. No gazing
wistfully at the empty spot in the bed.

"This other one," Rita asked slyly. "The fling, is he a
dish?"

Rita and her quaint phrases. "Yeah, the fling is a dish,"
Darcy said, giving in as she always did to Rita's unique blend
of callousness and caring. "He's a regular bowlful of lobster
bisque."

"Mmm, my favorite. Oh, honey, by all means, stuff yourself silly, but always come back to Peter. Remember, he is
your bread and butter."

The analogy might be forced, but Rita was more than
right—she was living proof of the danger of indulging yourself too often. Darcy didn't need any Steves or Chucks or
Simons screwing up her life, no matter how much fun they
were, or how good to look at. She didn't want to find herself
ten or twenty years down the road with a string of divorces
behind her, listening to her own daughter ask if there was any
such thing as love.

"Don't worry about me," she assured Rita before she hung
up. "Have you ever known me not to do the sensible thing?"

Rita rang off, content that she'd said her part, obviously
anxious to get back to her own budding romance. Hanging
up the phone, Darcy tried to shake off her resentment. Whatever her own irresponsibilities, Rita had a point. Darcy would
be a fool to base a future on the sublimely delicious night
she'd shared with Mitch. Life was a matter of day-to-day

coping, requiring money and stability, neither of which she would get by indulging herself between the sheets.

Still, it didn't help that Mitch was the first one she ran into coming out of the phone closet.

Literally.

His hands gripped her arms to steady her, reminding her forcefully of how they'd felt last night caressing her body. She wanted to melt against him, to lose herself in his kiss, but he obviously had other things on his mind. Dropping his arms immediately, he turned to call out to Mel as if he hadn't even noticed Darcy. "Can you take over in the kitchen? I've got to get outside and start nailing down those shutters."

"But Daddy—"

"Mel, no arguments now. Can't you see I've got a million chores to finish before the storm hits?" Taking a step forward, he seemed surprised to find someone in his path. "Darcy," he said, his tone softening as he focused on her face. "I thought you were still sleeping."

Avoiding his gaze, she glanced back at the phone closet. "Actually, I was just making plans to leave."

"You can't leave now." That was more like the Mitch she was used to, autocratic and demanding.

She responded accordingly. "I can't? And why not?"

"Because you won't get far in this storm," Gramps answered for him, coming up behind her. "Weather service says the hurricane is heading our way, gaining speed with every hour. They're closing down airports and evacuating the coast. You'll have to sit tight and wait it out with us."

Remembering how hard the wind had been blowing on her walk to the house, Darcy could well imagine how bad it could be when the hurricane finally hit them. Deep down, she might know she wouldn't be going anywhere for a while, but she didn't want to admit it to Mitch. She didn't like him thinking Rose Arbor was still her only option.

Conveniently, the phone chose that moment to ring. "That's probably Peter," she said brightly, turning for the closet.

Mitch grabbed her hand. "Darcy, we have to talk."

She felt a glimmer of hope. "Now?"

Clearly torn, he glanced over his shoulder. "I've got a lot to do right now, but later—"

"Go on, get to work," she told him, knowing there was really nothing left to talk about. "I have to answer the phone."

He didn't stop her when she pulled her hand free. Muttering an oath, he stamped out the front door.

"Poor Mitch," Gramps said. "That boy's worked too hard on this place to watch a hurricane destroy all his efforts."

Poor Mitch? Annoyed, knowing Gramps could have answered the phone for her, she left the old man standing in the hall. Thanks to him, Peter would be in a fine snit when she finally picked up. The stupid thing must have jangled a good dozen times already.

Closing the door behind her, holding the receiver to her ear, she winced. "Doesn't anybody ever answer the phone down there?" Peter squawked. "Would you please tell me what the hell is going on?"

Darcy lost what little was left of her temper. "In case it's escaped your notice," she snapped, "we happen to be sitting right in the path of a rapidly approaching hurricane."

"Escaped my notice? Who do you think has been on the phone all morning, trying to find a way down there? I can't book a flight and I'm told even the buses aren't running. It's been a nightmare."

Ordinarily, Darcy would have made soothing noises, but she was glad he'd had a hard time of it. Had he made his arrangements yesterday, instead of putting her off, he would be here with her now.

And last night would never have happened.

"But listen to me, ranting on about my problems," he said, no doubt uneasy with her silence. "How are you holding up, babe? Are you going to be all right with those people?"

She hated the way he said "those people," as if the Roses were some insects to be exterminated. "I'm fine. It's a sturdy

house and we should be far enough inland to escape the major
brunt of the storm.''

"We?''

"There's a houseful of people here,'' she told him irritably.
It wasn't her safety that worried him, she realized, as much
as the possibility that she'd be "fooling around'' with Mitch.

Which, of course, she had been. One day she'd have to tell
Peter all about her idyll at Rose Arbor, but she had neither
the time nor the stamina to tackle the confession now.
"What's happening with the Tavish people?'' she asked. "I
doubt we'll be having the meeting at Hilton Head tomorrow.''

"It's been rescheduled,'' he said distractedly.

"Really? When?''

"Listen, Darce, I'm sorry but I've got a million things to
do. Don't you worry, though. I'll be there on the next available flight and I swear, I'll make this up to you. We'll have
our vacation yet, babe. I promise.''

He didn't have to make the offer, she told herself as she
replaced the phone in its cradle. In his own way, he meant
well. Besides, as Rita pointed out, he was her bread and butter.

Too bad he left her craving lobster bisque.

Mitch strode to his workshop for his hammer and nails,
still cursing under his breath. Did even the weather have to
conspire against him? Waking early this morning, hearing the
wind outside the cottage, he'd known the hurricane would hit
them sooner than expected. It had been no easy thing leaving
Darcy alone in that bed, but he'd had to get Rose Arbor bat-
tened down for the storm.

He'd hoped she'd understand, but one call from Peter and
she was back to the prim and prissy executive, every strand
of hair, every stitch of her fancy work clothes, firmly back in
place.

Lord help him, but he kept seeing her as she'd been last
night, naked and joyful and responsive to his every touch.
Holding on to her hand just now, he'd wanted to run his

fingers through her well-groomed hair, to slide his palms under her silk designer blouse, but duty called him, and she'd gone so dutifully when called to the phone.

Only two things stopped him from marching back to the house and demanding she hear him out. One was that he had too much to do to delay even a second, but more important, he knew from the weather reports that she wasn't going anywhere just yet. Until this storm passed, Darcy was stuck at Rose Arbor.

And, he thought with a grin, a lot could happen in twenty-four hours.

Several hours later, Darcy paused to brush the hair from her face before bending down to the mattress again. She hadn't realized how heavy it would be when she'd volunteered to carry it to the back parlor. Maybe she should pool strength with Mel. She could hear the girl wrestling with her own mattress in the next room.

As Rita loved to say, there was never a man around when you needed one.

But that would be unfair to Mitch, she conceded. The poor man had been running around all morning, knowing that for every job he completed, another three waited. She'd heard him tell Gramps to stow candles and batteries in a centrally located room, either the back parlor or the dining room, so they could all gather to wait out the storm. As soon as he finished outside, then fixed the generator, Mitch planned to drag down the bedding. That was why she and Mel struggled with mattresses, to spare him the extra work.

Thinking of him outside, Darcy couldn't stifle a shudder. Though the windows were now boarded, she could still hear the wind, steadily picking up speed. If Mitch didn't soon get to the house, he might have to take his chances weathering the storm in the barn with Lester.

Thinking of the goat, she hoped the boys were done settling him in his stall.

"Darcy, I can't lift that stupid thing," Mel whined, appearing in the doorway between the two rooms.

Darcy kicked the mattress at her feet. "I know. You'd think they were made of lead. Come on, maybe we can work better together."

Putting their backs into it, as well as a lot of grunts, they were able to drag the mattress to the winding stairway, where gravity decided to take over, taking it down the steps in a bumping, snowball-effect motion. Surprised by the pull, Mel lost her hold. Darcy, in the lead, tried her best to steer the mattress, but halfway down, she, too, lost her grasp. Breathlessly, she watched the thing tumble past to the foyer below, landing on its side, teetering there until it fell with a loud thud.

"Tim-ber!" Mel called out with an infectious giggle.

Relieved that they hadn't killed themselves, Darcy began to chuckle with her. "Do you suppose we should try that again?"

"I'm game if you are."

Grinning, she climbed the stairs to the girl. "This time, though, maybe we should just ride it down."

"Are you serious?"

"As a kid, I tried it on a staircase like this. My stepfather was always thinking up games for us. Simon wasn't your run-of-the-mill parent."

"He sounds like fun."

He had been, Darcy thought. Too bad he hadn't been dependable.

Before they could collect the second mattress, the two boys came running from the back of the house, shouting Darcy's name. Since they both spoke at once, she had to stop them, demanding that they speak singly and a good deal more slowly.

"It's Lester," Ky said, panting, stirring her first pang of dread.

She really didn't need J.J. to add, "He's missing again."

* * *

Mitch looked around him as he opened the outside cellar door. Feeling the first drops of rain sting his face, he watched the branches of the old oak scrape against the house. He should have trimmed it back, he thought ruefully. At the rate the wind was picking up speed, the tree was liable to take off half the siding.

Yeah, and when did he have time to pull out the chain saw? The list of things to do was still a half mile long.

Anxious to get to the next item, he secured the door behind him and hurried down the cellar steps. Most of the outside work was done, but before he could tackle the indoor tasks, he had to get the generator up and running. With heavy rains, the cellar inevitably flooded and had to be pumped to prevent damage to the foundation. Unfortunately, the sump pump required electrical power, which often failed in a major storm. Mitch had been meaning to fix the generator for months now, but between one thing and another—like trimming the oak—he never seemed to have the time.

Time, he grumbled as he tinkered with the generator, aware of his minutes with Darcy ticking away. He should be charming her, showing her why she should stay at Rose Arbor, but instead, he'd been barking orders at her all day.

And she'd carried them out like a trouper, he thought. Watching her work with Gramps and the kids, noticing how they responded to her and she to them, he'd seen how it could be possible, the two of them sharing more than one night in a bed. If only she'd relax and let it happen.

He tried to picture her with his family, sitting down at the table for Thanksgiving, gathered around the tree at Christmas, but a niggling worry had begun to worm its way into his brain.

It's just the storm, he told himself. He had no reason to worry about his family, all upstairs snug and secure.

Yet the more he tried to dismiss the anxiety, the more it settled in and began to grow. He couldn't quite put his finger on what was bothering him, but the niggling became a pang, and then downright unease.

He tried to blame the rain slashing against the cellar doors, the wind howling through the cracks in the wall. No wonder he was getting goose bumps. All that was missing from making this a grade B horror flick was the haunting organ music.

Still, Mitch found it harder and harder to work. He had the same feeling he'd had before Darcy's accident, the sense that something was wrong. Very wrong.

Chapter Nineteen

"It's all right," Darcy said to the boys, trying to calm them. "Let's not panic."

"Panic?" Gramps entered the foyer from the back hall, his gaze going straight to the mattress on the floor. "Who got hurt?"

"Nobody. Yet." Mel frowned at her brothers who were dripping water all over the hall. "But Daddy isn't going to be happy when he finds out Lester is missing again."

Darcy shot her a look. "Melissa, please. I'm sure your father must have settled the goat in the barn by now."

"He told us to do it," Ky said with a hangdog expression.

"Only we got busy and forgot." J.J. looked ready to cry. "What if Dad didn't take care of him? What if Lester took off for Miss Macon's again?"

"He's out in this storm?" Gramps gazed at the door, his eyes narrowing. "Don't worry, boys, I'll go get Lester."

Darcy reached out to stop him. "Don't be cr..." She trailed off, seeing his frightened expression. Knowing that he believed his wife's spirit was somehow connected to that goat, she didn't feel right calling his offer crazy. For Gramps and the boys, she had to remember, Lester was far more than just a pet. He was part of the family.

"Let me go," she said firmly. "You stay with the kids."

Ky looked up at her, his serious face pleading. "When you find him, you're not gonna put him outside in the barn, are you?"

"Ky—" she started.

"Something bad could happen to the barn," J.J. interrupted, stepping up to tug on her sleeve. "It could blow down in the wind and then what? It will be just awful for everything if Lester gets hurt, if he—"

He broke off, unable to finish the thought, but Darcy could hear his desperation. Worse, she could see it in his brother's and grandfather's eyes. "All right, I'll go get him here," she found herself offering, "but you have to find a room he can't do much damage to, maybe the pantry."

Both boys flung their arms around her, but Mel was far from pleased. "Are you kidding me?" she asked in obvious disbelief. "Daddy will pitch a fit if you bring that mangy goat in this house."

"I don't doubt it." Grimacing, Darcy hugged the boys before going to the door. "But we all know nobody's going to get a wink of sleep tonight until Lester is in the house with us, safe and sound."

"You can't really mean to go out there for a stupid goat?" the teenager said.

Darcy couldn't blame Mel for being surprised. Less than a week ago, had anyone told her she'd be making this trek to the barn, she'd have laughed in their face. But here she was, for the third time in as many days, risking more of her wardrobe to chase after their wayward pet.

"Don't worry about me," she told the girl. "You just make sure you've got those mattresses set up in the back parlor when I get back. Your dad has enough on his mind without having to worry about setting up bedding, too."

"Forget Lester, Darcy. You could get hurt."

"I'll be fine," she assured the girl, but as she pulled open the door, and the wind rushed in to take away her breath, she suffered her own misgivings. Getting from here to the barn could mean risking more than her wardrobe.

And it was only the start, for not only was Lester *not* in the barn, neither was Mitch. Glancing around the dark structure, infected by the eeriness of the relative quiet of the empty expanse, she realized how much she'd been depending on him being there to help. Better to have Mitch shouting at her than be listed among the missing.

What if he was out on the road, looking for Lester? Surely it wasn't a good sign that he'd yet to return. A branch could have fallen, a wire could be down. *Mitch* could be hurt.

She ran outside, shouting his name, but her voice was lost in the wind. Glancing back at the house, so solid and safe behind its boarded-up shutters, she knew a strong urge to race up the porch steps and shove through the door.

The only thing stopping her was the look of disappointment she'd find on the boys' faces, and the thought of their father, lying unconscious somewhere in a ditch.

Bracing herself, she struck out down the road to Hester Macon's, still calling Mitch's name. As if trying to drag her back to the house, the wind tore at her clothes, her hair. She'd never known rain could hurt so much. It pelted her so hard, her face and bare arms felt bruised already. She'd done a stupid thing, coming out in this weather. How could she rescue anyone if she could barely hear or see two feet in front of her?

Still, she pushed on, shouting with all her might, "Mitch, c'mon, where are you?"

Down the road, she heard an answering, "Baaa."

With new life, she raced forward, finding the frightened, and very irate goat. Somehow, Lester had gotten himself caught in a tangle of rope, which in turn was snagged in a briar patch. What should have been a simple matter of disentangling the rope became a battle with the gusting wind, and the goat himself. Kicking out frantically each time Darcy tried to work him free, Lester did his best to make her work impossible. With a sinking feeling, she realized that even if she got Lester out of the rope, she still faced the ordeal of subduing him enough to drag him back to the house. The way this storm was progressing, they'd more likely be blown out to the Atlantic.

"Knock it off," she shouted at the blasted goat. "Are you trying to get us both killed?"

"I could ask you the same."

She turned at the sound of the voice and saw a rain-soaked Mitch marching up behind her. As he grabbed for the rope, efficiently slicing through it with the pocketknife he whipped out of his pocket, she realized how much of her anxiety had been centered around this man. Seeing him safe and miraculously unhurt filled her with such overwhelming relief, it was all she could do not to reach up and throw her arms around him.

Until he spoke again, shouting against the wind, "Are you out of your mind, coming out in this weather?" He punctuated each phrase by slicing at the rope. "Wasn't there enough excitement without risking your life for a stupid goat?"

"You think I *want* to be out here?" Her emotions stretched, Darcy was in no mood to be screamed at. "That 'stupid' goat happens to be the twins' security blanket, and I promised to bring him back to the house."

He gave a final tug with his knife. "The animal belongs in the barn."

"Maybe, but the boys will be up all night worrying, even sneaking out to check on him."

"We don't have time to argue about it." Pulling Lester free, Mitch yanked the goat up against his chest. "We've got to get back, now!"

He started down the road, Lester bucking in his arms. The sight would have made Darcy laugh if she weren't so angry at him. He glanced back, glaring at her in exasperation. "Move it!" he shouted. "Now."

She stepped forward, geared up for a fight, and as she did, a limb crashed down on the briar patch behind her. Seconds earlier, and she'd have been hit.

Shaken to the core, she conceded that Mitch was right. They had to get back to the house at once.

Shifting Lester to one arm, he held out his free one, drawing her into the shelter of his grasp. With his substantial bulk shielding her from the wind and rain, Darcy felt only relief and gratitude. If Mitch hadn't shown up when he did...

Not that she was foolish enough to try to thank him now. He was still cursing and struggling to hold on to the goat when they reached the house. To her surprise, instead of going to the barn, he went straight for the porch. He didn't wait for her to knock; he just banged on the door with his foot and barged inside with Lester the moment it opened.

It was up to Darcy to shut the door behind them as Mitch deposited the goat on the entrance rug. "Keep this mangy animal off the floors," he growled. "I'm holding you boys responsible if he gets into the least bit of trouble."

The twins answered by rushing up to hug Darcy.

Bending down between them, she felt the strangest urge to cry. She found it an incredibly wonderful feeling, hugging those boys as fiercely as they clung to her.

"Mel was right," Ky said, staring at her with a contrite expression. "We should never have made you go out there."

"We were so scared," J.J. added. "Mel, too, though she won't admit it."

"I was not."

"Was too."

"Kids, stop," Darcy interrupted before the verbal battle could escalate into war. "I'm okay, and so is Lester." She wanted to add, *Thanks to your dad,* but with Mitch still scowling, she blew at her bangs instead. "Nothing a towel and some dry clothes can't fix." She stood, frowning. "Oh, all my things are in the cottage."

"Mel will find you something." Mitch's gaze went from her to the boys. "Well, as long as everything seems to be back to relative normal, I'll get back to work on that generator.''

"You're not going back outside?" she blurted out. After their trek through the storm, battling the elements together, she found she was not yet ready to let him out of her sight.

"I'll be down in the cellar," he said over his shoulder as he headed for the back door. "Someone get this mattress off the floor. What's it doing here, anyway?"

"You said to gather up bedding," Darcy said, hurt by his tone.

He turned to her, exasperated. "I meant *air* mattresses, sleeping bags. Never mind, just push it to the side and I'll deal with it later. Gramps, you know where the camping gear is stowed..." He looked around, saw his grandfather wasn't there. "Don't tell me he went looking for Lester, too."

Mel shook her head solemnly. "He went upstairs to talk to Grandma Rose. Like us, he was worried about Darcy."

Mitch ran his hand through his hair, looking suddenly worn to the bone. "Yeah, well, everyone just stay put from now on, okay? No more unexpected excursions outside. I have to get that generator fixed before the lights go out."

Darcy could see the fear in his children's eyes, even if Mitch could not. "Mitch, wait," she called out, hurrying over to speak to him quietly. "Do you really have to leave right now?" she asked, drawing him out into the hall. "The kids are frightened. They need you here with them." She stopped herself short of adding, "So do I."

A good thing she did, for he rolled his eyes. "I'm not going down to that cellar for fun, you know. If the electricity fails, what do we do for power?"

Conscious of how physically close they were, yet so emotionally distant, she snapped, "You're a fraud, Mitch Rose. All that talk about the hustle and bustle of the city, yet here you are, burying yourself in work in the country."

"I'm just doing what needs to be done if we want to eat and have a roof over our heads."

"What does fixing that generator have to do with having

a place to live? Those kids of yours don't need electricity right now. They need their father."

His blue eyes glinted with frost. "I think I'm the better judge of what my children need. For your information, the generator will keep the sump pump working. If that cellar floods, there will be no foundation, much less a roof over anyone's head. Dammit, Darcy, give me some credit. I'm doing the best I can."

As if wary of saying more, he shook his head and marched off down the hall.

Darcy stood there staring after him, trembling, and feeling the biggest kind of fool. As he had so properly pointed out, she had no right to tell him how to treat his kids, no business getting involved at all.

It was the hurricane, she thought, biting her lips. The unsettled weather was wreaking havoc on her emotions, as well.

"He didn't mean to yell," Mel said quietly behind her. "Daddy gets like that when he's worried. He doesn't like being scared and I think you scared him a lot, going out in the storm."

Darcy stared down the hall where Mitch had gone, fighting the urge to go after him.

"Come on," Mel said, sounding far older than her sixteen years. "We've got to find Gramps, and we should be getting you into warm, dry clothing."

Nodding absentmindedly, Darcy went with the girl, reasoning that she'd accomplish nothing by talking to Mitch in her present mood.

Besides, she was worried about Gramps, too.

They found him upstairs, wandering around the left wing, mumbling incoherently. "I can't find her," he muttered in a rare case of panic. "Where is she? Where is my Rose?"

Darcy took his arm, unnerved at how fragile and pale he suddenly seemed. "It's okay, Gramps," she told him gently. "We found Lester, and the boys are settling him down in the kitchen right now. Why don't we go join them?"

He looked up at her, his eyes focusing on her face.

"Darcy," he said as if the name calmed him. "It's all right now," he said to himself.

"Yes, it is all right now, Gramps." Smiling, she tugged his hand. "You know what? I think we could both use a nice hot cup of coffee."

"I'll go get you some dry clothes," Mel volunteered, "then I'll meet you guys in the kitchen."

Nodding, Darcy led Gramps downstairs, watching him improve steadily by the moment. The sight of Lester with the boys put the twinkle back in his eyes. "I knew it," he said as if he'd just discovered a new continent. "I knew you were brought here for a reason."

What reason? she thought, watching him kneel beside J.J. and Ky. Sensing this was something she'd rather not discuss in front of the kids, she made a vow to ask him about it the second they were alone.

Shivering, feeling suddenly uncomfortable in her torn, wet clothing, she crossed the room to the counter and started shoveling coffee into the machine.

Mel arrived moments later, handing Darcy a pile of clothes. "I grabbed one of Daddy's dress shirts and a pair of his sweats," she said with an apologetic grin. "All I had that would fit you was a pair of slouch socks."

Chilled to the bone, Darcy took the bundle gratefully and slipped into the pantry to change.

Emerging a few minutes later, she knew she must look like something out of a sixties movie, clad in the overlarge shirt with the sleeves rolled up to her elbows, the tails reaching to her knees. The sweatpants she tossed over the back of a chair in case it got chillier. For the time being, she was warm enough in the bulky socks.

Pouring the coffee into cups, she listened to the wind howling outside, the branches scraping against the house. With the lights occasionally flickering, no wonder she felt on edge. Nothing bad had yet happened, but she had an underlying sense that all hell was waiting to break loose. She found herself glancing at the inside cellar door, wishing Mitch would come through it. She'd feel so much better if they were all gathered together in one room.

Which reminded her—they still had to set up the parlor. "Hey, kids, we've got to get the beds arranged."

"We'll do it," Mel told her, glancing at Gramps. "You two stay and get warmed up."

As the kids bounded off, Darcy sat down at the table opposite Gramps, handing him a steaming mug of coffee. Now seemed as good a time as any to ask her question. "What did you mean before, when you said I was brought here for a reason?"

He tilted his head, seeming almost amused by her question.

"Always so direct. Always in such a hurry. If you slowed down some and took time to look around you, you'd have your answer."

"I don't have time," she told him defensively. "I'm leaving just as soon as this storm is over."

Gramps merely shook his head, as if dealing with a stubborn child. "It takes some getting used to, our country pace. Mitch had trouble with it, too, you know, after years of all that rat race up north. You just have to slide into the rhythm of it, take things as they come. Let the pattern unfold like the petals of a rose."

"Nice analogy," she said, sliding back in her chair to sip her coffee. "You make it sound so simple, but it's not, you know. Most of us move at a far faster pace."

"Maybe, but where does it get you, all that running around? Ever think maybe you're just being sidetracked, distracted from the real and lasting beauty in life? How can you see the truth if you don't slow down and look it over?"

"The only thing sidetracking me is you." She was suddenly impatient with his vague ruminations. "I asked a question and you're deliberately not answering it."

"Oh, but I am. You young folks today expect an instant remedy for every problem. With your television and computers, you think all answers can be had with the flick of a switch." His broad smile took the sting out of his words.

"Sometimes, people need to talk to solve their problems. More important, they have to listen."

"I still don't see what this has to do with my being brought here for a reason."

He frowned, as if disappointed in her. "I'm talking about your special gift, my dear. If you think about it, you'll realize you've been listening to those kids since you got here. Mel's party, going out after Lester—you saw into their hearts and you've helped their father see, too."

"No, I—"

"You're the link between them, my dear. This family needs you."

She rose to her feet, knowing from his smug expression that he thought he had her cornered. "That doesn't wash," she said, pacing across the room. "You imply that I was brought here as some sort of interpreter, when all along you've been spoon-feeding me the information. *You're* the one who's overlooking the truth. Haven't you noticed that Mitch and I can't be in the same room for more than fifteen minutes without arguing? Face it, Gramps. We just don't get along."

He made a dismissive gesture with his hands. "That's just working out the kinks. It was the same with me and my Rose, at first. Oh, the spats we'd have, and then that wonderful making up. It wasn't always easy getting along, but we'll be celebrating our sixtieth anniversary, come next June."

"Anniversary? But she's—"

"Dead?" Gramps sighed, rising to come over to her, taking her hands in his. "My dear child, when you've lived as long as I have, you'll find you don't stop loving someone just because they're no longer walking and breathing. If you let it, love can grow far beyond physical bonding. When two spirits touch, no grave can keep them apart."

Darcy felt a tightness clamp her throat. "You really do talk to her, don't you?"

He nodded, patting her hands. "Every day. She likes you, you know."

She felt a chill, seeing in his expression what his words merely implied. Rose, the die-hard matchmaker, more than liked her. She'd handpicked Darcy for her grandson, to serve as the next grande dame of Rose Arbor.

It was crazy. Did she really believe a ghost could reach out from the grave and send her perfectly well-ordered life careening off in a different direction?

It was this place, and that storm raging outside, that made it all seem inevitable. Darcy was a grown, rational woman; she didn't have to do anything she didn't want to do. No ghost, or goat, or even grandfather could keep her here against her will.

It was then, of course, that she glanced up to see Mitch in the cellar doorway.

Chapter Twenty

Expecting to find his family safely ensconced in the parlor, Mitch was startled to step into the kitchen and find Darcy standing with Gramps, sharing a poignant moment. She looked more than ever like an angel, he thought, with the golden glow of the lamp backlighting her damp, curling hair.

Though there was nothing angelic about her outfit. His shirt had him remembering all too clearly what she hid underneath it.

Both she and Gramps turned to Mitch, Darcy's features taking on an edge of panic.

"Mitch, here you are," Gramps said, patting her hands before releasing them. "Got that generator going?"

Mitch shook his head, unable to hide his frustration. He'd wasted nearly an hour with the blasted machine, hearing an imaginary clock in his head tick off the fleeing minutes.

"I'll get to it later," he told his grandfather, but his gaze remained fixed on Darcy, who had turned pointedly away. "I, er, came up to check on the weather forecast. Hear anything new?''

"The radio is with the kids in the parlor. Sounds pretty fierce out there, though.''

Mitch nodded. He kept thinking about the shed he should have braced this summer, about the old oak brushing too close against the house. "Why don't you go get the kids and the radio?'' he suggested to Gramps. "We can wait out the storm in the kitchen, drinking hot chocolate. Like we used to do with Grandma Rose.''

Gramps smiled, clearly warmed by the memory, but Darcy looked more skittish than ever. "I'll get the kids,'' she said quickly, starting for the door.

Gramps held her back. "Let me. You stay here and help Mitch gather the stuff for hot chocolate.''

She turned to watch Gramps hurry through the swinging door, her back, stiff as a board, facing Mitch. He wanted to speak to her, to explain, but he knew she would only spin on him. With that ramrod posture, she was liable to snap her spine.

There was no denying she was upset. She made it even more obvious by stamping over to the cabinets, opening and slamming shut the doors. "I know what he's up to,'' she muttered. "And it's not going to work.''

"I'm sorry, all right?''

She glanced up, as if surprised to find him in the room.

Mitch felt at a loss. It was hard enough finding the right words without her watching him like a frightened rabbit. Apologies had never been easy for him anyway, and with Darcy he somehow always managed to say the wrong thing.

"I didn't mean to bark at you before. I was tense, and I have a habit of reacting wrong in tense situations. What you did, getting Lester...hey, I know I shouldn't have yelled at you. I was scared. It's no excuse, I know, but I was sick with fear. I just plain lost it.''

Her hands clenched around the pot she'd dragged out of the cabinet. "It doesn't matter.''

Of all the reactions he'd expected, it certainly wasn't a blithe dismissal of his feelings. "You put me through the wringer, tore me inside out with worry and now you say it doesn't matter?" he asked, striding over to her. "Dammit, woman, do you do this with everyone who loves you?"

She went absolutely still.

What lousy timing. They had to be standing in his kitchen with that pot and the storm and a worldful of differences between them, for Mitch to finally realize that here was the one he'd been waiting for all his life.

He loved her. It made no sense, given the short time they'd known each other, but as if his grandmother had whispered the words in his ear, he suddenly knew that Darcy wasn't only the right woman for him and Rose Arbor, she was the *only* woman.

Mitch stared at her, willing her to speak, hoping she'd give him somewhere to go with this. "Did I miss something?" he asked quietly when she remained silent. "Am I wrong in thinking that what you and I shared last night was something pretty special?"

"No." Her voice seemed so small, he could barely hear her.

"No, I'm not wrong, or no, it wasn't special?"

"Oh, Mitch." Her somber expression filled him with dread. "That was just a—"

"Dammit, Darce, I care about you." He took her by the arms. "God knows how or why, but sitting down there in the cellar, all I could think of were the moments I was wasting, precious moments that I'd rather spend with you and the kids. You were right. There's more at stake here than a flooded cellar. It isn't walls that make a home. It's people, and like it or not, Darce, you're one of us."

She refused to look at him, but she did speak, with a quivering voice. "You're talking crazy."

She wasn't just angry; she was scared of him, afraid of what he was asking her to feel. Maybe he should back off a bit, give her time to get used to it. Hell, he himself was still reeling from the discovery.

"We don't even get along," she went on. "When we're in the same room, it's like that hurricane out there. Every conversation we ever have turns into a tempest."

"Yeah, I noticed that about us," he told her, releasing her arms and leaning back against the counter. "The question is, what are we going to do about it?"

She really was cute when flustered, Mitch thought. Obviously, she'd expected him to argue.

"We don't have to fight, you know," he said, pressing his point. "If we try, I'm sure we can find other ways to pass the time. Among his other oddball theories, Gramps believes you can achieve anything in a relationship if both people work at it."

"Gramps."

He had to grin at her disgusted tone. "Obviously, he's done something to upset you, but take it out on him, not me. How about you and I call a truce? As long as we're stuck in this house together, let's forget there's a past and a future. There's just you and me and the kids. And of course, Gramps."

He reached out for her hand, but while she let him take it, she didn't move closer.

Stubbornly holding her ground, she spoke in a deliberately cool, even tone. "It's too easy to play pretend at Rose Arbor. I've been doing it from the moment I arrived. But it's not real, Mitch. The ghost, the magic, none of it's real. It's a dream, and come morning, we'll have to wake up."

He tugged, forcing her closer. "Unless Gramps is right," he said, pulling her against his chest, "and love is a matter of two people dreaming together."

"Yeah. We both know how you feel about his oddball theories."

He might once have scoffed, Mitch realized, but over the weekend, he'd come to think of grandfather as one wise old codger. "Give it a shot, Darce," he said into her hair. "What can it hurt? One night and we can see how we feel in the morning.''

She pulled back, frowning up at him. "Mr. Rose, that has to be the most unusual line I've ever had thrown at me.''

He shrugged. "I'm out of practice.''

"Oh, Mitch—''

He put a finger over her lips. "Not now, remember? The object is not to argue. Let's try this instead.'' He leaned down to kiss her, a sweet, gentle mingling of the lips that swiftly escalated into hunger.

"You pack quite a wallop into a kiss, ma'am,'' he told her huskily, running his hands along her sides. "Gramps would also say a lot can be built on that.''

"C'mon, what we have is just physical and we both know it.''

"Is it?''

She stared at him, into him, as if hoping to find answers in his gaze. But before he could offer his reassurance, the floor beneath them rocked with a tremendous crash. With a sizzle and pop, the lights went instantly black.

Darcy froze, too frightened to argue when Mitch ordered her to "Stay there!'' The entire house seemed to be reverberating still. All she could think of was, please, not the parlor. Don't let the kids be anywhere near that crash.

She heard the rasp of a match, then saw Mitch lighting a candle from the counter and jamming it into an antique candlestick straight out of a haunted-house movie. It made for an eerie light, casting strange shadows on his face, which did nothing to improve her nerves. "Let's go check the parlor,'' she whispered as if afraid to talk aloud.

He nodded. "I hope it wasn't that old oak,'' he muttered grimly.

Alarm bells went off in her head as she thought of the tree towering over the left wing. "The boys' bedroom,'' she said in the same, raspy whisper.

Before they could reach the swinging door, Gramps and

the kids burst through it brandishing flashlights, all very scared, but all unharmed.

As if sensing her relief, Mitch reached out to squeeze her hand.

It was a simple gesture, unnoticed by everyone else, but long after he moved away to reassure his children, Darcy felt warmed to the core.

"I'd better go investigate," she heard him tell Gramps as he grabbed the older man's flashlight.

"You're not going out there?"

Everyone turned to her, clearly surprised by the vehemence in her tone. Mitch strode over to put a comforting arm around her shoulder. "If the power line went down, it could start a fire. I need to check it out. Trust me, I won't take any unnecessary chances."

Trust me. Odd, to find that she did.

It was hard not to, she realized as she set about preparing the hot chocolate, knowing he'd be wet and cold when he returned. All day she'd watched Mitch take charge, putting them to work, getting the most out of them, yet making them feel that through their efforts everything would turn out okay. Even now, facing possible disaster, he made it seem like business as usual, a case of just one more task to be completed.

Working with Mel, Darcy made sure they had the drinks steaming and ready to pour when Mitch tramped in through the pantry, shaking the rain off his hair. "The house is fine," he announced as they crowded around him. "But we've got a fairly large gap on the side of the barn."

The boys looked instantly to Darcy. "See," Ky said in an awed tone. "We knew we were supposed to bring Lester here to the house."

"That Lady," J.J. said with the same hushed voice. "She sure knows what's what."

"I can't be certain, but the storm seems to be tapering off a bit," Mitch added as he stripped out of his wet shirt, leaving his chest bare. "We could just be hitting the eye, but I'm hoping I can run out soon and get some feed. We don't want

Lester getting sick on those flowers." He gestured at the pots
the boys had dragged in from the porch.

"Why is everyone always rushing to do things for them
and that stupid goat?" Mel snapped, flopping into the nearest
chair. "I wish I were a boy. Then maybe people around here
would start worrying about me."

"Relax, Mel." Mitch reached behind him into the pantry.
"I brought your rosebush in hours ago." He plopped the
Darcy Rose, still in its wrapping, onto the floor in front of
him.

"Oh, Daddy!" Mel leaped up, throwing herself into her
father's arms. "You're the best."

"I try."

Yes, he did, and he kept trying, over and over. Watching
him hug his daughter, then both his boys, Darcy granted that
this was one arena where Mitch put his stubbornness to good
use. It took a strong person at the core to keep all parts of a
family working together, and at the nucleus of this clan,
through good times and bad, stood Mitchell Allen Rose.

He looked at her then, extending an arm to invite her to
join them. She found it hard to resist, especially with the
children adding their smiles of welcome. With a pang, she
acknowledged how very much she wanted to be part of this
family, even if for only one night. As Mitch had coaxed, what
could it hurt?

Yeah, the tiny voice said. *That's what you thought in Virginia.*

"This chocolate is getting cold," she told them, gesturing
them all to the table. "And we need to get your father
warmed up."

Mitch shook his head with a grin, as if knowing she was
stalling, yet momentarily content to play along. Coming up
behind her, he took her by the shoulders. "I know a better
way to get me warmed up," he whispered in her ear. "It
involves taking that shirt of mine back."

He got too much enjoyment out of teasing her. She tried

hard not to react to the feel of his bare chest pressed up against her, with only thin cotton between them.

"My sweats!" he said suddenly, sounding like Lord Stanley finding Livingstone. "Mind if I take these? I can't tell you how good it will feel to slip into something a tad more comfortable."

"You're not going to change in here?" she said.

He looked like a wolf when he leered like that, she decided. The man got too much pleasure out of backing her into a corner.

"Sorry to disappoint you, but no, me and the Darcy Rose are going to the pantry. Try not to miss us."

Conscious of the others watching, Darcy refused to bite at that bait.

Yet, later, sitting around the table with his family, sipping hot chocolate, Darcy let herself get lost in the fun of listening to Mitch banter with his children and grandfather, watching the affection they so blatantly shared. And the relief, when they heard on the radio that it wasn't the eye passing over them, but rather the hurricane losing steam.

"Now that the storm's winding down," Ky said in his solemn little voice, "it's kinda like the night Lady's daddy shot Captain Allen."

"It was storming then, too." J.J. finished the thought for his brother. "Wanna bet Lady shows up tonight?"

"Not again." Rolling her eyes, Mel turned to her father. "Darcy's last night, and they have to start this up."

"You know, we've never actually told Darcy Lady's story," Gramps said.

Mel groaned, and Mitch's jaw tightened, but the other three vibrated with badly contained excitement. "C'mon, everybody, let's go to the foyer and Gramps can tell it there," Ky suggested, tugging Darcy's arm.

"We see her coming down the stairs a lot," J.J. explained, taking her other hand.

"You can't leave without seeing her," Ky added matter-of-factly. "You'll never believe in her then."

"Daddy, aren't you going to stop this?"

"No, the twins have a point," Darcy told Mel. "I did promise to stay up and watch with them before I left. Maybe we can all sit on the mattress while Gramps tells his story. With all the excitement, I don't imagine you got around to moving it?"

Three guilty faces proved that once again they'd neglected to do what their father had requested.

Mitch rose from the table with a sigh, but rather than chastise them, he looked straight at Darcy. "Good idea. It's time I took the opportunity to sit up and watch for Lady myself."

"Daddy, not you too!"

Mitch reached out to pull his reluctant daughter to her feet. "Don't be such an old scrooge, Mel. It could be fun, telling ghost stories in the dark." He held up the candle under his chin, making weird noises.

"Some fun," Mel muttered, but she filed out of the kitchen with the rest of them, plopping down on the mattress, leaning back on the wall next to her brothers, who had cuddled up next to Darcy.

Mitch settled in on Darcy's other side, his warm solid form reminding her that he still hadn't put on a shirt.

Huddling together in the dark, they listened while Gramps, the old ham, stood at the foot of the stairs with the only candle, weaving his tale with a well-modulated voice and dramatic gestures.

Keeping her eyes on the darkened stairway as she listened to Gramps begin his tale about star-crossed lovers, Darcy almost wished she'd see this Lady, or at least Gramps's beloved Rose. She was no longer afraid of ghosts, she realized. Hearing Gramps talk about his wife earlier, Darcy found herself wishing love truly could reach out from the grave, that it could prove so enduring.

"Nathaniel Rose might as well have put that bullet in his daughter's heart," Gramps said in conclusion, "for when he shot her Yankee lover, poor Lady all but died herself. She pined away, passing on exactly one year to the day after her

Allen, never marrying the wealthy foreigner her daddy insisted upon. She told her sister, my mama's grandma, that she would always regret not going off with Allen when he asked her, for she'd lost him forever, and all the money in the world would never bring him back. 'Don't make my mistake,' she told Grandma Susan on her deathbed. 'Don't ever mistake security and convenience for love.'"

Gramps paused to set the candle down on the table next to him. "And ever since that night," he went on, coming over to join them on the mattress, "Lady has roamed these halls, making certain that those she loves and cares about are blessed with the one rare treasure she let slip through her fingers. Jewels and gold might never line the coffers here at Rose Arbor, but the one thing we have in abundance is strong and abiding love."

Abiding love. Stealing a glance at Mitch, smiling beside her, Darcy was filled with a deep longing. As a kid, spinning dreams with Gran in her dreary apartment, this was exactly how Darcy had pictured her life. A good man, a bunch of kids, all gathered together for fun and laughter.

Even when Mel grumbled that Lady couldn't be much of a ghost if she didn't rattle chains or ooze slime, and countered with a far more gruesome story of her own, Darcy reveled in the magic that this place—these people—could weave around her. For a dream, she conceded, it was certainly a good one.

Too bad dreams couldn't last.

The children seemed determined to go on all night, though. They kept trying to top one another, each with a tale more supernatural than the last, even though both boys were yawning and Mel had mellowed to a dreamy tone. Gramps finally suggested that since it was late, maybe it was time they went to bed.

She listened to the expected rounds of protests, the boys not wanting to give up until they'd all seen Lady, until Mitch, ever the voice of reason, rose to his feet. "Let's go, kids. I'm going to need you guys working your butts off tomorrow helping clean up the mess this hurricane's dumped on us. And don't forget, school starts on Wednesday.''

The way they groaned, you'd think he'd threatened them with loss of life and limb.

Gramps rose, going for the candle. ''Come along, children, I'll help you get settled in.'' Grabbing the antique candlestick by its brass-ring handle, he gestured at Darcy and Mitch. ''I'm sure these two have things they wish to discuss. Alone.''

His attempt at matchmaking couldn't have been more clumsy if he'd dropped a brick on their heads. Embarrassed, Darcy opened her mouth to protest that she was going to turn in like everyone else, when Ky suddenly grabbed her wrist.

''Look, that light,'' he whispered, pointing down the hall.

J.J. had a death grip on her other arm. ''It's...it's Lady!''

Chapter Twenty-One

Mitch did a double take, spinning in the direction they pointed. It all rushed back to him, being their age, hoping against hope to see the ghost. Funny, but he'd forgotten how important it had once been to him. And in so doing, he'd overlooked how important it must be to his kids.

"It's not Lady," Mel announced. "It's just a reflection in the hall mirror."

She was right, but it didn't make the disappointment any less keen. For any of them. Gazing at the glum faces, Mitch realized they must all have their reasons for wanting to see the ghost. "Lady might have showed up," he said. "We were so caught up in our stories, we stopped watching."

"She wouldn't stay long on a night like this," Darcy added, her gaze sliding to his conspiratorially. "And you know, I...I do think I felt a chill."

And no wonder, Mitch thought, considering her long, bare legs.

"Yeah." Eager to believe, J.J. pulled on his brother's

sleeve. "Remember how she always disappears when Gramps finishes the story?"

Ky nodded sagely. "It's probably what happened. Still, I wish she could have stayed around longer. We want Darcy to really see her."

"Yeah. And Dad, too."

"I already have." Mitch could see he'd shocked everyone, himself not least of all, but something about their closeness tonight had him opening up in ways he'd never before imagined. "Do you think I could live in this house so long and *never* see Lady?"

"You actually saw her?" J.J. asked, his jaw hanging open.

"And didn't tell us?" Ky seemed affronted. Mel, Mitch noticed, eyed him suspiciously.

"It was a long time ago, when I was about your age, boys. It was only once, though I stayed up watching for years. I can tell you about it while I tuck you in. Gramps, if you still have that flashlight, maybe we should leave the candle for Darcy."

She stood abruptly. "Oh, no, actually, it's time we all turned in."

"It's okay," J.J. said, smiling at Darcy. "We don't mind if you guys stay up talking. Who knows, Lady might even come back."

"We owe it to the boys to watch for a while," Mitch said in mock seriousness. "Wait for me?" he added when she opened her mouth to argue. "Even if we don't see the ghost, I think it's time you and I talked."

She seemed reluctant, but she sat on the mattress. Herding the kids down the hall and into the parlor, Mitch took her compliance as a good sign.

Sitting in the candlelit hallway, Darcy found her compliance to be a very *bad* sign. She was looking for trouble, waiting for Mitch like this, but heaven help her, he had a way of smiling at her that turned both her logic and resolve to mush. Waiting for him was like her drive to Rose Arbor, letting herself take that extra curve, that one more hill, insisting the view ahead would be well worth the trouble.

Yeah, she thought, and she'd ended the drive with a crash.

Yet, though she told herself to get up, to go burrow into her sleeping bag, she couldn't find the will to move. She was no more able to turn away from the promise in Mitch's gaze than she'd been able to resist the lure of Rose Arbor. She thought of Gramps's claim and wondered if it could be true. Did some unseen force draw her, and keep her here against her will?

Shivering, she glanced up the stairway, but the foyer remained quiet and empty. Nothing stirred or hovered over her, spiritual or otherwise, dissolving that excuse. In theory, she should be quite free to go.

Still, she couldn't bring herself to leave the mattress. A little voice in her head insisted that she owed it to herself to see where this road would lead her.

Yet the moment Mitch appeared out of the dark, and the throbbing started again in her veins, she saw it all too clearly. Who was she kidding? From the start, she'd known where they'd be going with this.

Mitch must have known, too, or he wouldn't have brought the blanket and pillows. *We really should talk*, he'd said, and of course they *should*. Trouble was, they had too much pent-up emotion between them, and knew only one way to express it.

The moment he reached the mattress, Darcy fell into his arms.

Warning words tumbled through her brain, even as he pulled at her shirt and she yanked off his sweats. Making love with Mitch was foolish, insane—the children could walk in on them at any moment—but it felt so good to have his hands on her, his lips on her, and she hungered for more.

Their coming together was as tumultuous as the storm still raging outside, as if like the weather, they'd been building to this for days. She touched him everywhere, holding nothing back. Stroking the taut muscles of his back and thighs, tracing the work-roughened lines of his limbs, she marveled at how physically beautiful Mitch was, how strong and noble and good. Holding him, exploring him, it was all too easy to pretend she could forge a life with this man. That she could give and give and give of herself, and never be afraid he would leave her.

And Mitch helped foster the fantasy by tenderly caressing her, by worshiping her with his tongue. Rubbing against him like a cat, writhing beneath his touch, she groped and stroked and ached to get her fill of him. She crossed over the line of logic, surrendering to the dizzying, intoxicating world of emotion.

For the first time in a very long while, Darcy threw caution to the wind.

Opening herself to Mitch, she took him into her heart, even as he entered her body. Holding him, clinging to him with wild abandon, she knew, in a heady moment of exhilaration, how beautiful it could be when two people dreamed together.

Exploding inside her, all around her, her passion burst into a thousand blazing pieces. She felt so powerful, so good and right. Clutching Mitch, aching to give him yet more, she saw in an instant of piercing clarity that nothing would ever be the same again.

And as the real world slowly sifted back to her, the realization of how much had changed frightened her to death.

"Whew," Mitch said, rolling off her. "I guess that pretty much proves last night wasn't a fluke."

That was the trouble with rising to too great a height, she realized. Inevitably, reality intruded, and you fell back to earth with a thud.

What had she been thinking? By opening up her heart, she was leaving herself wide open to disaster. "It was all a mistake," she said quickly, moving away to snatch up his shirt. "Last night was bad enough, but this...I should never have let it go so far. I'm just not the kind of person to have an intense physical relationship."

Leaning on his side, propped on an elbow, he stared up at

her as she dressed, clearly mystified. "We just shared what I thought was a fairly intimate moment. Are you trying to tell me it was nothing but sex?"

"No. I mean, yes." Stabbing her arms into the sleeves, she hastily did up every last button. "C'mon, Mitch, what else could it be?"

"You don't feel it, Darce? This thing between us? I once thought it was physical, too, and I hoped our coming together would get you out of my system, but it's obvious it's not going to work that way. You've wedged your way into my life. You belong here now."

Belong. The word touched a raw nerve. She'd spent most of her life searching for a place to call home. She'd thought and planned and oh so carefully arranged things so she could buy that impressive condo in the city. At long last, she would have her own place, her own future, and she'd be out of her mind to give anyone the chance to take it away.

"You're wrong, Mitch," she told him, shaking her head. "I don't belong here. I have a career and a life in the city," she added, beginning to feel as if she were speaking from rote. "I have to go back to New York."

"Do you?" Angrily, he rolled onto his back to stare up at the ceiling. "Are you sure you're not just retreating into your shell, pretending the world and its realities can't reach you? Maybe you're running so fast and working too hard so you don't have to face life. Peter isn't your boyfriend, he's your sedative, something to keep you from feeling anything more than the occasional disappointment. From recognizing who you truly are inside."

She sat hugging her knees, wincing as each word he uttered hit home. "Be that as it may," she said with forced calm. "He's coming for me in the morning."

Offering marriage, Rita had warned. A safe, stable future.

"And you'll go with him?" Mitch narrowed his gaze, but kept it trained on the ceiling. "Just like that, you can forget about us?"

"There is no *us*, Mitch," she said, hearing the hysteria

creep into her tone. "That implies both a you *and* me, but let me assure you, that wasn't me, Darcy MacTeague, just now in that bed."

"Really? It sure felt like you."

All at once, his sarcasm was too much. The conflicting emotions of the past few days threatened to bubble up and spill out of her, and she clasped her knees tighter, trying to hold it all in. "You keep talking about Rose Arbor being a place to find yourself, but I just keep getting more and more lost. I haven't been myself since I got here, since I heard that voice on the road. *Help us,* the voice said, like I was hand-picked to come save you people. Like I'm just some stupid little puppet, with your ghosts and grandparents pulling the strings."

He sat up slowly, studying her as if she'd just lost a screw. "What are you talking about?"

"I don't know." Mortified that she'd babbled out such nonsense, she hugged her knees so hard they hurt. "Everything seems to be shifting, sliding out of focus. I feel like I'm not in charge of my own life any longer. Like I've lost all control."

"Honey, where I come from, they call that falling in love."

"No," she protested, shaking her head. "I don't believe in love."

Holding her gaze, he moved to sit beside her, his hand stroking her cheek. "Then I'd say we're in a heap of trouble, because that's what's happening between us and it's not going to stop just because you want it to. We have something here, and if you weren't so busy denying it, so scared of failing, we just might create something special."

"Stop it. You can't change my mind."

"No, I can't. Only you can do that." His voice gentled with regret. "I don't know who hurt you so bad, Darce, but you can't go on hiding forever. You're going to miss a lot of life that way."

"Funny, that's what Simon said," she said, the bitterness spilling up and out of her.

"The woodworker?"

"He was Rita's third. He came right after Chuck, a cold, selfish creep who lasted only a year, but long enough to make Simon seem like the answer to our prayers. He had this way of teasing a smile out of me, Simon did, always urging me to lighten up, to open up. He wanted us to be one big happy family, Rita and I, he and the kids his ex-wife let him take for the summer. Have you any idea what a temptation that was for a lonely kid? A big, old wonderful farmhouse, other children to play with and tell secrets to, a dad I could finally love and rely on..."

She paused to regain her poise. "I had three glorious months to fall hook, line and sinker, until one morning I woke to silence, an unnatural quiet for that busy house. I found Rita in the kitchen, staring at a note on the table. Simon was gone. He was driving the kids back to his ex before heading for the West Coast. To find himself, was all the note said. I ranted and raved at Rita, accusing her of chasing him away, her with all her fighting and nagging, but she just shrugged. 'All the love in the world wouldn't keep that one to home,' she told me, and I knew she was right. I'd loved him completely, but it wasn't enough. Would never be enough."

"Oh, Darce."

"Hey, I learned a valuable lesson. Rita got married again soon after, to a nice guy named Steve, but I vowed I'd never again give my trust blindly. Let Rita fall in love and have her heart broken. I'm better off married to my work."

She threw the words out to act as a barrier between them, but how like Mitch to ignore that she'd uttered them, to slip a comforting arm around her shoulders instead.

Mitch held Darcy close to him, feeling helpless. Listening to her talk about her stepfather made him realize that the odds had been stacked against him before he could even get into the fight. After such a miserable childhood, no wonder she found it hard to trust in something as elusive as love.

Gazing down at her, he found nothing to encourage him in her body language. Stiff and tense, curled up as if squeezing her knees with her arms could hold her together, she'd even put his shirt back on to serve as a shield between them. While here he sat, naked and wide-open to her, aching with love and ready to slay all her dragons. If only she'd let him.

He had to find some way to show her that she'd be making the biggest mistake of all if she went back to New York with that jerk, Peter.

Relax and stop stewing, Gramps would tell him. *Let love find a way.*

Perhaps the best he could offer was honesty, the true, inner Mitch, the part no one else ever saw. "In some ways, I know how you feel," he told her quietly. "My grandparents never knew, but my folks had every intention of splitting up, too. The night before they left on their trip to hash out the details of their separation, I went to my father, lashing out, blaming him for everything. I know now that it takes two people working all the time to make a marriage, but I wasn't much older than the twins then. I was angry and scared, and...well, they died in the accident before I could take the words back."

"Oh, Mitch. I'm sorry." One arm left her knees to slip around his waist.

Encouraged, he went on. "I was here with my grandparents, up in bed the night we got the call. I was thinking about what I'd said to my dad, regretting it, when I saw a faint glow in the darkness. Oddly enough, I wasn't frightened, not even when I felt something brush my cheek, a gentle touch, almost reassuring. Seconds later when the phone rang, I already knew what had happened to my parents."

She pulled away, turning to look up at him. "Are you saying their ghosts visited you?"

"I know it sounds far-fetched. Worse, I never did see that light again, though not for lack of trying. I was as bad as the boys, staying up all hours, searching everywhere, but after a while, I guess I got embarrassed by it, and over the years, I convinced myself I'd dreamed up the whole thing. I put the incident in the back of my mind, but every now and then..."

He paused, wondering if maybe this was being *too* honest with her.

"Mitch, what?"

"You're going to think I'm crazy."

She shook her head. To Mitch, she'd never looked lovelier, sitting there in his shirt, tears glistening in her eyes. He fought the urge to roll her back down to the mattress, to show her his love in time-proven fashion, sensing it was far more important to tell her the rest.

"All right. I don't know how or even why, but it's like I get this inner nudge, as if someone or something is urging me to act."

"Like a premonition?"

"I guess. Only it feels like the touch on my cheek that night."

"Is it..." She paused, looking up the stairway. "This nudge, is it like a...whisper?"

Her own voice was so hushed, he could barely hear her. Edging over, he put a reassuring arm around her. "Kind of. I suppose I should learn to trust it, because when I act on it, everything turns out okay." It had brought him out to the accident site, he realized, and it had sent him into the storm tonight to bring Darcy safely home.

She was shaking her head. "You really believe in all this? I mean, who is this ghost of yours? Your parents, your grandmother, Lady?"

A good point. "I don't know. Maybe it's whoever you need it to be."

"This is beginning to sound like a "Star Trek" episode."

He laughed, snuggling her closer. "How about this, then? What if my ghost is a combination of everyone who's ever loved in this house? A sort of manifestation of all that caring."

"And what would you call it? Lady Love?"

"Don't be such a cynic. It's a pretty powerful lure, when you think about it. All of us living here, joined together in a common bond of emotion. No wonder no one ever wants to leave Rose Arbor.''

"Lester does."

"Unless you were right, and he has an ulterior motive for his escapes. It could be our ghost thinks you belong here. Just like the rest of us."

She stiffened. "Mitch, don't start this again."

"Tell me you didn't have fun tonight. "Tell me..." He paused, glancing down to the mattress. "Look me in the eye, Darce, and tell me Lady doesn't have good reason for wanting to keep us together."

She wrenched away, rising to her feet. "Remember? I don't believe in ghosts, and I don't believe in love."

He too stood, taking her by the arms. "Dammit, what do you expect me to do? Let you walk off and leave me to spend the rest of my life pretending the last few days never happened?"

"Well, what do you want me to do? Pretend the rest of *my life* never happened? You're always saying how it's important to have roots. Well, mine are planted firmly in the city, Mitch."

"We should at least talk about it, try to compromise."

"How? Would you move to New York? Or do you plan on maintaining a long-distance relationship? Can you really tell me that makes any sense?"

For Mitch, their staying together was the only thing that made sense, but talking to her now was like facing a brick wall. Releasing her, he reached for his sweats, stabbing his legs into them as he tried to think of yet another way to reach her.

"I'm going to turn in," she said flatly, rubbing her arms as if to find warmth. "You coming?"

He stood three feet away, staring at her, feeling as if a million miles stretched between them. "I need to make a tour of the house. Make sure everything's okay."

It wasn't true. What he needed was to sink back down to the mattress with her, to spend the rest of the night—the rest of his life—in her arms. But she was doing it again, holding herself in, putting up barriers, and they were both too tired to get anywhere tonight.

Yet when she didn't move, he decided to give it one more shot. Crossing the three feet between them, he wrapped his arms around her. "Relax, Darce. Can't you see I've got enough belief for both of us? After Simon, I guess there's no use in making promises, but we can at least try this out for a while. And keep trying, until we get it right."

"What about the kids? After what they went through when you and Beth split up, would you really want to put them through that again?"

"Stop making excuses. This isn't about the kids, and you know it. You're scared. Hell, I am, too, but where have you gotten, playing it safe? A car, a condo? Things can't take the place of people who care about you. Take a chance with me, Darce. I'll do my best to see you never regret it."

She looked up at him, her big, brown eyes glistening with indecision. "Oh Mitch, I ca—"

He put a finger over her lip, not wanting to hear her denial. "You can at least think about it, can't you? Tonight, before you drift off to sleep, and tomorrow before you waltz off with Peter, give a thought to the fact that no one will ever love you like I do."

Leaning down, he kissed her then, a soft, gentle salute that said more than any awkward words he could manage.

All things considered, it was the hardest thing he had ever done, leaving her there where she stood, and trusting that love indeed would find a way.

Chapter Twenty-Two

The next morning, Mitch strode through the garden to survey what was left of it. With all the debris, he found it hard to follow the paths. Broken branches lay everywhere, most of them from the rosebushes, though two cracked limbs came from the old oak. One trellis still stood, but it had been battered enough to warrant tearing it down, and the latticework was a disaster. Searching for the hole they'd dug for the new rosebush, he found it buried in an avalanche of mud. The bright, blinding sunlight was an added insult. No doubt Mother Nature wanted to be certain he saw every last detail of the havoc she'd wrought.

He tried not to feel discouraged, but Rose Arbor was a wreck. He'd been to the barn to assess the damage there, and guessed it would run in the tens of thousands. It would cost him to fix the roof on the back porch, too, but there wasn't enough money in the world to salvage the shed. He supposed he should be grateful the cellar hadn't flooded.

Righting an overturned bench and setting the Darcy Rose

on it, he rolled up his sleeves, determined to plant the rose-bush, anyway. *New beginnings,* Gramps had said. Mitch understood it was late in the season to be planting roses, that they'd have to watch over it and give it special care, but he needed to see this bush standing solid in the ground—as living, visual proof that they were all moving forward. By planting it, by establishing its roots, he'd symbolically be giving Darcy a reason to stay.

He hadn't talked to her since he'd kissed her last night. She'd been conked out when he'd finished his tour of the house, and when he got up this morning, she'd been curled in her bedroll, making soft little whimpering sounds in her sleep.

As he dug, he wondered what she was doing, if she was up and drinking the coffee he'd made for her. Imagining her chatting with the kids, plotting with his grandfather, he felt a spurt of envy. He wanted to be there, too, talking to her, learning everything there was to know about her.

And on that thought, he glanced up to see her walking to him.

Nature had nothing on Darcy, he decided, for she seemed a beam of blinding sunlight. Granted, there were smudges of mud on the yellow T-shirt, and a slight tear on the hem of the matching shorts, but Mitch had never seen anything lovelier. He stopped digging to lean on the shovel and smile at her approach.

With a lurch, he noticed she didn't smile back.

Be patient and gentle, he told himself. *She's scared and needs to be coaxed out of it.*

"You're looking chipper this morning," he said as she neared. "Get a good night's sleep?" He just loved it when she blushed.

She gestured down at her clothes. "I went to the cottage to get my things. You'd never guess I'd had a shower, would you? I helped the kids get Lester out of the house."

"I hope you didn't try to put him in the barn."

She made a feeble attempt at a smile. "It's amazing how

relatively untouched the cottage was, compared to that disaster. Or this.'' She looked around them with a pained expression. ''Poor Gramps. This will break his heart.''

''It's just the tip of the iceberg. Did you see the back porch?''

She took time to look at him then, really look at him. ''Oh, Mitch, I'm so sorry about what's happened here. I only wish there was something I could do to help.''

He didn't have to hear the unspoken *but.* He could see it in her eyes. ''You're not staying?''

She glanced to the right. ''Peter is here. We'll be leaving soon for New York.''

Soon? Focusing on the word that hurt the most, Mitch gripped the shovel, trying to hide his reaction. As fast as possible, she was leaving him. ''New York, huh?'' he said tightly, poking the shovel into the wet dirt. ''What happened to the rendezvous in Hilton Head?''

''There's been a lot of damage, I hear. The Tavish meeting will be in New York. I have to go, Mitch. It could mean my promotion.''

''And who can resist a promotion?'' Hard not to sound bitter. Harder yet to give up hope. ''No chance for us then?''

She shrugged halfheartedly. ''I could come back. For a visit.''

Flinging the mud behind him, he shook his head. ''The last thing I want to do is push you, but we both know if you run away to the city now, you'll get caught up in the rat race and you won't ever come back.''

''I'm not running away,'' she protested angrily. ''I'm running *to* something. Up there, my job, my life—that's the real world.''

''You want real?'' he said angrily. ''Look around you. See all the hard work and rebuilding we're facing here? It doesn't get any realer than that.''

She did look around her, unable to hide the grimace. ''What you're asking is impossible,'' she said flatly. ''I can't just throw away years of sacrifice and hard work. It's too impulsive, too spontaneous, like something Rita would do.''

"Dammit, forget your mother. You're not her, Darce, any more than you're Beth or I'm Simon. We're talking about you and me, and our fresh start. We just have to grab it, and try our hearts out to make it work."

She looked at the rosebush, biting her lip. "I have to go back." She sounded ready to cry. "It's the only place I feel safe."

"Safe? That was Lady's problem, remember? Mistaking convenience for love."

She turned to face him with her wide, pleading eyes. "It's not the same, Mitch. Lady was part of Rose Arbor. I'm not."

He watched her lift her chin, determined to hide behind her stubborn wall of protection. If he thought it would help, he'd grab her and kiss the fear right out of her, but being who she was, Darcy would require logic. Gripping the shovel, he searched for the words to convince her. "I'm thinking we were wrong, blaming a ghost for extending your one-night stay into a four-day weekend. Maybe it was just your own subconscious. Ever think that you *want* to stay, Darce? That deep down you know what Lady and Lester and the rest of us already figured out? You're part of us now."

Her eyes went wide, drinking him in. For a heady moment, he truly thought he had her, that he'd won her over.

Until her gaze shifted behind him.

He turned to see a male rendition of Darcy when she'd first arrived, from the silk Armani to the gleaming leather shoes. Mitch eyed the gold watch and slicked-back hair with a sinking feeling.

Mitch didn't need her to call out to a name to know this was the infamous Peter. If what Darcy wanted was hardedged ambition cloaked in flash and polish, Mitch could never compete with that.

He suffered through the introductions, wishing he wasn't wearing his muddy jeans and flannel shirt, knowing that even in his best suit, he'd never have the mind-set to compete with a shark like Peter. Listening to Darcy, hearing her talk about their plans in that clipped, no-nonsense fashion, Mitch saw the writing on the proverbial wall. He'd never had a prayer.

Watching them stroll off arm in arm, he told himself to face facts. He'd given it his best shot and lost her.

He flung the shovel to the ground. The worst of it was, how could he fault Darcy for her choice? Looking around at the ruined garden, he knew things around here would be dicey at best for the next few months. He couldn't compete with the life Peter could give her. Hell, he couldn't even afford the repairs to her Lexus.

His heart heavy, he made his way back to the house. If nothing else, he still had his manners, and he meant to make good and certain that he and his kids were in the driveway waving farewell to her. As Mel would say, they had to show Darcy, just in case, that there would always be a welcome here at Rose Arbor.

So much for two people dreaming together, he thought angrily. So much for legends, and ghosts, and believing in magic. What good was fantasy if it didn't show up when it really mattered?

Seeing Lester in his pen, he glared. "Stupid goat," he growled as he strode past. "Now, when we really need it, couldn't you do something to stop her?"

Climbing the porch steps with Peter, Darcy felt battered by a mass of swirling emotions. She'd spent a nerve-racking morning waiting for Peter's call, fearing the lure of Rose Arbor would yet wear her down, only to have him show up unannounced, appearing at the front door just as she'd been on her way out to go looking for Mitch.

Talk about two worlds colliding.

It had been no easy thing, standing between him and Mitch, craving lobster bisque, knowing she must take the bread and butter. Safe, logical, unemotional Peter.

Too bad, though, he had to be so annoying. Nobody understood better about disrupted schedules and mud-ruined clothing, but Peter had been here less than an hour and he'd already worn her out with his complaints. How petty his constant griping seemed in the face of all this destruction.

She had the mental image of Mitch, all alone with his shovel, still fighting to keep the place going.

"Why don't you wait here on the porch while I gather my things?" she suggested, suddenly anxious to escape his petulance. "I'd bring you inside, but the kids will probably pester you with questions."

His swift compliance proved she'd taken the right tack, but his eagerness to avoid the boys merely irritated her further. She would have liked him to meet everyone, to see how at home the Roses made her feel, but she feared he would say something obnoxious to ruin the memory for her.

Especially since a memory was all she'd have left.

Pushing the thought away, she hurried inside. Seeing the mattress propped up against the wall, she was doubly happy Peter hadn't come in with her. When she thought about what happened here last night...

No, she insisted to herself. Something that wonderful couldn't possibly last. Such emotions were too special, too fragile, and besides, she knew better than to believe in love.

Instead, she focused on the concrete and solid—the presentation, the commission that would buy her new condo, her own home, at last.

"Darcy, please, tell me it's not true," Mel cried out with her best theatrics as she raced down the stairs. "Swear to me you're not really leaving with that...that wimp!"

Darcy had imagined a few tearful hugs, but she now saw the goodbyes would prove far more difficult. Mel might sneer with patented bravado, but Darcy recognized the look in her eyes. Hadn't she felt the same, gazing at that callous note from Simon?

"I have to go," she explained, telling herself it was not the same at all. She was leaving *before* the kids got too attached to her—and she to them. "You've known all along I'd be returning to New York."

"But I thought...after last night..."

Darcy tried not to look at the mattress. Mel couldn't know about her and Mitch. She must mean the fun they'd had braving the storm together. "I'm not falling off the face of the earth, you know. I'll be back for a visit."

Mel's snort proved she wasn't buying it, any more than her father had. "Well, since everyone else is deserting the sinking ship," she said, crossing her arms over her chest, "maybe I'll go to Philadelphia."

"You can't leave your dad now. He needs you more than ever."

"You're leaving him, aren't you?"

"It's not the same—"

"You're right. It's not. Kids are supposed to grow up and leave, but two people who love each other should stay together forever, like Gramps and Grandma Rose. I used to think you were smart, Darcy, but you're acting dumber than Lady. At least she knew she was making a mistake."

"Mel—"

But the girl was already flying out the front door, slamming it shut behind her.

"Poor thing," Gramps said quietly, appearing at her side. "Never been much good at saying goodbye."

"It's been an emotional morning."

"Talked to Mitch, have you?"

It never ceased to amaze her how the old man could read her thoughts. "I tried. Please, Gramps, help him understand."

He shook his head sadly. "Can't do that, my dear, when I don't understand myself. I look at you both and see only that you belong together."

Hard? These goodbyes were proving impossible. "Don't do this to me. I'm trying to be sensible. I'm just not that impulsive. I haven't known Mitch long enough to take such a risk."

"Sometimes, all it takes is a moment. A glance."

"'Strangers In The Night'? This isn't some song, Gramps. This is real life, and we're both wearing too many scars to take such a leap of faith. You can't base a future on a mere four days.''

He took her hands, squeezing them, staring intently into her eyes. "Listen to me, child, and listen well. Every so often, life offers a quiet moment of vision, a stunning instant where we can see ourselves with heartbreaking clarity. Don't waste it, Darcy. Seize your moment.''

"Darcy!" Peter called out suddenly from the porch. "Come out here. Quickly.''

She wrenched her gaze from Gramps to the door. With a sigh, he released her hands. "Go on, then,'' he said wearily. "I'll fetch your bags.''

"Oh, Gramps,'' was all she could say, throwing herself in his arms and hugging him fiercely. It struck her hard how much she was going to miss his gentle, albeit offbeat, wisdom.

He held her a long moment, patting her back. "It'll be all right,'' he told her soothingly. "When your moment comes, you'll know what to do.''

It seemed an odd thing to say, but before she could react to it, he was pulling away and nudging her to the door. "You go on, go save your young man before Mel chews him up for dinner.''

Hurrying out to the porch, she found it wasn't Mel accosting Peter, but rather the boys, pelting him with the questions he'd hoped to avoid. Serves him right, she couldn't help thinking as she stepped up to join them.

"Good, here you are,'' Peter said, cutting Ky off midinquiry. "Hurry, or we're going to miss our flight.''

"Gramps is bringing my luggage,'' she told him, turning to the boys. For once, their blond hair was perfectly combed, their freckled faces scrubbed and shining, as if they'd dressed up special to bid her goodbye. "Besides, before I can leave,'' she said, feeling the lump rise in her throat, "I want to tell these two how much fun I've had hunting for ghosts with them. I guess I'll have to come back, won't I, if I ever hope to see Lady?''

"If she's still here," Ky said with a noncommittal shrug. "We think she's gone."

"What's this?" She looked from one boy to the other.

J.J. seemed suddenly as solemn as his brother. "We think she gave up on us now that you're leaving."

Shaking her head, she realized not even the twins would let her go easily. "I have nothing to do with Lady appearing or disappearing," she insisted. "She'll be back, guys. You can't keep a good ghost down."

Ky tried to smile. "We're going to miss you, Darcy."

"Yeah," J.J. seconded, his little-boy voice sounding strained. "So will Lester."

"Yeah, well, I brought him to say goodbye," Mitch said behind them, walking up to the porch leading the goat by a leash. Glancing at the rental car, he held up his end of the rope. "I'm not taking any more chances with my insurance bill."

She smiled weakly, feeling that painful tug again, that lurch in the pit of her stomach at the thought of leaving him.

But Gramps appeared with her suitcases, signaling that the time had come. All but snatching her bags out of the old man's hands, Peter tossed them in the trunk of the rental, leaving Darcy to stare one last time at the Roses. Mel had joined them, everyone minding their manners, standing together as a unified front. A family.

"Darcy? Can we leave some time today?"

Peter was right. Getting in the car beside him, she knew she'd just been delaying the inevitable. Sparing a backward glance at the house as they drove off, she could understand now why a ghost would haunt Rose Arbor. It was, as Mitch had predicted, a hard place to leave.

Throat clogging as they drove off, she twisted her head for a last, lingering image of the Roses, etching the memory into her brain.

"As I said on the phone," Peter was saying as they left the driveway and hit the road. "Binch is ecstatic about the Beverly account. Did I tell you he mentioned you by name?"

He went rambling on, detailing the strategy and all the hours they would spend chasing that account, but Darcy's attention faded. It seemed so distant, the world he described, especially when she thought of the roof that needed repair, the bushes to be pruned, and Mitch, at the end of each grueling day, dropping exhausted into his big, empty bed.

"But enough about the office," Peter said suddenly, turning to glance at her. "Poor Darcy, just look at you. What an ordeal it must have been, staying with those people."

"What do you mean, *those people?*"

"Isn't it obvious? The shabbiness, that dirt. Not exactly the environment we're accustomed to. And the way they stared at you when you were leaving..." He paused for a dramatic shudder. "It makes one wonder if maybe there's been a bit too much inbreeding."

"Why, you snob," she said, amazed at her anger. "Maybe they seemed shabby and dirty and a little dazed, but so would you if you'd been out all morning trying to salvage what you could from disaster. You're right, it isn't the environment we're used to. Nobody here runs off for a love affair or business meeting, not without first thinking about how it will affect those around them. Did you happen to notice that, Peter? Did you see how they think about each other, not themselves first and foremost?"

"Good heavens, there's no need to get hysterical." He gazed at her as if she'd grown an extra nose. "What has gotten into you?"

What indeed?

He stared at the road ahead, one hand on the wheel, the other reaching out for her. Instinctively, she recoiled from his touch.

"If this is about the Tavish deal..." He frowned as he returned his hand to the wheel. "I mean, what else could I do? I was there, with everything set up and waiting, and you were here—"

"Whoa, go back. What is this about the Tavish account?"

He wouldn't look at her. "They wanted to move fast. Get things set up for the Christmas season."

"You went ahead without me." It was a statement not a question. She realized it was exactly what Peter would do.

"Ah, babe, don't you see I did it for us?" Again, his hand slid over toward hers. "I didn't get the chance to tell you yet, but Binch was so pleased, he gave me my promotion. Soon, we can afford to get married."

Nails digging into her palms, Darcy thought of her own promotion, the condo that was to be her home, all wiped away in the wake of Peter's ambition. *Trust me,* he'd said, all the while stalling to put her off. "You snake. You took all my hard work and gave me no credit for it."

"Hey, I covered for you." He always attacked when he felt defensive, she realized. "You had big holes in your presentation."

"There were no holes, Peter, and we both know it. You stole that account right out from under my nose."

Staring at his profile, she watched his jaw tighten, not with strength, like Mitch's, but with anger. "We were facing a crisis," he said crisply. "I was there when they wanted to close the deal. You were not. You were down here playing footsies with your farmer."

Yes, she had been, and she was suddenly glad for her time at Rose Arbor. Had she not watched Mitch with his family, had she not seen the tenderness with which Gramps continued to adore his wife, she might never have known how deeply a man could care about those he loved.

Gazing at Peter, she recoiled from more than his touch. Even without proof of his treachery, how could she ever consider marrying this cold, uncaring person? After Mitch, she couldn't imagine kissing him. Thanks to Mitch, she knew how it could—and should—feel when two people touched.

Nor, as he'd warned, would such feelings go away. A relationship didn't vanish merely because the person no longer stood beside you. Thoughts of loved ones were like ghosts, popping up when you least expected, forcing you to remember. Only look how long she'd carried the bitter memories of Simon with her, perpetuating the pain, until here she was, running away from something rare and special, just in case it too might someday disappoint her. Who did she hope to protect? Whether she was left behind, or she did the leaving, the ache would be the same. In truth, she had nothing to gain by leaving.

She glanced back down the road toward the house, remembering how drawn she'd been to it from the moment she'd seen the sign on the highway. Had Lady been at work even then, luring in the next mistress of Rose Arbor? Or had it been Darcy's own instincts, long buried under hurt and bitterness, trying to tell her that here was where she could grow and prosper? That here, with these people, was where she belonged.

It didn't make sense to run back to New York; it would do her no good to leave the Roses. Like vibrant ghosts, they would stay alive in her mind and heart, haunting her the rest of her days.

Mitch, most of all.

I *love* him, she thought, stunned to find that she really could believe in that emotion.

All at once, she felt a chill seep into the rental car, a curling mist that no longer unnerved her. She waited, ready for the whisper, but this time, she heard no *Help us.* Instead, she could have sworn she heard, *Help yourself.*

Even as she shivered, Lester leaped in front of the car.

Peter slammed on the brakes, bringing the rental to a skidding, shuddering halt, while the goat skipped off down the road to Hester Macon's.

"Stop the car!" Darcy cried out in a burst of exhilaration.

"For heaven's sake, Darcy, we *are* stopped."

"I know," she said, laughing and crying at the same time. "It was just such a dramatic moment, it seemed to require it. Oh, Peter, I'm sorry, but I'm not going with you."

"Are you serious?" Gaping at her, he watched her grope

at the door handle. "Or more to the point, have you lost your mind?"

"Actually, I think I've *found* my mind. Gramps was right. I was ready when the moment came, and now I'm going to seize it. Or I will, if I can ever get this stupid door open."

He leaned over to yank up the handle, muttering about the dregs of the rental-car stock. "Go then, if you must, but I warn you, Binch is expecting you in the office first thing in the morning."

She paused outside the door, leaning in, wanting him to understand. "I'm not going to the office. I don't belong there anymore. I'm beginning to wonder if I ever did."

"Don't you think you're overreacting? Be sensible and get back in the car. We can discuss this on the way home."

"New York is your home, Peter, but mine is here, with the Roses. I now know I'll never be happy anywhere else."

"You're talking rubbish." Tight-lipped, he ground the ignition until the engine leaped to life. "Your mother will be calling, you know. I hope she can talk some sense into you."

"I doubt it." That had been her mistake all along, she realized, letting Rita influence how she thought and felt. Mitch was right about that, too. She wasn't like her mother and he wasn't like Simon. They were Darcy and Mitch, and it was time for new beginnings.

Patting the door, she stepped back from the car. It was a good thing she did, for without a word, Peter jammed on the gas and sped off down the road. His anger, she suspected, had less to do with losing her than the time he'd wasted on this trip.

She should probably be livid with him—really, he had been an absolute slime about the Tavish account—but all she could summon at the moment was gratitude, since he'd helped open her eyes. Laughing to herself, she realized she wasn't even angry that he'd driven off with her luggage. She felt like dancing with overwhelming relief. For the first time she could remember, she felt suddenly, blissfully free.

Turning back the way she had come, her heart leaped at

the thought of the night ahead, the years ahead. Sighing happily, she said a quiet, "Thank you, Lady."

And she liked to imagine she heard an answering sigh in the trees overhead.

Chapter Twenty-Three

Hearing the screech of brakes, Mitch started running, swamped by déjà vu. The nudge, he thought. Please let Darcy be all right.

When there was no resounding crash, he glanced back over his shoulder at his family. "Go," they shouted in unison, gesturing him forward with wide, beaming smiles. "Go on, go get her."

As if he needed the encouragement.

For Darcy, the closer she got to Rose Arbor—now that the first few moments of exhilaration had passed—the less certain she became of finding a welcome. They'd all been so upset with her, Mitch especially. She kept seeing him in her mind, glaring at her as he held tight to the goat. Nor could she truly blame him. The way she'd left, after all he'd said and done to convince her to stay, was hardly an auspicious start for a relationship.

But going back to him now was just that, a start, the first

building block in establishing trust. From now on, she would learn, and not hide from her mistakes. With Mitch's help—with his love—she'd just keep trying harder.

As if in reward for finding the right answer, she looked up to see Mitch running toward her. The relief on his face, the joyful speed with which he swept her up into his arms, let her know that he'd come just for her.

As he kissed her, a long, hot, hungry declaration, she knew that Gramps was right. In the end, everything would somehow turn out all right.

"That's it," he said breathlessly, pulling back to look at her. "No more taking chances. We're getting married."

The man sure knew how to pull the rug out from under her feet. "My goodness, Mr. Rose. You don't waste time."

"Why wait? I know we belong together, and if you're here now, I'd say you have to know it, too." He reached up to touch her face. "Though you gave me quite a scare, right up to the last minute. I don't ever again want to have to rely on a ghost."

"How could you know..." In her mind, she saw Lester leaping in front of them, the same goat Mitch had been clutching as if his life depended on it. The very same Lester who should still be attached to the rope he still held in his hands. "You did it on purpose? You let Lester go?"

He looked like his sons when they knew they deserved a scolding. "I had to risk it. I had to do something, Darce. I'd run out of words and you were leaving."

"You're too much, Mitchell Allen Rose," she told him, touched by the gesture. "It will serve you right if Hester socks you for a hefty marigold bill."

He drew her closer, kissing her hair. "Maybe you're worth it. Have I told you yet how much I love you?"

She clung to him, awed by how lucky one woman could be. "Not nearly enough, but you've certainly shown me. Oh, Mitch, I'm still scared to death of the future, but I'm willing to take the chance."

He grimaced. "We certainly have our work cut out for us.

I was thinking, maybe we should do some advertising. I haven't got much in the budget, but with your talent for organizing things..."

He paused, tossing the ball in her court and waiting to see what she'd do with it. Touched that he would offer this compromise, that he would show such trust, she felt her throat tighten. "We'll have to be careful. We wouldn't want anything that would spoil the aura of the place."

He smiled as if she'd just given him the world.

She wanted to give him more. Touching his face in wonder, she thought of Gramps and Grandma Rose and the love they continued to share. "Oh, Mitch, I want to grow old with you. From now on, let's do all our dreaming together."

He answered by kissing her fiercely.

"Looks like we'll have plenty of company," he told her hoarsely, pulling away as the boys came barreling down the road in their direction.

"Dad," they called out. "Is Darcy okay?"

"What are you two doing here? Didn't I tell you to fix that pump?"

"We're gonna," Ky said.

"But we wanted to welcome Darcy back, too."

Nor were they alone. Mel, and then Gramps, came around the bend, all of them joining in one big embrace when Mitch announced that he and Darcy were getting married.

Mel started on about the dress she'd wear to the wedding, while the boys offered excuses about the pump, but Gramps just gave Darcy his shrewd expression. "What was it?" he asked. "What changed your mind?"

A tiny smile played at her lips. "It was like you said, the moment came, and I just knew. I was sitting there staring at Peter, wondering how I wanted to spend the rest of my life, when I suddenly remembered something Mitch told me."

Mitch tilted his head. "Yeah, and what was that?"

"It must be the Roses."

He grinned back at her. "All five of us?"

"Every last one." Studying each face, she knew a wave

of gratitude that she'd found them, that they had invited—no, welcomed—her into their family circle.

"Come on," Mitch said, taking her hand. "Let's get back to the house."

Linking arms with him, joining the Roses as they walked down the drive, Darcy knew she'd found more than her future at Rose Arbor.

At long last, she was home.

* * * * *

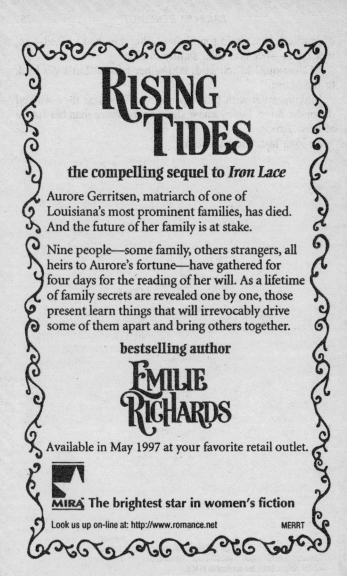

Take 4 bestselling love stories FREE

Plus get a FREE surprise gift!

As seen on TV!
Free Gift Offer

With a Free Gift proof-of-purchase from any Silhouette® book,
you can receive a beautiful cubic zirconia pendant.

This gorgeous marquise-shaped stone is a genuine cubic
zirconia—accented by an 18" gold tone necklace.

(Approximate retail value $19.95)

Send for yours today...
compliments of ▼ *Silhouette*®
™

To receive your free gift, a cubic zirconia pendant, send us one original proof-of-
purchase, photocopies not accepted, from the back of any Silhouette Romance™,
Silhouette Desire®, Silhouette Special Edition®, Silhouette Intimate Moments®
or Silhouette Yours Truly™ title available in February, March and April at your favorite
retail outlet, together with the Free Gift Certificate, plus a check or money order for
$1.65 U.S/$2.15 CAN. (do not send cash) to cover postage and handling, payable
to Silhouette Free Gift Offer. We will send you the specified gift. Allow 6 to 8 weeks for
delivery. Offer good until April 30, 1997 or while quantities last. Offer valid in the
U.S. and Canada only.

Free Gift Certificate

Name: _____

Address: _____

City: _____ State/Province: _____ Zip/Postal Code: _____

Mail this certificate, one proof-of-purchase and a check or money order for postage
and handling to: SILHOUETTE FREE GIFT OFFER 1997. In the U.S.: 3010 Walden
Avenue, P.O. Box 9077, Buffalo NY 14269-9077. In Canada: P.O. Box 613, Fort Erie,
Ontario L2Z 5X3.

FREE GIFT OFFER   084-KFD
ONE PROOF-OF-PURCHASE
To collect your fabulous FREE GIFT, a cubic zirconia pendant, you must include this
original proof-of-purchase for each gift with the properly completed Free Gift Certificate.

084-KFD

And the Winner Is...
You!

...when you pick up these great titles
from our new promotion at your
favorite retail outlet this June!

Diana Palmer
The Case of the Mesmerizing Boss

Betty Neels
The Convenient Wife

Annette Broadrick
Irresistible

Emma Darcy
A Wedding to Remember

Rachel Lee
Lost Warriors

Marie Ferrarella
Father Goose

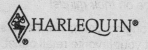 

**This summer, the legend
continues in Jacobsville**

*Diana
Palmer*

A LONG, TALL
TEXAN SUMMER

Three **BRAND-NEW** short stories

This summer, Silhouette brings readers a special
collection for Diana Palmer's LONG, TALL TEXANS
fans. Diana has rounded up three **BRAND-NEW**
stories of love Texas-style, all set in Jacobsville,
Texas. Featuring the men you've grown to love from
this wonderful town, this collection is a must-have
for all fans!

*They grow 'em tall in the saddle in Texas—and
they've got love and marriage on their minds!*

Don't miss this collection of original Long, Tall Texans
stories...available in June at your favorite retail outlet.

Silhouette®